A Little Nigh

This time, he initiated the kiss.

This time, she knew what to do.

After all of the flirting and teasing, she wouldn't have thought a mere kiss could do so much. But the touch of his lips against hers added fuel to the embers, and heat flared.

Heat, and burning desire.

He caressed, teased, and then deepened the kiss, claiming her. Her hands splayed across his strong back, pulling him closer. Their bodies molded together. She met his tongue, and all she could imagine was it elsewhere on her body, urging her to higher levels of passion and need until she . . .

He drew away. She could feel his heart pounding, knew he was just as aroused as she. Good. It gave her a moment to recover. She licked her lips, and his eyes followed the movement.

'You see what I mean?' he asked. 'Can we work effectively if we're constantly . . . distracted?'

'I can see where it might become a problem.' Hannah nodded slowly. Light from a nearby street lamp threw silver into his hair, made shadows pool in his eyes. 'So, you're suggesting we should get it out of our systems?'

'Exactly.'

A Little Night Music

Sarah Dale

In real life, always practise safe sex.

First published in 2007 by
Cheek
Thames Wharf Studios
Rainville Road
London W6 9HA

A catalogue record for this book is available from the British Library.

www.cheek-books.com

Typeset by SetSystems Ltd, Saffron Walden, Essex

Printed and bound by Mackays of Chatham PLC

The paper used in this book is a natural, recyclable product made from wood grown in sustainable forests. The manufacturing process conforms to the regulations of the country of origin.

ISBN 978 0 352 34110 5

To the boys in the band:
Chuck, Dennis, Glen, John C., John P., JY, Lawrence,
Ricky, Todd, and Tommy.
Thanks for the inspiration . . . and for keeping the
dream alive.

Prologue

Hannah put the finishing touches on her hair, trying to tuck the last corkscrew curl into the upsweep at the back. It persisted in sticking out of the side of her head, looking like an auburn antenna tuned to a bad station. She couldn't do anything about the braces that had cursed her throughout high school, so she promised herself she would smile as little as possible. Keeping her mouth closed would also prevent her from saying something stupid.

The glasses, however, she could fix. She took them off and her image in the mirror immediately blurred. She squinted at her reflection. That was no good. What was the point of not being able to see him? She slipped them back on and left her dressing room.

The poster pinned to the Laura Ashley wallpaper next to Hannah's bed drew her attention and she sighed. It was a wistful sound, and she firmly told herself there would be none of that during dinner, either.

The thought of sitting at the same table as Nathaniel Fox made her knees weak, so she sat on the edge of her wide canopied bed, bouncing on the hated floral bedspread in the vague hope that the rough treatment would somehow destroy it. She'd lobbied for vivid colors and clean lines when her suite had been redecorated but her mother and the interior-designer-of-the-year had overruled her. Instead, her suite of rooms had been filled with soft pastels, stripes and florals, and – nightmare beyond nightmare – a canopy bed.

Her black crushed-velvet skirt hiked up too high, and

Hannah firmly tugged it down over her thighs. If she'd only had some warning, she could have lost that last twenty pounds she was battling and fit into the cute Gucci sundress that she and Gina had found at a vintage shop.

How could her mother have forgotten to tell her until casually, this afternoon, 'Oh, by the way, that singer you like so much will be at dinner tonight. What's his name again – Cougar? Wolf?'?

Fox, Mother. Nathaniel Fox.

Fox's face grinned down at her from the wall. Hannah had been a fan ever since she'd first heard his husky voice coming out of her radio. The fact that he was just about the sexiest man on earth made her pulse rate climb. The life-sized picture caught him mid-leap from the top of a drum riser, the leather pants pulled tight across his thighs. His dark hair flew around his face, highlighting the lean cheekbones, the wide mouth. She wondered what it would be like to press her lips to his, to feel that mouth moving on hers. It certainly wouldn't be like that awful Spin-the-Bottle game on her class trip to Yosemite. An unfamiliar ache settled in her stomach and she wondered how close it was to dinner.

A glance at the clock on her nightstand showed Hannah just how late it was getting. Taking her courage firmly in her hands, she stood up. She'd heard a car door slam half an hour ago and had peeked out of her window to see a dark-green Porsche that could only belong to Fox parked in front of the house. She was, regrettably, too late to catch a glimpse of the man himself. Instead, she watched as her father's chauffeur slipped behind the wheel and drove the car out of sight, no doubt parking it out by the garage. It had taken her this long to get her nerve up to go downstairs and meet her father's guest.

Everett Forbes was a big-name music producer, and Hannah had grown up with musicians wandering in and out of her house, treating her like some adorable little mascot. But this was different. Very different.

None of the others had inspired whispered midnight conversations with her best friend, Gina. None of the others made her body fluttery when she looked at them.

She pressed her shaking hands to her cheeks, willing herself not to blush. 'I will not make a fool of myself,' she swore aloud. Oh God, her voice was shaking. She repeated the phrase, this time going for a sexy rasp. It didn't work. She left the bedroom, giving the cute sundress a last longing look, and passed through her sitting room.

The wide marble stairway seemed a long way down in her new shoes. The spiky heels and straps had looked so good when she'd bought them. Wearing them was a whole other story.

Grasping the banister, she caught sight of her chewed nails and grimaced. Something else she hadn't had a chance to fix. She started down the stairs, trying not to totter.

The sweeping staircase led to the black-and-white tiled entrance foyer of their Hollywood mansion. Hannah stayed close to the banister, watching the steps as she descended. She wondered how presenters at award shows were able to glide down the middle of a staircase without looking down. Surely she'd fall on her ass.

'Hey, can you tell me where the bathroom is?'

The voice interrupted her concentration. Hannah looked up from where she was watching her feet, and saw him. Nathaniel Fox, all six glorious feet of him, standing there, expectantly waiting for her to answer his question as if it were the most normal thing on earth.

Her foot missed the next step, and she toppled forward.

He caught her before she hit the floor, hauling her up against his hard chest. Her fingers dug into his shirt as she struggled to regain her balance, gripping the soft black linen like a lifeline. Beneath it, his chest was hard, the heat of his skin warming her. He smelled of smoke and something undeniably male, something she'd never experienced before, and it made her feel even more giddy.

His eyes really were the most incredible shade of blue, fringed by the longest lashes she'd ever seen on a man. Hannah admitted almost hysterically that her experience with men's eyelashes was remarkably slim.

'Are you OK?' he asked. His fingers still gripped her upper arms, sending shivers of excitement along her skin.

Hannah nodded, not trusting herself to speak. Her hands drifted up to touch the silky ends of the hair that fell over his shoulder like a raven's wing. It was as soft as it looked in the poster on her wall. A gold hoop in his left ear glinted through the dark strands.

Oh God, she was touching Nathaniel Fox! He was holding her in his arms . . . and he was close enough to kiss.

Her gaze settled on his mouth and, before she could talk herself out of it, she wound her fingers in his hair, yanked his head down and kissed him.

His mouth was hard, warm. Hannah felt dizzy with pleasure and pressed herself against him. For one brief, sweet moment, he kissed her back, his lips caressing, teasing the curves of hers. Then with a soft groan, he gently put her away from him.

'Whoa, honey, that was nice, but you need to grow up a little bit first,' he said. His fingers touched her cheek, the pad of his thumb skating lightly across her bottom lip before dropping away.

'I'm sorry,' Hannah blurted, raising her hand to her mouth. She could feel the hot color in her cheeks, and knew she was as red as her hair. How awful.

Fox grinned, that slow grin that set her heart to

pounding every time she saw him in concert. Only now it was directed at her. 'It's OK,' he said. 'I didn't mind. Now where's your bathroom?'

Hannah pointed down the hall. When he turned away, she ripped off the stupid high heels and fled back up the stairs to her rooms. Once there, she fell onto the bed and pressed one of the pillows over her head, trying to blot out the memory of what had happened.

Well, most of it. The embarrassing parts. The kiss, however . . .

She threw the pillow onto the floor and grabbed the phone. She'd called her best friend, Gina, right after Mom had told her Fox was coming to dinner. Of course she'd promised to call Gina back with all the details. She'd known Gina since second grade and had gotten her hooked on Nathaniel Fox, too.

'Is he there?' Gina demanded. 'Is he as gorgeous in person? Omigod, tell me *every*thing!'

'I have just made a total, complete and utter fool of myself,' Hannah wailed. 'My life is ruined.'

Gina made appropriate soothing noises, gasps, and finally a long squeal when Hannah got to the part about the kiss.

'I cannot *believe* you did that,' she said. 'I am so totally jealous. I hate you.'

A knock sounded at Hannah's door.

'It gets worse,' Hannah said. 'Hold on a sec.' She padded into the sitting room, the phone held to her side. To the door, she said, 'Yes?'

'Miss Hannah?' It was Maria, their maid. 'Dinner is being served.'

There was no way she could go back down there, not after the humiliation of rejection. 'I'm not feeling well,' Hannah said.

'Oh no, dear! Would you like me to have your mother come up?'

Dear lord, no.

'No, I'll be OK. It's just a headache. I want to take a nap. Thanks, Maria.'

Back on the phone with Gina, she relayed the rest of the awful story.

'But you *kissed* him,' Gina said. 'That's so awesome.'

'And then he threw me back into the pond for being too small.'

'I don't know,' Gina said, ever the optimist. 'It sounds to me like he'll be back to fish again later.'

'Do you think?' Hannah asked, perking up slightly. 'Really?'

'What did you say he said? You need to grow up a little? That kind of makes sense. I mean, we *are* still jailbait, at least until next year. You don't want to be responsible for the downfall of his career.'

'I suppose not.' Hannah got up and paced through the room, unable to sit still with a fresh wave of excitement surging through her. 'You think I still have a chance? When I'm eighteen, or older?'

'Totally,' Gina said. 'I mean, your dad's just produced his second album. You'll get to meet him again.'

Hannah couldn't stop a grin from slowly curving her mouth. 'I'll need to have a plan. I have to be ready next time.'

They spent the next two hours on the phone, formulating the plan, hashing out the details. Giggling, imagining what it would be like. Hannah turned on her computer and typed as they talked.

Finally, Gina said, 'Have you started the social studies paper for tomorrow?'

'I wrote it last week.'

Gina snorted. 'Oh, stupid, me, of course *you* did. But I haven't, so I've got to go. Call me back if you start to freak out again, OK?'

'OK. Or I'll call if I get any more ideas about the plan,' Hannah said, and hung up. She replaced the cellphone in its charger and wandered back into her bedroom. The window seat was padded, one of the few places in her room that she actually liked. Leaving the lights off, Hannah sat, pulling her long legs up and smoothing the skirt over them. The wide circular driveway outside was currently flooded with light. Fox's Porsche was back in front of the door, so he must be getting ready to leave.

A pang twisted her chest. She'd blown it. He was going to leave and she hadn't even been able to put together a coherent sentence. Not to mention that she'd been the ultimate klutz.

But you kissed him, a little voice reminded her. *And you're going to kiss him again one day.*

Hannah opened her window, letting in the mellow southern Californian spring air scented with night-blooming jasmine. Maybe she'd get to hear his voice one last time before he left.

Waiting patiently, Hannah was rewarded when she heard the front door, below and to her left, open. She couldn't make out the words, but she guessed that her parents were saying goodnight to Fox. Hannah watched, secure in the dark, as he strode to his car.

Her heart pounded. He looked so hot in the tight black pants that her mouth dried up. He was so close and yet so unattainable right now. He'd made that clear.

Fox opened the door to his dark-green Porsche, then paused and looked up at the house.

At Hannah's window.

She shrank further back. If he saw her watching ... She couldn't bear to add to the embarrassment. She heard the car engine purr to life, and when she furtively glanced down again, Fox was gone.

Hannah stayed at the window for a long while, watching the lights of Los Angeles twinkling down the hill, hardening her resolve.

One day, so help her, she was going to make love to Nathaniel Fox.

Chapter One

Nine years later

'Are you ready for the meeting?' Sam asked.

Nate looked up, his fingers paused momentarily on the strings of his guitar. Distracted, he tried to remember what meeting he was supposed to be ready for.

'Oh, the new publicist, right,' he said finally. He strummed the guitar strings, stopping to tighten a tuning peg. A single plucked string filled the studio with monotonous sound before he stopped to make another minute adjustment.

'Ms Montgomery will be here in half an hour,' Sam said, not moving.

'Fine,' Nate answered. He swung around on the stool, putting his back to his manager. He could still see him in the floor-to-ceiling mirror on the opposite wall. 'You know where to find me.'

'Why are you being so difficult?'

Nate leaned over the instrument cradled in his arms. 'Publicists aren't high on my list of favorite people right now, Sam.'

'I know you had a problem with the last one –'

'He offered me drugs, Sam,' Nate said, his voice low and tight.

Unbidden, the memory of that moment swam up into his consciousness. The smirk of the weaselly little man, so sure that Nate would take him up on the offer. The moment of indecision, what had only been a few seconds but had felt like a lifetime as he'd battled the craving, the yearning to give in.

His hands tightened on the neck of the guitar, compressing the strings and drawing a low strangled sound from it. With effort, he let go.

The only good part of the memory was the expression on the weasel's face when Nate had answered by grabbing him by his shirt front and telling him where he could put his drugs.

'And you said no,' Sam said.

Nate gritted his teeth. Put that way, it sounded like his refusal had been easy.

Sam continued. 'That's great. You're clean now and I'm proud of you, but the fact is that you fired him. He was doing a hell of a job on publicity for the tour.'

'That layout in the *Weekly Word* wasn't publicity, it was character assassination.' Nate swung back to face Sam. His manager's hair had started to grey, the thick curls drawn back from a sharp face. Almost against his will, Nate felt his anger drain away. Sam had always been there for him, an odd cross between friend and father figure.

'Hannah Montgomery's good, and we're lucky to get her.'

'I know.' Nate scrubbed a hand over his face. 'I'll make nice with the publicity. I'll even smile for the camera when I have to.'

'No, don't make nice,' Sam said. 'We don't want nice. We want reformed bad boy. But still a bad boy.'

Nate grimaced.

'It's what your fans expect,' Sam said. 'Your image sells, and you know it. And let's face it, after your last album, it's your sex appeal we're banking on.'

The words were a knife twisting in Nate's stomach, but he said nothing. Only Sam could get away with a statement like that, because of everything that had gone before.

'Think about what I've said,' Sam said. 'Hannah will be here soon, and we're going out to dinner.'

'Dinner? Why?'

'To celebrate.' Sam pinned him with what Nate assumed was supposed to be a stern look. 'You're going to behave, aren't you?'

'Like the devil that I am,' Nate promised.

Sam snorted, but the look in his eyes told Nate that some of his worry had been eased. 'Half an hour, Nate.'

Nate waved him out of the rehearsal room. He stood, stretching the kinks from his spine. The piano to one side of the room beckoned, and he sat down at its bench, poising his fingers over the keys. After a moment, he hung his head, letting one finger plink a key. It had always been about the music, but after the cataclysmic flop of his last album, and everything that had happened after, even that was in danger.

This new publicist had better work out.

He rolled his shoulders and once again put his fingers to the keys. He transferred his tangled emotions into what he'd always done best. Music flowed, filling the room. The guitar would always be his stage instrument, but the piano filled a different need. He'd done some of his best writing on its keys.

The fact that he hadn't written a single new note in the last two years was something only he and Sam knew.

And now here he was on the cusp of a tour for an album of cover tunes – and terrified of all the temptations waiting on the road.

He had to relax. T'ai chi helped but it wasn't enough to smooth the tense ache in his shoulders, not enough to ensure he slept through the night.

Maybe he needed to get laid, he mused. He let his fingers play across the keys, stroking them as if they were a willing woman. Still, casual sex with some random bimbo had ceased to appeal, which left him very short of options.

He could only imagine how the tabloids would spin that one.

This was getting him nowhere, and he had work to do. There were a million details to pull together, and the tour was due to start in less than a week.

Despite himself, Nate found he was actually looking forward to meeting the new publicist. He'd liked her when he'd interviewed her over the phone. She had some good ideas, and her previous record spoke of her capabilities. She'd done a great job with the fallout from Jenna Glenn's stage fright. This could be his opportunity to take control of his publicity, rid himself of some of the bad-boy image, which Sam seemed to think was so important, but which had led to such problems.

In spite of himself, he grinned. Maybe she'd even be cute.

Hannah presented her ID to the young man behind the desk while gracing him with a warm smile. 'I'm here to see Sam Granby.'

'Of course, Ms Montgomery,' he said. 'Mr Granby is waiting for you. Take the elevator to the fourth floor. He's in conference room forty-two.'

'Thanks,' she said. Pocketing the ID, she headed toward the elevators, her heels clicking on the marble floor. She gave a quick glance to the oversized bronze sculpture rising up into the atrium on her left. Something about its flowing lines suggested the passion of music, the freedom of movement.

It made her think of Nate Fox, and sex.

It wasn't helping.

She pushed the elevator button. What was taking so long? She glanced at her watch. The flight had been late getting into San Francisco, and the car Sam Granby had sent for her had gotten stuck in traffic. The universe was obviously conspiring against her, right down to the slow elevator. She pushed the button three more times for good measure.

Her cell rang. She switched her briefcase to her other hand and answered it.

'Where are you?' Gina demanded.

'Elevators,' Hannah said.

'And how many times have you pushed the button?' Gina asked.

A smile quirked Hannah's mouth. Her best friend knew her too well. 'Only four. I think.'

'Calm. Down.' Gina said. 'Take a deep breath, or I swear I will bitch-slap you when I see you tonight.'

Hannah's tension bubbled out as a giggle, and she felt a little better. Thank God Gina was there to ground her. Gina had juggled her schedule as a fashion photojournalist to be available to take shots of Nate for concert publicity.

'I'm sorry,' Hannah said. 'I'm just nervous.'

Gina snorted.

'I don't want to come across as a rabid fan.' Hannah fiddled with the earpiece of her sunglasses, realized she was doing it, and shoved them into her briefcase.

'But you *are* a rabid fan,' Gina said with a laugh. 'You still have that poster of him hanging in your apartment.'

'But it's not in my bedroom anymore,' Hannah pointed out.

'Only because your last boyfriend complained that he felt like he was being watched in bed,' Gina said. 'Good thing you're past him now – he'd get in the way of your vow.'

Her vow. To have her night of passion with Nathaniel Fox, the man she was now working for.

Gina had been the first person she'd called after she'd gotten the offer from Sam Granby. And, of course, Gina had immediately asked if she remembered what she'd sworn as a starstruck teenager.

Oh, Hannah remembered it all right. When Sam had made the initial contact about working for them, it was the first thing that had gone through her mind.

She'd seen Nate Fox a few times over the years at industry parties. Had even spoken to him a few times. He'd never connected her with the gawky teenager who'd fallen into his arms – or if he had, he hadn't mentioned it. He'd always had some svelte and gorgeous model or starlet on his arm, a drink in his hand. He'd been a hard partier, on the A-list, in demand for every opening at every new hot spot.

And then he'd fallen.

Here it was, nine years later, and, despite his history and the scandal, she still got hot and bothered when she saw him in concert. 'Pavlov's bimbo,' she and Gina called the phenomenon. The sound of his voice coming through the microphone was all it took to get her panties wet.

'I know what you're thinking about!' Gina said with a laugh, breaking into Hannah's thoughts.

'Don't be ridiculous,' Hannah said. 'I'm a professional and I'm here to do a job.'

'Uh-huh,' Gina said dubiously. 'And you're a rotten liar.'

The elevator pinged, saving Hannah the need to answer. Inside, she pushed the button for the fourth floor. Once.

She pressed a hand to her stomach, unsure if it were butterflies or the airplane coffee that was responsible for the state of her stomach.

Of course, if she were being honest, she would admit that it was entirely due to meeting him again. She could close her eyes and picture the midnight silk of his hair brushing against his shoulders. The thick fringe of lashes that threw his dark-blue eyes into shadow.

The curve of his mouth that spoke of hot passion.

This time, she knew what to do with him. She was no

longer small enough to be thrown back into the pond. The glasses were long gone, banished by Lasik surgery. Her Bozo the Clown curls were gone, too. It had taken years and the aid of a pricey hairdresser, but she'd finally learned to tame the frizz, smoothing the curl into sleek waves that flowed down her back.

Hannah had dressed carefully for this meeting, searching for a combination of utterly competent businessperson, gracefully creative publicist and sexually confident woman. The pale-green silk noile of her suit highlighted her complexion and outlined her curves without being tight or obvious. The skirt was professional but short. A hint of dark-green lace at the V of the suit jacket was the only indication of the stretch lace camisole beneath.

'I have to go,' she told Gina.

'OK. The captain just said we'll be landing in half an hour. Call me when you find out where we're eating, and I'll meet you at the restaurant. And remember not to be tongue-tied when you meet him. You can put your tongue to better uses when you seduce him.'

Hannah hung up, still laughing.

The elevator let her out into a long hallway, the cream walls lined with framed posters of the stars who'd recorded at the studio. Hannah recognized all of them, having met a good many of them over the years. Her career had taken off in college when she'd turned a young college band into a regional, and then a national phenomenon.

With the intimate knowledge of the music business gained from watching her father, and the contacts she'd made from her work with Konfused Khildren, Hannah had worked her way up until she was one of the best PR people in the music business. She'd been using her mother's maiden name since college, and most people didn't even realize she was the daughter of Everett Forbes, producer extraordinaire.

And now here she was, working for her idol.

The first thing that Hannah saw when she walked into Sam Granby's office was the poster of Nate Fox on the wall. It had been taken a few years after the one she had hanging up in her apartment. His guitar was slung at his side, an extension of his body, one hip propped lazily against a stone wall. His arms were crossed over his chest, and he looked dark and dangerous. The leather that clung to his thighs was pulled taut, outlining lean muscles.

She wondered what it would feel like to run her hands along the material, feeling the hardness beneath. To follow it up to where the cloth clung, cupping his crotch. She felt an ache between her own thighs, making her aware of how the thong she wore rubbed against her, heightening the feeling of arousal.

Hannah tore her eyes from the poster, belatedly aware that Sam Granby had extended his hand and was waiting for her to take it.

Lovely. Caught fantasizing about Nate Fox in front of his manager like some starstruck groupie. Squaring her shoulders, Hannah gathered her professional persona and met Sam's hand with her own.

'Sam, it's a pleasure to meet you again,' she said. He was a compact, barrel-chested man, making up in strength what he lacked in height. His curly hair, once dark, was salted throughout.

Sam motioned her to a seat. 'I'm thrilled you've agreed to work for us, Hannah.'

Hannah deliberately chose a chair that placed the poster at her back. There was no sense in tempting her eyes to seek it out. She didn't need to make a fool of herself by drooling. 'Now that you've hired me, I have to admit that I've wanted to work with Nate for years.'

'You're a fan, then?' Sam asked.

Hannah laughed. 'Guilty as charged. Since I was a teenager,' she admitted. Opening her bag, she drew out a file, placing it on the desk. 'I've reviewed the material you sent and everything looks fine.' She slid a sheet of paper across the desk. 'I've written up a press release based on what we discussed over the phone. I'll get that out to all the majors as soon as you approve.'

'Nate's the one who signs the checks,' Sam said. 'He gets the final stamp of approval.'

Her stomach fluttered at the sound of his name, at the reminder that she'd meet him again soon – really meet him this time, on her own terms, and not as a palm to be pressed at an industry party.

And definitely not as a gawky teenager.

'I've let it leak that we'll be shooting publicity shots at Fisherman's Wharf tomorrow afternoon. I want a crowd there. I want people talking about how good he looks. I want fans to spread the word that Nate Fox is back.'

'That sounds good,' Sam said. 'I'll meet with our security guy tonight after dinner and make sure he's prepared.'

'Good,' Hannah said. 'I've arranged for Gina Salvatore to take the photos. You'll meet her at dinner tonight. She's going to do some digital work for us, even though she usually works in film. It would be great if she could get some shots of him with fans, signing autographs, that sort of thing. I want them posted on his website by tomorrow night.'

Sam nodded, scribbling a note on a piece of paper. 'If you get the digital pics to me after the shoot, I'll send them to our web master.'

'I'll give you the memory card,' Hannah assured him.

Sam leaned back in his chair, restlessly turning a pencil between his fingers. 'I'll be frank with you, Hannah. Since the accident, he hasn't done well dealing with the publicity. The new album, *Cannibal Eyes*, is a covers album – well, you know all that. You also know that sales aren't great. We did it to fulfill Nate's production contract, and the label doesn't feel like investing much money in promoting it. With the tour due to start, I want to flood the market with his image and sound. I want this tour to be his comeback. I want you to show the world that he's back in top form.'

'To show them that he's not a drugged-out, used-up has-been?' Hannah asked.

Sam's mouth tightened, but he answered easily enough. 'Yes. That's why I want you on the road with us, Hannah. I know that's not a publicist's normal job, but it's important to me that you keep on top of every little development, and spin it the way we want.'

She leaned forward, her grey eyes holding his. 'Is he clean, Sam? And will he stay that way?'

'Yes,' he answered. 'He will.'

'Good. I've cleared a huge block of my time, for which you are paying me nicely,' Hannah said with a quick smile. 'I'll be on the road with you as long as you need me. I may have to spend some time working with my other clients, but Nate will be my first priority. We'll put him back on top, and make sure he stays there.'

Sam spread his hands, giving her an easy grin. 'What more could I ask for?'

Hannah crossed her legs, smoothing her skirt over stockinged thighs. 'You've been with him a long time.' She knew he had: he'd been Nate's manager all those years ago when she'd met Nate so briefly.

'Yeah,' he said. Sam's ankle rested on his knee. His foot bounced restlessly. 'Ever since I heard him sing in a little bar in Redwood City. The band he was with was mediocre, but he stood out. Women swooned whenever they heard his voice, and the music he could pull out of his guitar showed me he had true talent. The rest is history.'

'Hardly,' Hannah said with a laugh. She twisted a lock of hair back from her cheek. 'It was two years before you got him a recording contract.'

Sam's eyebrows arched. He gave a rueful smile. 'I knew you'd do your homework. Nate's music was just out of the mainstream, always has been. Boy bands were in and Nate just didn't fit the image. He's never been the innocent charmer that mothers would accept on their daughters' walls. He's the one who steals their daughters' hearts, makes them hunger for something forbidden. And deep down, where they'll never admit it, the mothers want him, too.'

Hannah suppressed a shudder at the thought of her mother and Nate. 'Women love a bad boy,' she said.

Wasn't that the truth.

'Your work paid off,' she said. She liked Sam Granby, she decided. He was blunt and focused, but there was an energy about him that came out in small ways, in the twitch of his foot, the play of his fingers. His enthusiasm filled the room, and she sensed that he used it as a tool to get what he wanted.

'Yes, it did,' Sam said. 'But there were days I'd have gladly gotten him a choreographer and taught him some dance moves to get him noticed.'

Hannah laughed at the image. She had a great imagination, and Nate had long featured in it, but there was no way she could stretch it to include him in a trendy hat and earnest expression, bopping across the stage.

'He got his first hit off the CD we were marketing at the clubs,' Sam said. He used the pencil to point at one of the records framed on the wall.

'"Strange Desires",' Hannah murmured.

Growing up in an industry household, she'd actively avoided a real interest in popular music. The artists who came to her house for meetings or parties were just her father's colleagues and business associates, nobody special. They treated her like the little kid that she was, or ignored her, and if she heard their music on the radio, it was with little more than a passing note.

Until one day, hanging out with a friend, she caught the 'Strange Desires' video on MTV.

Her adolescent hormones flared, her heart fluttered and an hour later she was at the Galleria, intent on finding the CD. The band was named Fox, but it was Nate's show all the way. He was the only one she had any interest in.

So she hadn't really had to research the nuances of his career for this job. She could, in fact, recite them by heart.

A local DJ had picked up 'Strange Desires' and played it on a show featuring new music, and the song took off. That led to a recording contract and Fox's first platinum album. He won Best New Artist that year, and his second CD showed that he wasn't a one-hit wonder.

'He was riding so high,' she said to Sam. 'What happened to him, Sam?' She was aware of the almost wistful tone in her voice.

Sam gave a short laugh. 'He took to the life like he was born to it. Started believing too much in his own PR. Too many long nights, too much partying on top of a brutal schedule. He started with a few pick-me-ups and it all went downhill.'

'And now we have to get him back on top,' Hannah said. 'Luckily, bad PR isn't the death knell it used to be. If we do it right, we can turn it around and he'll be the golden boy of the music business again.'

'That's what I want,' Sam said. He glanced at his watch. 'Why don't you see if you can track down Nate and then we can get out of here and get some dinner?'

'Sounds great,' Hannah said. 'I'll have to call Gina and let her know where to meet us.'

Sam named a restaurant and Hannah made a quick note of it before standing up. As she stood, her eyes wandered once again to the poster.

She was about to meet him again. That thought made her mouth dry up. Other parts of her weren't so lucky.

Just looking at a picture of him had her hot and needy. How on earth was she going to be able to handle him in the flesh?

The fantasy of handling him in the flesh was not helping her state of mind.

But she had to. She was a professional. She was going to represent him, and she was going to do a damn good job. And then, after she'd gotten him back to the top of the charts, she was going to seduce him and give him the most mind-blowing night of his life. And hers, too.

First, though, she had to get through meeting him again, and dinner. One baby step at a time.

Sam had said the studio that Nate was in was down the hall and to the right. She stopped in the ladies' room first. A swipe of dark-red lipstick and a dab of powder and her confidence was restored. She made a quick call to Gina who had just landed and was dealing with her camera equipment. Her friend promised to be at the restaurant in time for dinner.

A last look in the restroom mirror and she was as ready as she was going to get.

Hannah peered through the glass in the studio's door. The recording booth was empty, but through the window that separated it from the performance room, she saw Nate Fox again.

He sat at a piano, his back to the door. That surprised her. She'd have thought he would be playing his guitar. Her heart gave a curious thud and she felt adrenaline shoot through her body, heightening her senses. Glossy black hair fell over the collar of his teal-blue shirt, shorter than it used to be, but still long enough to wrap around her fingers. The muscles of his shoulders moved easily beneath the shirt as he played, and she imagined running her fingers up his back, over his shoulders . . .

Music spilled out when she opened the door. It was one of his older songs; she recognized it immediately. She closed her eyes, letting the music wash over her, absorbing it through her pores. It reminded her of thunder on a sunny day, coming unexpectedly, promising rain and wind and raw power.

Hannah slipped inside to stand unobtrusively just next to the doorway connecting the rooms. She knew in theory what all of the knobs and levers and lights did – she couldn't have grown up the daughter of a producer without picking up a few things – but it had never been where her interest lay. She was fascinated by public versus private persona, by media, by the psychology of it all.

And she was fascinated by Nate Fox.

She was within a few yards of him, but he hadn't seen her yet. He was obviously lost in the music. He leaned back so far she thought he'd tumble over except for the fact that she'd seen him perform the maneuver in music videos and on stage.

He played the final few notes, then his hands stilled on the keyboard. For a moment, he sat, arched back, eyes closed, listening to the music fade away.

Then he opened his eyes and saw Hannah.

Chapter Two

Nate stared. Even upside down, the woman standing by the door was a knock-down, drop-dead stunner. He hadn't heard anyone come in ... Maybe the blood had all rushed to his head and was making him hallucinate? It had never happened before, but if this was a hallucination, he was perfectly happy to have it continue.

He sat up and spun around on the stool. The vision was still there, which implied she wasn't a mirage. Even better.

She had long red hair that looked as though it would feel like fairy gossamer if he touched it. She had a redhead's creamy skin and a pair of amazing grey eyes.

And then there were her legs. Oh my, her legs. Her suit skirt was tasteful even though it was short, and her strappy high heels accentuated the line of her calf and the strength of her thighs. He imagined running his hands along those legs, and felt his cock stir. It took all of his concentration to wrest his mind away from the lustful thoughts, before his leather pants announced to the world what he was thinking.

The woman took a graceful step away from the wall. 'Nice performance,' she said. 'I hope I'm not interrupting.'

'Oh, not at all,' he said. He stood and held out his hand. 'Nathaniel Fox. But you can call me Nate.'

'Hannah Montgomery.'

His hand tightened on hers. The bones of her hand were delicate, but her grip was strong. The gaze that met his was confident and assessing. An exotic scent, light and heady, stole around him. He found himself wanting to breathe it in and wondered if it would be stronger there at the soft skin beneath her ear. 'The infamous Hannah. I'm honored.'

'I'm infamous?' she asked. Her voice was just the tiniest bit husky, which he found incredibly sexy. He'd liked it on the phone. He liked it even better in person. He wondered how it sounded when she cried out in passion.

'Of course,' he said, forcing himself to stay with the conversation. 'The woman who saved Jenna Glenn's ass? Who rejuvenated the career of Simone DePaolo? Who helped take Double Zero out of the realm of boy bands and into the adult market?' He was suddenly glad he'd paid attention to Sam's list of her credentials. 'We've all been intrigued.'

She smiled, just a little, revealing a dimple in her left cheek. 'Intriguing. I like that.' She trailed her tongue across her bottom lip, moistening the curve.

Nate wanted to follow the path of her tongue with his own. His grip on her hand loosened, but only to trace his fingers on her palm. He wondered how far she would allow the flirting to go. 'So do I,' he said. 'I hope I'll get the opportunity to get to know you better.'

Hannah grazed Nate's palm with her fingernails, smiling appreciatively when she saw him draw in a sharp breath. 'You will. Sam wants me to be hands-on with the PR. We'll be seeing a lot of each other.'

'I'm looking forward to it,' he said.

'So am I,' she purred, and finally let go of his hand. He still felt the tingle of her sharp caress on his palm. And it had shot all the way to his cock, leaving him uncomfortable and suddenly looking forward to what he'd previously expected to be a boring dinner.

'Sam sent me to fetch you,' Hannah said, and the thought of being fetched by her sounded amazingly kinky, the way she said it.

Nate spread his hands. 'I'm at your mercy.' He wondered if she knew how much he meant it. Nate picked up his jacket and gestured for her to precede him out the door.

Which he did not only out of politeness, but also because it provided him with a fine view of her ass.

The sway of Hannah's hips masked the shaking of her knees. Dear Lord, he was flirting with her. She hadn't expected that to happen quite so fast. Was he like this with every woman?

Then she decided that it didn't matter. He was flirting with her, and she was going to take every advantage of it. The fact that he showed an interest would make her goal that much easier to attain. She would tease him into insanity, make him long for her the way she'd always wanted him. Then, after she'd repaired his image and got him back into the realm of rock gods, she would have him. *After* her job was done. She'd better keep reminding herself of that.

Still, the fact that he showed such a strong interest – as evidenced by the clear outline of his thickening cock against the line of his pants – thrilled her to the core.

It was all she could do not to touch him in the elevator. Nate dominated the small space, filling it with his warmth and deep earthy scent. Her heels brought her closer to his height, but there was something about him that made her feel petite, delicate. She felt the pull of him, felt it down deep inside where it made her blood rush. And he did it all without even trying. He just leaned casually against the wall, making the silk of his shirt stretch against his chest, widening the V above the buttons at the top. Blue eyes edging into black watched her with an intensity that made her very aware of herself as a woman.

The sweat on his neck looked very enticing. Hannah wanted to run her tongue along it. His black leather pants laced up the front, and she ached to unlace them with her teeth. She wanted to hear his reaction to that.

But she behaved. There would be time enough to seduce him, even if she had to wait. She'd waited all these years. She understood patience. Hannah smiled at that, feeling a great sense of satisfaction when Nate's gaze went to her mouth.

The elevator seemed to be heating up. If there had been mirrored tiles on the walls, Hannah was sure they'd be steamed. Of course, she might not have been able to keep her hands to herself if they had been. The urge to see herself wrapped around his semi-naked body would have been too much to resist.

His reaction to her now more than made up for his reaction all those years ago at the bottom of her stairs. If he'd looked at her then like he wanted to push her up against the wall and bury himself inside of her, she wouldn't have had a clue what to do.

Now she'd have no problem thinking of a response.

The elevator jerked to a halt, the doors hissed open. Nate straightened, pushing one hand through his hair, disheveling the already tousled strands. He gave her a smile that made her thong damp, and then followed her into the foyer where Sam was waiting for them.

Hannah smiled at Sam when they joined him. She had to pull herself together. Had to stop mentally peeling the clothes off of Nate and urging him to touch her.

She was a professional. She could do this.

Sam had made reservations for them at a Japanese place, one of Nate's favorites. Gina walked in while Sam was speaking to the hostess. She gave Nate a slow once over and then greeted Hannah with a hug, pausing long enough to whisper, 'He's hot!'

Oh yeah, Hannah thought. And he was going to be hers.

She introduced her friend to Nate and Sam, and then the solemn hostess led them to a private room, separated from the main area by sliding shoji screens. An American-style table surrounded by four chairs was a concession to the clientele, but it was decorated by a simple spray of blossoms in a pottery bowl, an arrangement displaying the traditional feeling of *shebui*. Hannah found herself at one side of the table, with Nate just around the corner.

Oh yes. Perfect.

He seemed pleased by the arrangement, too. He held out her chair for her, and afterwards let his hand trail along her shoulder before he sat down. When he did, his leg brushed against hers beneath the table, the contact lingering for a moment. She sensed he was still close, an inch from her.

The gentle notes of a samisen fell into their initial silence, joined by the haunting tones of a wooden flute as they perused their menus. Hannah found the music somewhat wistful, and took a deep breath, letting it out slowly. The server poured green tea into fragile porcelain bowls for them, and the fragrance joined the assault on her senses.

She had to remember the plan. The job came first, and then she would be free to seduce Nate Fox.

She darted a glance at him and found him looking back at her. A smile quirked his mouth, only for her, and heat pooled at the juncture of her thighs. Maybe the plan needed to be rethought. Maybe she'd do a better job working with him if she weren't so tuned to his body. Get the lust out of the way, then settle down to business. It was so hard to concentrate when every nerve in her body hummed with awareness.

The petite server, dressed in a pale-rose kimono, took their orders. Gina and Sam ordered teriyaki. Hannah rolled her eyes, called them wimps, and ordered sushi. Nate followed suit, obviously knowledgeable about the cuisine.

'One of the things I love about San Francisco is the fresh seafood,' he said. 'I miss that when I'm on the road.'

'It must be tough, being away from home so many days out of the year,' Gina said.

'It can get tiring,' Nate agreed. 'Sometimes it's a struggle to keep up the energy and enthusiasm.'

It was an obvious reference to his past drug use. Was it also a warning that he was afraid he would succumb again?

It wasn't her job to be his therapist or his mother. It was her job to make him look good, no matter what. She'd dealt with this before, with clients who were determined to destroy themselves. She'd hated every damn second of it: of watching them fuck up, again and again; of struggling to find some way to downplay it or hide it or make some big commotion over here to distract everyone from it.

Early in her career, when she worked for a label, one of the artists had OD'd, found with the rubber strap still digging into his flesh and the needle still in his hand. He hadn't been her client, but she'd helped with his campaign.

She closed her eyes. If Nate was headed in that direction, maybe it was better to leave him as her teenage fantasy, as a poster on her wall. Just do what she'd been hired to do, and if he imploded, she'd just move on to the next job.

But when she opened her eyes again, he was watching, and she had the sense that he knew what she'd been thinking. She shivered under his gaze.

'I imagine touring has its perks as well,' she said, making an effort to lighten the mood.

'Room service,' he said with a slow smile, his eyes never leaving hers.

The words conjured up a specific image: Nate, naked and sleep-tousled, groping for the phone to order up morning coffee and croissants. Hannah ran her tongue along her lower lip again.

'Yes, there's definitely something to be said for someone bringing you breakfast in bed after a long hard night,' she said, and took a slow sip of her tea, her eyes teasing him over the bowl's rim.

'My parents and I did some traveling when I was young, and I loved it,' Gina said. 'Europe was spectacular. I'd love to go back.'

'It's certainly more interesting than Bays Junction, Wisconsin, or Willington, Kansas,' Nate said. 'I spend a lot of time in places like that – although I think I spend even more time on the tour bus.'

'The thrilling life of a rock star,' Hannah said with a laugh. 'What about the image of the fancy hotels, the parties, the champagne luxury? Don't burst our bubble.'

'The beds in the tour bus, the tiny bathroom, no privacy,' Nate put in. The laughter in his eyes told her he was teasing her now, understanding her worry and trying to get a rise out of her.

Hannah had fantasized enough over the years about a narrow intimate bunk on the bus, the swaying motion of the moving vehicle urging them closer ... She swallowed hard, struggling to maintain a professional demeanor. Throwing him onto the table and ripping open his shirt was not the image she was going for.

'Funny you should mention that,' Sam said, the upward quirk of one eyebrow showing he wasn't oblivious to the undercurrents of the conversation. His porcelain chopsticks clattered faintly as he played with them, his fingers constantly moving. 'I hope you're comfortable with the idea of being on a tour bus with a bunch of male musicians.'

'Isn't that every woman's fantasy?' Gina asked. Her raised eyebrows told Hannah that she was well aware of what Hannah had been fantasizing about. 'Having a bunch of rock stars all to yourself ...'

'I'm sure it will be fine,' Hannah assured Sam. She was just not going to look at Gina again. Nope. 'We're all professionals.'

'I'm not so sure it's a good idea,' Nate said. She heard his reluctance, saw the look he shot Sam.

'It's part of the game,' Hannah said. She looked at him, her eyes lingering on the lean planes of his face. His mouth was sensually sculpted, the bottom lip just a little fuller. Yum. 'I can put out a thousand press releases that tell the world you're back on top, but they're all just words – let's *show* everyone. I can do that best by being right there, ready to put the spin on everything that happens.'

'Everything?' he asked softly. His eyes glittered with a look that was just for her. Oh my, the man knew how to flirt.

She found herself getting excited by the prospect of going on tour with the band, and not just by Nate's proximity and those enticing leather pants. 'Think of it as your opportunity to redesign your image. I'll be there to guide the publicity in the direction you want it to go. Show how this tour's not like the excesses of the past, how you're no longer the type to get high and throw TVs through the window or have a string of groupies lined up outside your hotel room door.'

'Are you sure about that?' he asked, a glint of amusement in his dark eyes.

'Well, we'll have to negotiate about the groupies.' Hannah's stomach twisted uncomfortably. She didn't want to think about the groupies. Fact was, they had little or nothing to do with Nate's former drug habit. If he wanted to flaunt them, that was his decision.

She just knew she couldn't compete with the skinny, barely dressed types that followed rock stars around. Much less the gorgeous starlets and supermodels he'd been seen with in the past.

'So, you tell me,' Hannah said. 'What's the image that you want to portray?'

'What do you think?' he asked. His eyes challenged her to answer.

Her head tipped to one side while she considered. 'I think there's a difference between how you want to be seen and what the public expects to see. If it's a primarily male demographic, then the groupies and the parties let the boys fantasize about the perks of being a rock star. A little T & A always boosts sales. But if we're marketing more toward your female fans, that's not what they want to see. They want the fantasy that they might be the one you pluck out of the crowd, the fan in the fourteenth row who gets noticed.'

'So the possibility is that some fans get to ... meet me ... might fuel *their* fantasies,' Nate said.

'Do you want to be someone's fantasy?' she asked, realizing too late that he might see it as a come-on. She felt her cheeks flush.

'Speaking as a woman as well as a visual artist, I'd say there's a fine line,' Gina said, smoothly filling in what might have become an awkward silence. 'Capitalizing on a female fan's fantasies is good, but too much of a bad boy, the sense that they just wouldn't be able to hold onto you, is too much. They'll feel inadequate.'

Hannah sent a mental note of relieved thanks in Gina's direction for filling the void Hannah's temporary panic had left.

'Gina's right,' she said. 'The bottom line is that the music is what ties it all together. We feed the fantasies of both sides: the bad boy rock star who walks a little on the wild side, and the dark brooding musician who can be caught and tamed. But it's your music that spans both of those visions. And your music has always been your real love, not the fame or lifestyle. Am I right?'

He nodded.

'Then we need to show that. We need to show that you're clean again, that the wildness of your past is gone, but not completely destroy the mystique of the musician's life. We want the men to want to be like you and the women to want you.'

There was respect in his eyes. The sudden realization that he appreciated her business sense was more of a turn-on than she would have thought possible. It shocked her.

'So what do you think, Nate?' Sam broke in. 'Hannah's right about the positive look at a drug-free but still exciting life on the road. You can be the bad boy that your fans expect, while showing them that you take your music seriously. Your fans will find you hot *and* inspirational. It's a winner of a publicity concept.'

'It's an interesting idea,' Nate conceded.

Hannah, however, wasn't finished. 'No matter what you decide, Nate, there's one thing that we have to be completely clear on. You need to be one-hundred-percent honest with me. I need to know what you're thinking, what you're doing and what you're going to say. There can't be any surprises, or I won't be able to do the job you expect.'

He started to speak, but she held up one hand, stopping him.

'I know you're clean now, but I've seen a lot in this business and I know that the pressures will pile up. If you feel the need for a pick-me-up, I want to know. If you get drunk and pass out in an alley, I want to know about it before the press does. And if you stay sober, I need to know that too. I can't work for you if I don't know what I'm going to get hit with.'

The world tightened to a single point of contact with his eyes. 'I need honesty, Nate, and I won't settle for anything less.'

The moment stretched, and she felt certain that he was going to get up and walk out. But he didn't. He gave a tiny, almost imperceptible nod. She nodded back, relieved more than she'd expected to be. They'd reached an agreement.

A shoji screen slid soundlessly back, admitting the server with a tray of miso soup and the bottles of wine and saki that they'd ordered. She began to ladle the soup into individual bowls, the steam sending tantalizing wafts of spices into the room.

Nate leaned toward Hannah, taking the opportunity to speak quietly while Gina and Sam were occupied with the woman's motions. 'You impress me.'

'What is this with "i" words?' she murmured, taking another sip of tea and keeping eye contact with him. 'I'm infamous, intriguing, impressive . . .'

He moved so that his lips were next to her ear. His breath was warm, raising goosebumps along the sensitive flesh of her neck. She had to put her tea down so he wouldn't see her hands shake.

'Intoxicating,' he said. 'Igniting.' His tongue flicked out and slid against her earlobe. 'Impassioned.'

Hannah stifled a whimper by biting on her lower lip, which, she realized, was probably even more enticing.

Nate Fox was coming on to her. To *her*.

She hadn't anticipated the tables being turned on her. She'd figured she'd do her job, get to know him and seduce him at some point along the way. Ideally, she'd tease him until he was a helpless slave to her desires.

The fact that he was seducing her was an incredible aphrodisiac. She shifted in her seat so that her leg was brushing against his again. The nylon of her stocking slithered against the leather of his pants.

'You can tell all that from just one meeting?' she asked. She was trying not to think about sliding under the table. She loved the smell of leather.

'First impressions are crucial,' he said, pressing his thigh against hers. 'Plus, you're infamous, remember? You have a knack for turning the bad into something good, and you seem to bring out the best in people. You inspire musicians. There's another "i" word. I'm sure people have been dying to know how you do it.'

'Music is a passion of mine, but I'll freely admit I'm crap at it,' Hannah said. 'Can't sing, can't play an instrument. The best I can do is dance to it. But I knew I wanted to be a part of it somehow. I realized that there are so many incredible musicians and bands out there that never get a break, despite their talent, and I wanted to help. Plus –' she lifted one shoulder in an artless shrug '– I'm good at what I do. I can think fast, talk fast and put a spin on something so fast it'll leave you breathless.'

She wanted to make him breathless. She wanted him gasping her name as she – oh no, not going there. She had to get control of this or she would lose her mind.

She shifted away just a little. She had to catch her breath, and Gina had turned to look at her, curiosity in her green eyes.

'I've always been curious about the song "Winter King" from your first album,' Hannah said, grabbing at the first thing she could find. It was true she'd always wondered about the song. 'I absolutely love the time change in the chorus. What prompted you to write it that way?'

The amused glitter in Nate's eyes told her he knew exactly why she'd changed the subject. One long finger traced the weave in the linen tablecloth, while his leg continued to press against hers beneath the table. 'I wanted the feeling of melancholy that winter brings out in so many people. I wanted to keep the listener unsure of what was coming next. I wanted them haunted by the images of ice and death.'

'That's a good image,' Hannah said. 'I always felt a little sad listening to it.' She scooped a generous amount of wasabi into the small ceramic bowl in front of her, then added just enough soy sauce to make the concoction liquid. She stirred it idly with one blue-painted chopstick. She noticed Nate watching her actions.

'I like it this way,' she said. 'Very refreshing.' And very hot. But saying that would be just too over the top, wouldn't it? The motion of his thigh was maddening. He had so much energy ... She imagined that sex with him would be the same: relentless. The dull ache between her legs throbbed with her heartbeat.

Thankfully their meals arrived, before she took the thought any further and had to go to the bathroom to wring out her thong. She sighed at the plate full of California rolls and spicy crab rolls.

She reached for one. 'I never could handle chopsticks,' she said conversationally as she picked up a roll with her fingers and dunked it generously into the bowl. Raising it to her mouth, she bit into it, swallowed, then slid the second half into her mouth. She let a soft sigh of gratification break from her lips.

It had the intended effect on Nate. When she licked the wasabi off her fingers, he looked away, ducking his head so that his dark hair fell in his eyes. She saw his throat convulse as he swallowed.

'So, Gina, what got you into photography?' Sam asked.

'I wanted a backstage pass to an N'Sync concert.'

Sam sputtered into his sake.

Gina laughed. 'No, really. I talked my way backstage with a camera I borrowed from my dad and a press pass a friend copied from one he saw online. I was lucky that security sucked. No one bothered to look too closely. I got to meet the band, I got some cool shots.' She shrugged. 'I was hooked.'

Sam raised his cup. 'Here's to ingenuity.'

They joined him in his toast, enjoying the easy laughter.

Hannah found herself relaxing, the tension of the day slowly seeping from her shoulders. Things were going to be OK.

Then Nate's hand came to rest on her knee, lingering a moment before starting a slow trip upward. She forgot how to breathe when he found the lace edge of her stocking. If he kept that up, she would never be able to keep her hands off of him. Then his fingers started to move again, exploring along the edge of the lace, slipping just underneath, running his fingertips along the sensitive flesh of her upper thigh. The sensation turned her bones to liquid, and she had to bite her bottom lip to keep from moaning.

Hannah gripped the stem of the wine glass to keep her hand from trembling. She took a hefty swallow. If his fingers drifted any higher, if he touched the place that ached for him so badly, she was going to come, right there at the table. Gina would never let her live it down.

Besides, they had to leave something for later. And she was very much afraid that later would come sooner than she'd planned.

She'd known all along that where Nate was concerned her common sense went right out of the window, and it was beginning to look like her professionalism was going to join it.

Hannah refused to let him know just how tempted she was to ask the others to leave so that she could climb onto his lap and taste his mouth with hers. She pressed her thighs together, hard, trapping his hand, and blithely ate another piece of sushi. She covered his fingers with hers, boldly sliding his hand farther up her thigh, to a point where he could feel the heat radiating from her crotch. She could hear his breathing change, a little more ragged now, though he tried to cover it by wiping his mouth with his napkin.

Placing his hand firmly back on his own lap, Hannah curled her fingers into the lacing of his pants. She tugged gently. He was hard and thick beneath her fingers, and she smiled appreciatively. Then it was his turn to grab her wrist and remove her hand.

She retaliated by offering him a piece of sushi. He somehow managed to trap her fingers in his mouth, sucking gently before letting her go. Her nipples tingled, wanting to receive the same attention. The way he flicked his tongue against her fingertips was a promise of things to come. Namely her.

Gina coughed, and kicked her in the side of her foot. Heat slipped into Hannah's cheeks as she realized she and Nate had become the entertainment portion of the meal. But she still couldn't keep from smiling, even as she deftly found something else innocuous to talk about.

The dinner meeting ended soon thereafter. As they walked to the front door, Nate put his hand on Hannah's arm and slowed her pace. He drew her close to his side, taking possession of her space.

'How about a nightcap?' he asked. 'I know a great wine bar a few blocks away.'

A chance to have a private drink with Nate Fox? Like there was any question.

Hannah leaned into him a little, and nodded. Slipping out of his grasp, she walked out the door that Sam was holding for her. She snagged Gina and drew her to one side, whispering the change of plans.

'Oh, there's a *big* surprise,' Gina said.

'I'll let you know just how big tomorrow,' Hannah said giddily.

Gina snorted and got into the limo that was waiting curbside.

Hannah and Nate stood outside the restaurant and watched the limo pull away. She shivered a little. A hint of fog had rolled in, cooling the night air.

'There's no wine bar, is there?' Hannah asked, tipping her head back to look at him.

'Nope,' he confessed. His arm was around her waist,

his fingers resting warmly against the underside of her breast.

'We're going to your place, aren't we?'

'Yep.'

'Your intentions with me aren't at all honorable, are they?'

He smiled, left eyebrow arching.

She couldn't help but smile back, even as she said, 'Do you sleep with all your publicists, Mr Fox?'

'Only the intoxicating ones.'

'And how was your working relationship with them afterward?'

'I don't usually think that far ahead,' he said. 'I tend to act on impulse.'

His thumb slowly stroked the curve of her breast, a light touch, but one that made it hard for her to concentrate.

'Well, I'll still be working for you come tomorrow,' she managed, trying desperately to talk them both out of this. 'It's my job to think ahead.'

He moved in front of her, tipped her chin up with gentle fingers so there was no way for her to escape his gaze. 'It's obvious that we're attracted to each other. See?'

This time, he initiated the kiss.

This time, she knew what to do.

After all of the flirting and teasing, she wouldn't have thought a mere kiss could do so much. But the touch of his lips against hers added fuel to the embers, and heat flared.

Heat, and burning desire.

He caressed, teased, and then deepened the kiss, claiming her. Her hands splayed across his strong back, pulling him closer. Their bodies molded together. She met his tongue, and all she could imagine was it elsewhere on her body, urging her to higher levels of passion and need until she . . .

He drew away. She could feel his heart pounding, knew he was just as aroused as she. Good. It gave her a moment to recover. She licked her lips, and his eyes followed the movement.

'You see what I mean?' he asked. 'Can we work effectively if we're constantly . . . distracted?'

'I can see where it might become a problem.' Hannah nodded slowly. Light from a nearby street lamp threw silver into his hair, made shadows pool in his eyes. 'So, you're suggesting we should get it out of our systems?'

'Exactly.'

She took a deep breath. She hadn't intended for it to happen so quickly.

But she'd been planning this, waiting for this for nine years. Waiting and wanting.

Now *want* was rapidly turning into *need*.

She reached up and toyed with the silky strands of his hair. Nine years. 'Then what are we waiting for?' she asked.

Chapter Three

His house was a short walk away, in a tree-lined district of Victorian homes. Inside, Hannah got a brief glimpse of the décor – red walls and wooden beams, stained-glass panels above the doors. A music room was visible through an archway, complete with a black baby grand and a row of guitars. Nate led her, unprotesting, up the sweep of stairs, his fingers linked with hers.

Hannah was so aroused that she was breathless by the time they reached the second floor. Part of her kept insisting that it was too soon, she needed to keep her professional life in focus. The other part of her, the part that was panting with hunger, could only think of Nate, and the teenage vow she'd made so many years ago. They were just at the doorway to his bedroom. She caught a glimpse of a wide four-poster bed before he pushed her against the doorjamb and kissed her.

Hard.

Hannah knew, vaguely, that it was the final test. Her last chance to protest, to back out. Say the word, push him away, and that would be the end of it.

The wooden edge of the door pushed into her back, sharp and unyielding. Nate's body was just as solid, his heat warming her, causing flames to lap at her self-control. He wanted her.

Nate Fox wanted her.

Anyone else and she could have maintained her professional decorum, but the heady realization of his desire for her had shut down her thought processes.

The shaggy hair at the sides of his head was soft, and she wove her fingers through it to pull him deeper into the kiss, just as she'd done as a teenager. This time, however, he kissed her much harder, until he was bruising her lips. She matched him, kiss for kiss, curling one leg around his calf. She could feel his arousal pressing into her stomach, and she rocked her hips to pleasure them both. The low growl he made was gratifying, the hands that tightened on her hips even more so.

They broke apart, gasping. 'Breathe,' Nate crooned. His mouth was temptingly close, and she leaned forward to run the tip of her tongue across his bottom lip.

'Why?' Hannah asked, his taste lingering in her mouth. Spices and desire. Sin and satisfaction. 'Aren't you trying to make me pass out?'

He laughed huskily. He nuzzled her throat, teeth scraping gently just above her pulse. 'Not just yet,' he said. 'There's a lot more I intend to do to you before I let you rest.'

'Promise?'

'Hell, yes.' He dragged her into the room. A tall lamp in the corner was lit, illuminating the bed with its headboard and footboard of wrought-iron vertical posts, the corners ending in what looked like crystal balls. The sheets and bedspread were pristine white.

Hannah clawed at the buttons on his silk shirt, opening it nearly to the waist before pressing her lips to the smooth flesh that was revealed. A light dusting of hair swirled around his nipples. Her fingernails trailed through it, following it down to his belt. He pulled the rest of the shirt out of his waistband and tore it off over his head. It caught on one of his wrists, and he brought the silk up to rub against her cheek. She moaned.

Nate's fingers fumbled with the tie at the back of her jacket, and when it fell apart he ripped the garment off her shoulders, dragging it down her arms. It flew, landing somewhere on the floor. She didn't care. The evergreen lace cami followed, eased over her head with a speed she found exciting. He took her breasts in his hands and pressed his mouth to them, nuzzling the deep valley between.

Hannah tipped her head back, her eyes closed as she savored the sensations. Her body demanded more, moving restlessly in his hands. She was desperate for his mouth to give her what she needed, and she was shocked to hear herself beg. Nate's thumbs flicked the nipples that were outlined against the lace. Before she could react to the liquid ache his caress sent curling through her veins, his mouth closed over her, suckling her nipples through the material. The sensation filled her with heat.

Hannah grabbed his hair again; it seemed like the only thing holding her up as her knees started to buckle. He realized, and caught her, only to slide down the zipper of her skirt so that it parted and fell to the floor. She managed to kick it away.

He backed up then, just a few paces, and stared at her, his eyes dark with appreciation – no, downright lust – as he took in the lacy bra and thong, stockings and heels. The look he was giving her made her thighs tremble.

She wasn't going to be able to stand up much longer.

So, she took matters into her own hands. She flashed him a smile, then turned and sauntered over to the bed, giving him a full view of her ass framed by the thong. Then she sat on the bed and crooked her finger at him. She didn't have to do it twice. Nate hurtled across the room and dropped to his knees in front of her.

Hannah leaned back on her elbows as he slowly ran his strong hands up her legs, from ankles to calves to thighs – where again he toyed with the edges of her stockings – and back down again. Deftly he slipped her shoes off and tossed them aside. She ran her toes across his chest, sliding over his nipples. He grabbed her ankles and set them on his shoulders, and began tracing the route his hands had taken with his tongue.

Up her calves ... her thighs ... along the edge of the lace, on the sensitive bare skin of her legs close to her crotch. Her thighs quivered and she could smell her own arousal. Her clit throbbed as he gently sucked her skin into his mouth. The fantasies she'd had about him had been numerous, but not a single one had even come close to this. She wanted to fall back on the bed, but she wanted to watch even more.

As if reading her thoughts, he looked up at her, his wicked smile a promise of things to come. Hannah didn't have to try to look seductive. She knew her eyes revealed exactly how she felt. She wanted him.

Nate gave a low laugh and tugged at the edge of her thong. She raised her hips obligingly so he could slide it off. His eyes darkened when he noted that she shaved, then he dipped his head back down and blew warm air across her crotch. Hannah moaned. His breath added heat to the fire that was already raging.

She reached out with one hand to pull his face closer, but he resisted. Instead, he stood and reached behind her to unsnap her bra and fling it; she was vaguely aware of it catching on a bedpost and dangling there. He pushed her back on the bed and straddled her legs, the leather that covered his thighs cool against her heated skin. He leaned over and scraped his teeth across one of her nipples. At the same time, his fingers did similar things to her other breast. Lightning shot through her.

Hannah squirmed her hips, clutching at his muscular shoulders, unable to move very far. God, she didn't think she'd ever been so aroused. He was making her feel things she hadn't thought her body was capable of.

'Please,' she moaned, and he laughed softly again. The velvet sound of his voice wrapped around her, almost tangible in the pleasure it gave.

Hannah arched up a little, brushing against his leather pants, gasping with triumph when his hands clenched convulsively. But he didn't stop what he was doing, didn't stop the scrape of his teeth, the tantalizing draw of his mouth. A sizzling line of fire was trailing from her breasts, down her body to her crotch.

When it reached her clit, the dynamite went off. Hannah cried out, her eyes closing as pleasure exploded, her body fragmenting as the waves continued with each lazy pull of his lips.

The fire slowly faded, the twitching subsided.

This had never happened before. What was he doing to her? She stared at him, gasping, astonished and drippingly aroused. If that's how she reacted to him playing with her breasts, what was going to happen next?

'Breathe,' he said again, placing a trail of sharp bites down the side of her neck. 'I've only just gotten started with you. I wonder . . .'

'What?' Hannah gasped. She looked up into his midnight-blue eyes and felt herself falling.

'I wonder how many times I can make you come tonight,' he said, and slid down between her legs.

Before she had time to fully process the weight of what he'd said, he flicked his tongue against her nether lips. Instantly, the languorous feeling of satisfaction dissolved, sending her spiraling again toward pleasure.

He traced the cleft between her thighs, easing away when she arched closer, teasingly light in the contact. Using his thumbs, he separated her folds and his tongue sampled the rich cream within. Hannah almost came unglued. He caressed her in maddening circles, tasting her everywhere except where she desperately needed him to be. Her hands clenched the soft comforter into mounds, her hips arching. His laugh rumbled against her, vibrating, sending waves of pleasure through her lower belly.

But it always took her forever to come again this way . . .

Then his tongue found the sensitive nub of secret flesh, swirling a slow caress across it.

This time, she screamed.

'Lie up across the bed,' Nate said after she stopped hyperventilating.

'I can't,' she said. 'My legs don't work anymore. I'm not entirely sure I even have legs.'

'Oh, believe me, you do. Luscious, incredible legs. Legs that have been driving me wild all evening. I can't wait to feel them wrapped around my neck.'

Hannah whimpered. Her fantasy had escalated beyond her wildest imaginings. And never in any fantasy had she given him such complete control over her.

Nate helped her lay back so her head was cradled by the fluffy white pillows. He stood on the bed over her, and she reached up for the laces of his leather pants. She sat up and pressed her face into the crotch, inhaling the scent of leather and feeling his erection press against her cheek. He watched her intently as she fumbled with the knot, his breathing rapid. The fabric parted, and she saw that he wasn't wearing underwear.

Hannah leaned back, admiring, as he slowly peeled off the pants and tossed them away. She reached out a hand but he shook his head. Eventually she dragged her eyes away from his impressive cock and looked up. When she caught his gaze, he smiled.

And did one of his famous leaps into the air.

Hannah shrieked, instinctively stiffening, half-expecting him to land on her. But he bounced on the bed on his hands and knees on either side of her, laughing at her fear. Before she could react, he kissed her, his mouth possessive, allowing no room for any coherent thought. She tasted herself on his tongue, a mixture of his mouth and her juices.

'I was right,' he said when he drew away. 'Intoxicating.'

His tongue began a maddening exploration of her neck while his hand trailed down over her body. He pinched her nipple; paused to cup the curve of her hip; slid lower. Her hips flexed as he dipped a finger inside her, then drew it back out.

His hand moved back down, toying at her outer lips until she thought she'd have to ... well, do something drastic ... before, finally, he drove it inside of her.

His fingers, so talented on the keyboard, proved their talent here. They thrust to the rhythm of her heartbeat, slow at first, and then quickening as her passion mounted. Hannah clutched his shoulders, her fingers digging into the muscle. He was her lifeline and her tormentor and she loved every second of it.

'You just don't know when to stop, do you?' he growled, when the last quivers of her pleasure faded away.

'Not a clue,' she said, gasping for breath. Her hand closed around him, enjoying the feel of smooth skin wrapped around his iron length. She explored with her fingers, rubbing the droplet at the tip of his cock with her thumb. She watched his face, seeing the clenching of his jaw when she teased his sac with her nails.

He rolled away abruptly, and reached to open the nightstand drawer. A foil packet was tossed to the floor as he quickly rolled the condom on. He positioned himself between her thighs, his hand sliding along her body. He cupped her ass and Hannah lifted her legs, pulling them back so that they rested on his shoulders. She was completely open to him.

'Oh yes,' he murmured. 'Wrapped around my neck. Yes.' His pupils were so large that his eyes looked black with desire.

He rested the head of his cock at her slick entrance. Hannah tried to wiggle her hips, tried to take more of him in, but she was in no position to move very far. Her stockinged legs skidded along his shoulders.

'How many was that?' Nate asked. The roughness of his voice gave away just how slender his control was. He rested on his hands, gazing down at her from a matter of inches. The look in his eyes was pure heat.

'How many *what*?' Hannah demanded, frustrated.

His teeth flashed white in his grin. 'How many times have you come so far? Weren't you keeping count? Don't tell me we have to start over.'

Hannah took a deep breath to scream 'Aaaargh!', but the sound was choked off when he thrust into her. He filled her, and she molded around him.

God, but he felt exquisite inside her.

That was her last coherent thought as he moved hard and fast. Clutching at his arms, feeling the rigid muscle of his biceps beneath her palms, Hannah let herself be swept away by sensation. His weight pushed her into the bed, the rocking of his hips swept her along a path of pure sensation.

Then she felt his muscles tighten, felt him tense, and she urged him on, feeling him swell just before he came. The last frantic thrust triggered her yet again.

Nate collapsed on top of her, but kept just enough weight on his elbows so as not to crush her. His breath was hot against her shoulder, his hair tickled her skin. Finally, he rolled to one side, dragging her with him, and draped a leg over hers.

'It's really hard to count,' she said. She gave in to her inclination to nuzzle the skin of his jaw, to breathe deeply of his scent, all warm and clean and male.

'Hmm?'

'Well, I mean, was that a whole bunch of orgasms, or was it one long one with a bunch of peaks?' She waved one hand vaguely in a peaks-and-valleys-type motion. She was vaguely surprised she had the energy left to lift a hand.

Nate opened one eye. He trailed one hand down her side to the damp cleft between her thighs. 'If you don't hush,' he threatened, 'I'll keep going until you pass out.' To prove his point, one finger slid slowly inside of her.

Oh dear Lord . . .

Hannah woke the next morning with sunshine in her eyes. It fell in a shimmering path through the window and across the bed. At some point they'd crawled under the covers and curled together in a warm, sated mass.

Now she stretched, reacting in surprise when she realized Nate was no longer in the bed. His pillow bore an indentation of his head. She rolled over and buried her face in the pillowcase. It smelled like him, warm and intrinsically male. Reluctantly, she eased away from it and crawled out of the bed. Stupid bladder.

With a wry grin, Hannah realized she was still wearing her stockings. She peeled them off and tossed them in the general direction of the rest of her clothing, which was scattered across the hardwood floor. She headed toward the door, then paused. His silk shirt lay at her feet. Biting her lip, she grabbed it and slid it on. It slithered around her, caressing her thighs, reminding her of his touch.

Thankfully, the bathroom was attached to the bedroom; she didn't have to go stumbling through the house to find it.

She sat on the toilet, head in hands, and thought. Her work here was done. She'd fulfilled the promise she'd made to her seventeen-year-old self nine years ago. She'd had her night of passion with Nate Fox.

And *damn*, it had been *good*. It had, in fact, exceeded her expectations. It had been the most mind-blowing, teeth-tingling, toe-curling sex of her life.

Hannah washed her face and peered at herself in the mirror. Her hair was tousled, her natural curls beginning to spring to life. She found his comb and smoothed her hair the best she could. Hopefully, she would look sexy and not frizzy. She fully intended to put on her wrinkled suit and leave. She'd find Nate, give him a kiss to thank him for a wonderful evening and ask him to call her a cab. She'd promised herself one night of passion. Now she'd gotten him out of her system, she could be his publicist without all the sexual tension getting in the way.

But then she sniffed the air, and her stomach growled in response to the wafting odor of bacon. Like the enthusiastic dog in a Beggin' Strips commercial, she followed the scent downstairs. She didn't even bother removing his shirt.

The house had retained its Victorian flavor, right down to the William Morris acanthus-leaf wallpaper. The traditional furniture added to its warm appeal. But the house didn't look lived in. Hannah paused in the living room, glancing around for anything that seemed to be uniquely Nate, and found nothing.

Following her nose, she found Nate in the kitchen. Here at last were the modern additions that made life bearable. Appliances and utensils reflected the best in cooking techniques, designed for style and ease of use. She took it all in with a brief glance before her gaze settled on Nate standing at the stove. He was wearing only an apron, and she was treated to a back view of the big bow framing his tight ass.

Buns for breakfast, anyone?

He must have heard her giggle, because he turned his head to look at her sideways. A tiny smile lifted his mouth and his left eyebrow raised slightly. 'Good morning,' he said.

It was a snapshot straight from one of his videos, a moment she had drooled over repeatedly, hitting the VCR's rewind button over and over again. Now, like a Pavlovian bimbo, her knees went weak in response.

Oh this was not good. He was supposed to be out of her system.

'Good morning,' she managed. 'Nice, ah, apron.'

'You think so?' He turned to show her the front view. It was embossed with big red lips and the words 'Kiss the Cook.'

Of course it was. Hannah fought the urge to laugh hysterically. Low blood sugar. Surely that was it.

'You know,' Nate said, 'I thought you couldn't look sexier than you did in your underwear, but seeing you in my shirt . . . well, damn.' He removed the frying pan of bacon from the heat. Already on the table sat what looked like eggs Benedict and hash browns. That was all Hannah managed to notice before he covered the distance between them with quick strides and swept her up into a kiss.

Chapter Four

His hands gripped her bottom as he pulled her hard against him. She slipped her arms around him, enjoying the feel of smooth hard muscle beneath warm skin. She returned the kiss, sliding her tongue between his lips, losing herself in the sensation of his body against hers. Nate's low growl of approval made her dizzy. She thought she was going to pass out because her heart and lungs just didn't seem to want to work in tempo anymore.

She hadn't intended to get into another clinch, but his presence was just too intoxicating. Nate touched her, and everything but the thought of sex fled from her mind. And it wasn't so much *thought* or *mind* that was involved, really. Just pure animalistic reaction.

Nate picked her up and bodily carried her a few steps to the counter, swiping some dishes into the sink before depositing her on the granite surface. She yelped as her butt hit the cold counter.

'Sorry,' he said. 'Let me distract you.' His teeth grazed the side of her neck. His morning beard abraded her skin. She found it highly erotic. Her shirt fell away from one shoulder, and he nipped her collarbone. In response, she wrapped her legs around his waist. His hips were lean and hard between her thighs, and she slipped forward so that he pressed against her, only the cloth of the apron separating them. She was already wet with arousal.

His hands slid up her sides and onto her breasts. He rubbed the silk over her nipples. When they hardened against his palms, he teased them with his fingers, and Hannah moaned. The mesmerizing sensation was sending slow waves of pleasure through her, all of them ending up in the spot pressed so tightly against his erection.

Reaching up, she latched her hands onto the cupboard handles. Her breasts spilled out through the front of the half-buttoned shirt. Nate didn't need any more invitation than that. His mouth captured one nipple while his fingers pinched the other. Hannah closed her eyes, her breath coming in short gasps. Each slow suckle pushed her closer and closer to the edge. She involuntarily moved her hips in a circular motion, giving in to her arousal. He was hard against her, and when she started grinding against him she felt his teeth clamp down. The flash of pain made her cry out.

'Too much?' he gasped.

'No,' she managed. Borderline, but not too much. The sharpness had intensified the need that pulsated in her clit.

He drew back slightly and slid a hand between them. She moaned again as his fingers found her wet core. He moved his hand lazily, teasing, not bringing her over the edge like she craved. 'I guess so,' he said, displaying his now-glistening fingers. He ran them across her lips, then kissed her again so they could both taste her arousal.

Nate repeated the motion, dipping into her and this time tracing her moistness onto her nipples, then greedily sucking it off. The relentless attention to her breasts was bringing her close to a peak again, and she wondered if she would repeat last night's incredible experience.

She didn't get a chance to find out. Nate continued to nuzzle her breasts as he pulled a condom from his apron pocket. A moment later, the head of his cock nestled at her slick entrance.

She closed her eyes, but Nate's husky 'Look at me' caused her to open them again. They stared at each other as he slowly, steadily entered her, not breaking visual contact even when he was sheathed completely and deeply inside of her.

Was he the one throbbing or was she? She flexed her muscles and was gratified to hear him gasp. So she did it again. And again.

He lost the staring contest. His eyes lost all focus as he began moving, plunging into her. Seconds later the world spiraled red as she came, and on the heels of that she heard him cry out as he did the same.

For a moment they rested, her arms around his neck, his head on her shoulder and his breath rasping in her ear.

Wow. Just ... wow. She hadn't made any plans beyond a one-night seduction. It thrilled her to know he was still so interested. Thrilled her – and scared her. She was in unplanned, uncharted territory now. She'd lost her chance to make a clean getaway.

And she still had the photo shoot this afternoon. And after that, the tour and her job as his publicist. Oh yeah. Her job.

'I'm sorry you had to wake up alone, but you were sleeping so peacefully,' he said. His eyes were the most mesmerizing blue. 'I was going to bring you breakfast in bed. Room service.'

'I think the kitchen service has sufficed just fine,' she said. Her mouth sought his in a long slow kiss before she slid off the counter. Amazingly, her knees managed to hold her up. Her fingers still trembled when she tried to button the shirt. He pushed her hands away, deftly slipping the buttons into each hole. Oh my. Amazing sex, breakfast and he was still coordinated enough to help her dress.

She was in so much trouble.

Nate stood in the doorway and watched Hannah run lightly down the front steps to the waiting cab. Even though he knew he'd see her again in a few hours, at the photo shoot, he found himself missing her already.

When the cab pulled away, he closed the door. He needed to shower and change as well before the shoot, but that could wait. First he wanted to check out a very strong hunch.

He went into his study – a mess of papers in these final days of arrangements – and moved off the computer monitor a Post-it note reminder to call his accountant. A touch of the mouse and the Macintosh flared to life. A few keystrokes, a few Internet search queries and his suspicions were confirmed.

When he'd first kissed Hannah Montgomery, something had stirred in his memory. There was something about the way her mouth moved on his, about the way that her hands clenched in his hair that triggered a recollection that wasn't quite fully formed. At the time, he'd been distracted enough not to pursue the niggling memory, but it had continued to burn in the back of his mind the whole night. Then, when he woke up this morning and gazed down on her in something akin to wonder, the memory had again surged to the forefront.

In repose, with her hair sleep-and-sex tousled and her face mostly devoid of make-up, he'd caught a glimpse of what she'd looked like when she was younger.

Nine years ago, the awkward Hannah had surprised him with her boldness when she'd kissed him in the foyer of her parents' Hollywood home. That kiss might have been spontaneous and clumsy, but the underlying emotion had affected him deeply, so much so that he'd never forgotten the kiss – or her.

She was so different now. Not just her looks – of course a coltish teenager would bear only a passing resemblance to the woman she was to become – but also her demeanor.

She wasn't shy anymore.

It was a huge turn-on.

Nate shifted in the office cha
No, she hadn't displayed any sl
morning. Now she was confic
walked into the studio, all he
peeling off her business suit.
woman in a suit intriguing, alwa
find beneath the professional ima

He'd found a hot, fascinating w

It had been a long time since h
get lost in a woman's body. To tot forget everything but sensations and needs. Passion and pleasure.

The need to control everything about his life was all that kept him from picking up a bottle of beer, a handful of pills on those days when he was feeling stressed, overwhelmed. During the nights when he struggled so hard to make music, to spill the songs he felt bottled up inside of himself.

The thought of trying to keep his hands off of her while she toured with him was daunting.

He wanted her again.

With a groan, he headed for the shower. So much for getting the attraction out of his system.

The knock at the hotel-room door came before Hannah could even slip out of her shoes. She knew without asking who it was. Hannah flipped the safety lock and wordlessly ushered her friend into the room.

Gina threw herself down on the bed, bouncing once before pushing herself up on one elbow to stare at her friend. 'So, how was the wine bar?' she asked. Her eyes were wide, feigning an innocence that Hannah didn't buy into for a moment.

Hannah couldn't help the completely goofy grin that curved her mouth.

Gina laughed. 'That wine bar excuse was so lame I don't know why you bothered.' She sat up and clasped her arms around drawn-up legs. She peered over the

nees, her fey green eyes wide. 'OK, I want
l. I was the one you called when you vowed
one night with Nate Fox, and I'm the one who
to hear about it first. So, spill. How was he?'

How was he? Hannah sank down onto the bed next to her friend. She closed her eyes, remembering the taste of the skin along his throat. The low husky groan she'd drawn from him time and again. She licked her lips unconsciously, reliving the pressure of his mouth on hers.

His mouth trailing downward, seeking treasures . . .

How was he? He'd been beyond words.

'Hello, remember me?' Gina waved her hand in front of Hannah's face.

'It's . . . strange,' Hannah said finally. 'For nine years I've been obsessed with the idea of sleeping with him. You and I have plotted any number of schemes; I've fantasized about every detail. But I never gave a single thought to what might happen afterward. It's as if I just assumed my life would go on as normal . . . that achieving my goal was somehow separate from everything else.'

'That's a hell of a mental block,' Gina agreed. She got up and helped herself to orange juice from the minibar. Further exploration revealed a wrapped Danish on another shelf.

'Isn't it crazy?' Hannah got up and paced the room. Realizing she'd removed only one shoe, she stopped and bent down. 'It's not as if I'm a virgin or have never been in a relationship. I know there's always a morning after.'

'How did the morning after go?' Gina asked.

Hannah felt the smile explode across her face. 'Um, is it still a one-night stand if breakfast gets a little heated?'

Gina groaned. She swallowed the large bite of cheese Danish, and waved the wrapper. 'You had a better breakfast than I did.' She peered at Hannah. 'You're not going to give details, are you?'

'No.' Hannah shook her head. 'It's still too fresh. And I still have to face him at the shoot today.' She sat down abruptly as fresh anxiety flooded through her. 'What was I thinking, having sex with him first? I have to work with him now. How the hell am I supposed to see him all the time and not want to climb all over him? Last night was the most unprofessional thing I've ever done.'

She leaned forward and rested her head on her knees. Dizziness washed over her, brought on by the mortifying feeling of guilt. 'Oh God, I slept with a client.'

Gina put an arm around her. 'You let nature take its course, sweetie. The sexual tension between the two of you at dinner was so thick I almost choked on it. You're both adults; you can figure out how to work together. As long as you use your PR skills to rocket him to the top again, there's shouldn't be a problem.'

'I've never slept with a client,' Hannah repeated. She looked up, catching a glimpse of herself in the dresser mirror. Did her mouth actually look swollen?

'Your client's never been Nate Fox before, rock-star fantasy and total hottie.'

Well, that was true, but it did little to alleviate the guilt she felt about violating her personal work ethic.

'Just ask yourself this – was it worth it?' Gina asked.

The smile came back, unbidden, as the memories flooded her brain and flushed her body with heat. 'Oh, yeah.'

'Whoa,' Gina said, frowning. 'I thought this was going to be just one night.'

'What makes you think it's not?'

'That look on your face,' Gina said. 'You're practically licking your lips. Don't you dare fall for him.'

'I'm not,' Hannah denied. 'That's ridiculous. Just because the sex was good –' incredible, stupendous, mind-blowing '– doesn't mean I'm imagining white picket fences and children.'

'Sure,' Gina said dubiously. 'So how are you going to make it through the shoot today?'

'Like the complete professional that I am,' Hannah said.

Like the basket case she was going to be the minute she saw him again, knowing that she was going to have to keep her hands to herself from now on.

The agreement had been one night to work the lust out of their system. It didn't matter that she was still feeling incredibly lusty.

Gina laughed. 'Yeah, and I'm going to capture every minute of your utter professionalism on film. You know, I'm really beginning to enjoy this assignment, even though I'm not the one getting hot sex.'

'I didn't say the sex was hot.'

Gina burst out laughing. 'Honey, the look on your face has told me almost everything! I still want details, but at least I know he blew your mind from here to next Tuesday.'

'Here to next *year*,' Hannah said. 'You're right. No matter what, it was worth it. It was definitely worth it.'

'Sometimes you just have to go with what your hormones are telling you to do,' Gina said. A slow smile curved her mouth, and she sighed. 'Remember that time in Phoenix? I met that guy watching the photo shoot? That still rates up there as one of the best weekends of my life.'

'Maybe so,' Hannah said. 'But you didn't have to work with him afterward, and have everyone wonder if he hired you because you were good in bed. I mean, will people think I'm working for Nate because we're having a relationship?'

'You're having a relationship now?' Gina asked. 'How did it go from one night with complimentary breakfast to a relationship?'

'That's not what I meant,' Hannah said. 'You know, if you weren't my best friend, I'd have to fire you.'

'Yep,' Gina agreed.

'We're going to have to keep what happened to ourselves. He just doesn't need that kind of publicity.'

'If someone finds out, so what? It's the music business, babe. Everyone thinks rock stars sleep around.' Gina ducked away from the pillow Hannah tried to throw at her, and got up, stretching languidly. 'I need to check the equipment and make a few phone calls. I'll meet you at Fisherman's Wharf.'

Hannah had a long list of things she had to do, too. Top of it was figuring out how to build a working relationship with a man whose tongue had traced all the intimate spots on her body. A man she wanted again.

Poor planning, that's what it had been. Note to self: next time, job first, sex fest afterward.

Wait. That *had* been the plan. But somewhere along the way, she'd completely lost focus.

Hannah peeled off her suit, trying not to remember how Nate had done it the night before. She failed. Every garment removed, every brush of cloth against her skin, reminded her.

Her shower felt really, really good, in more ways than one.

Towel wrapped around her wet hair, but otherwise naked, she opened the closet and surveyed the outfit she'd packed to wear today. She wished she'd brought something else. Something a little sexier. The plain black pants, while elegant, were not what she really wanted to be wearing when she saw Nate again. The sweater she'd packed in anticipation of San Francisco's cooler climate was neither clingy nor low-cut.

And there were going to be groupies. Let's not forget the groupies. They wouldn't be wearing black pants and sweaters. She just knew there'd be an excess of cleavage and high heels, come hither looks and offers of just about everything. She found herself suddenly regretting the phone calls that had leaked the shoot to the public.

She wanted Nate to notice her. She wanted him to remember. She was pretty sure that every second of last night was going to be etched in her memory until the end of time. She wanted him to remember her the same way.

Even if she couldn't rip his clothes off and devour him anymore.

Gina was completely wrong in her assessment. There was no way in hell that Hannah was falling for Nate. No amount of good sex could take the place of friendship, common bonds. Just because the thought of having to work with him chastely made her cringe, it didn't mean anything.

And her reluctance to share the details of last night with Gina had nothing to do with the desire not to reduce them to giggling anecdotes.

There were no deeper feelings, deeper longings. It just meant that she wanted to savor the memories a little longer, that was all.

The shot about rock stars sleeping around had gotten to her, though. She knew Gina hadn't meant it badly, but it made her wonder about Nate's agenda last night. Was she just another notch on his bedpost? An attractive woman he wanted to have some fun with? See if he could get his own publicist into the sack?

After all, it wasn't as if she had supermodel looks. He was known to date A-list celebrities, and she was pretty sure she wasn't on anybody's list. She couldn't compete with that.

She would be an idiot to fall for Nate Fox.

Everything had to go perfectly. It was her first day on the job, and how the photo shoot went could set the tone for the rest of the campaign.

Hannah reached the area of the Wharf where they'd

decided to do the photo shoot. At least the weather was cooperating. The sky was that certain shade of blue only achieved on the Bay in the spring. Not too windy, not too hot. Nothing to interfere with the shots.

With a practiced gaze she assessed the crowd that had gathered. Not too many media types yet, but there were enough to show that her emails and calls had gotten some attention. A local radio station had parked a van as close as possible to the cordoned-off area, music blaring from speakers. The gathering wasn't huge yet. Most people just glanced curiously at the roped-off area and, not seeing anyone famous, continued on. Enough stopped to swell the crowd, though, pushing its outer limits into a wider area. There was an undercurrent of excitement, almost like the first day of a fair, excited voices, restless fans.

With luck, the place would be mobbed by the time the photo shoot was finished. A controlled, non-threatening mob, impressive enough to make Nate look like an A-lister. She noted it all, filing it away for later.

An astonishing number of people milled around inside the cordoned-off area – Sam and an assistant; Gina and her cameras; the equipment guys; a huge bald black man in Armani and wraparound sunglasses who looked as though he'd snap Hannah's neck like a chicken's if she sneezed wrong.

Nate, however, wasn't there.

Hannah flashed her ID at a rent-a-cop and he let her past the temporary rope barrier.

'Hey,' Sam said, in what she'd already figured was his characteristic bluntness.

'How're things going so far?' she asked.

He turned in circles, making his own observations. He raised a hand in a quick wave and a woman behind the rope waved back. Her motion was seen and copied by about a dozen others.

'Friends?' Hannah asked.

'Some of the FoxFanatics,' Sam said. 'God, I hate that name.'

Hannah laughed, having to agree with him. She knew the president of the fan club, though, and had been impressed by the work the woman had done in keeping the fervor over Nate high, despite his two-year absence from the music world.

'Don't ever let them hear you say that,' Hannah told Sam. 'They're our hardcore audience, and we want them to keep spreading the word.'

'I know, but why couldn't they have called themselves something like the Vixens? Now that's sexy.'

'It sounds like a roller derby team,' she countered.

A gofer pressed a cup of coffee into Sam's hands, glancing apologetically at Hannah. The aroma was great, but the thought of caffeine on her jittery stomach made her shake her head.

'We need to have a meeting before this gets going. I want you to meet our head of security and make sure you two are on the same page about fan contact.'

'Ready when you are,' Hannah said.

'Gina!' Sam barked.

Gina looked up from the camera she was fiddling with. Sam tapped his watch, and she held up her hands to indicate fifteen to twenty minutes.

'I'll grab Andre and meet you inside,' Sam told Hannah.

He directed her to Castignola's, the upscale restaurant adjacent to the area of the Wharf on which they'd be doing the shoot. They'd rented out a private room and the restaurant manager escorted her back.

She didn't bother knocking, assuming Nate would be alone.

Her stomach lurched. A blonde woman, her back to Hannah, was bent over a seated Nate, their faces close.

Chapter Five

The woman leaning over Nate straightened, looking back over one shoulder to see who had come in, and Hannah choked back a laugh at her own jealous paranoia. A make-up artist, evening out Nate's skin tone with a brush of powder and adding a smudge of eyeliner to bring out those smoldering eyes.

She'd always found the concept of men with a bare hint of make-up unbelievably sexy.

Nate watched her with a lazy hunger in his eyes. He stood as she approached, his dark-blue gaze sliding slowly over her, from the tips of her shoes to the cling of material at her thighs. He didn't rush and, by the time his eyes met hers, she was having a serious fantasy about pushing him back into the chair and straddling him. Nate took her hand, fingers folding warmly around hers as he drew her close. He leaned in, his mouth skimming a hello across her cheek. Hannah forgot how to breathe – dammit! – when his lips brushed her ear.

'You look great,' he told her, his voice low, a husky caress that warmed her blood. He closed his teeth lightly on her earlobe, laughing very softly at the breathy sound that escaped her. Nate's hands caressed her shoulders for a moment, the heat of his palms going straight to her nipples. They tightened, puckering in the skimpy lace of her bra. Luckily, he removed his hands before she could cover them with her own and guide them downward to cup her through the soft sweater.

That would have made them very, very late for the photo shoot.

The stylist finished repacking her industrial kit. 'Don't mess up my hard work,' she said to Hannah, in a tone that clearly bespoke envy rather than any sort of real threat.

'Are they ready for me outside?' Nate asked as the woman left. He moved to the buffet set up along one wall. A variety of the restaurant's specialties were arrayed across the crisp white linen.

'Soon. Sam wants to have a meeting in here first; he's on his way.'

'How about you?' he asked in that same low voice. 'Are you ready for me?' He held a shrimp to her lips, the lazy glint in his eyes daring her to take it.

Oh God.

Hannah accepted the morsel, enjoying the fresh seafood texture and the spicy taste of cocktail sauce. 'I thought last night was supposed to have gotten it out of our systems.'

'Funny thing, that.' Nate stepped even closer to her, trapping her against the chair. He cupped her jaw with one hand, traced the shape of her lower lip with his thumb. 'We may have miscalculated. I'm pretty sure we're not finished yet.'

Her brain rebelled. She couldn't do this; she had to be professional.

Her body, tense and dampening, agreed with him wholeheartedly.

The door burst open and Sam entered, accompanied by the big bald man she'd seen earlier. Hannah stepped away from Nate, putting the table between them. She could tell from the purse of Sam's lips that their close proximity hadn't gone unnoticed.

She cursed her fair skin, knowing she flushed more than the sharp sea breeze outside would have caused. She wondered if Sam knew of last night's carnal romp.

If he did, he didn't mention it now. Instead, he indicated the large man at his side.

'Hannah, this is Andre, head of security and Nate's

personal bodyguard. Andre, Hannah Montgomery, Nate's publicist.'

'Hannah!' The looming man put his meaty hands on her shoulders. The bass rumble of his voice seemed to vibrate the floor. For a moment Hannah was sure he was going to press her down into a chair and interrogate her with a big light on her face.

Instead, he planted big air kisses near each of her cheeks.

'Great to meet you, darling,' he said. 'I adore your shoes, by the way.'

'Um, thank you,' Hannah managed.

'Have a seat, everyone,' Sam said. 'We only have a few minutes.'

They sat at one of the small round tables. Andre went to the buffet and poured everyone a glass of water. Hannah sipped, grateful for something to do with her hands. Outside the windows, gulls wheeled above moored boats.

Beneath the table, Nate apparently found something to do with his own hand. He stroked her thigh. She pushed his hand away.

He put it back.

Sam glanced at her, then at Nate.

Shades of last night. Hannah drew in a deep breath, forcing herself to concentrate. 'As Sam's probably already told you, I let Nate's fan club know about today's photo shoot. That'll show the media that there's still a lot of interest in Nate. Andre, most of these women are pretty reasonable, and I don't think they'll get out of hand.'

'Sam warned me to bring a few extra guards with me. Won't be a problem,' Andre said. 'Just let me know ahead of time when you do something like this again.'

Hannah nodded her assent. 'After the shoot, we'll take a few minutes with the media – soundbites, that sort of thing. Then Nate should mingle with the fans. Sign some autographs, pose for pictures with them, thank them for coming. Nate, you're good with that, right?'

Nate grinned. 'Hell, yeah. I've never had a problem being surrounded by beautiful women who worship me.'

He caressed her inner thigh, and she knew from the wicked twinkle in his eye that he was being cheeky. Still, she couldn't help wonder how much truth was in his statement.

Other than the past two years, when he'd pretty much been out of the media's radar, Nate had never seemed to have a shortage of women. The last girlfriend Hannah had heard about was Suzanne Cooper, who'd been killed in the accident that had forced Nate into rehab. Before her, there'd been a rotating supply of gorgeous celebrities.

She couldn't recall if he'd dated a fan before, but then again, she hadn't paid close attention. The fact was, she wasn't much different than the fans who were lined up outside, desperate for a glimpse of their rock god. She'd *been* one of them. It was only her job that put her on the other side of the security barriers.

'We also need to make sure the paparazzi are kept under control,' Sam said. His fingers played a drum solo along the edge of the table. 'They're going to be looking for any scrap or hint that Nate's slipping.'

Andre passed a hand over his shaved head as if to test for any stray fuzz. 'There's no such thing as a controlled paparazzi,' Andre said. 'The best you can hope for is to avoid the worst of them. My boys will keep an eye out. Hannah, give us a list of who's allowed and who's not.'

She made a note in her BlackBerry. 'Will do, Andre.' She saw Sam check his watch. 'Showtime?'

He nodded. They all rose, but before she could step

away from the table, the manager touched her arm. 'A word?'

They stepped to a corner while Nate and Andre headed to the door. Some of Gina's equipment cases cluttered up a table next to them.

'Here's the deal,' Sam said. 'Other than drugs, Nate's personal life is personal unless he chooses to talk to me about it. So I'm not going to ask for details.'

God, he did know about last night. Knew, or guessed. Plus, it wasn't as if Nate hadn't been obvious at the table.

'Sam, I –'

'Just keep your eye on the job, is all I'm saying,' Sam said, surveying her. 'No distractions, no interference.'

Hannah felt a tweak of annoyance. 'Absolutely not,' she said. She didn't bother telling him it was just a fling, anyway. He said he didn't want to know the details. 'I'll put him back on top, Sam. That's what I'm here for.'

'Glad we're on the same page.'

Outside, the crowd had grown in anticipation of Nate's appearance. A wave of shrieks swelled when the fans spotted him. Despite her experience, despite doing a lot of shrieking of her own at his concerts, Hannah still wasn't prepared for the reaction. At least it was gratifying that the info she'd leaked to the FoxFanatics bulletin boards had been noticed. Andre and the rent-a-cops scattered around stiffened, but the women – maybe thirty in total – didn't try to rush the flimsy barrier. They just pressed close, waving paper and Sharpies and CDs and posters, shouting Nate's name.

Nate turned the full force of his smile on them and the noise faltered, just for a second, before rising even higher. He raised a hand in greeting, then made a motion that implied signing an autograph, and mouthed, 'Later.'

Good. Every fan he could connect with was one who'd

spread the news to her friends. Who'd continue to buy CDs and concert tickets and anything else that featured Nate.

Hannah made a mental note to ask Sam if they'd ever worked with the FoxFanatics – maybe offer a limited edition fan club T-shirt, preferred seating at some of the concerts. Anything to entice them to spend more money on their hero.

She crossed over to stand with Andre and let Gina take over, then glanced back at the fans. They'd subsided in their squeals, enough so that Hannah could hear the barking of the hundreds of sea lions that made their home on floating docks just off the pier. The young women vibrated with excitement, flipping their hair and even touching up their lip gloss without taking their eyes off their idol.

Hannah put a hand to her own hair, which she'd pulled back in a big clip to keep it from getting in the way. Back at the hotel, it had looked artlessly tousled. Here, compared to the young women's coifs, it felt haphazard and boring. And she didn't even want to think about comparing her businesslike outfit to their casual, flirty ones. She might be wearing expensive pants and a silk sweater, but she knew it was dull in contrast to the fans' tight jeans and skimpy camisole tops, the thin fabric making it obvious how chilly the weather was.

Gina had started snapping shots. Hannah turned her attention back to Nate. He stood on the wooden boards scoured silver-grey by time and salt, casually leaning against the railing, dark hair whipping around his face in the wind.

Hannah watched as her friend coaxed the reluctant musician into posing for the camera. She could sense his discomfort with the posed shots, and knew instinctively that even after all these years, he still found being the subject of a camera's lens disconcerting. She couldn't think of too many pictures she'd seen of him that had affected her as deeply as the ones which had been taken when he was performing. Those captured a depth of passion that these maneuvered shots lacked. Still, she knew Gina was capable of coaxing even the most reluctant people into relaxing in front of the lens.

There was no denying that Nate looked sexy as the wind blew the neck of his shirt open, revealing the line of his collarbone, the edge of his neck. The way he leaned back against the railing pulled the soft denim of his black jeans tight over his thighs. Her hands clenched when she remembered the feel of those muscles beneath her palms.

Lord, but just looking at him made her horny.

'Finest ass in the business,' a deep voice rumbled next to her.

'Oh yeah,' Hannah replied wholeheartedly. She looked up at Andre, seeing herself reflected in his sunglasses.

'Oh, girl,' Andre said. 'It's a good thing I'm not the jealous type.'

She sighed. 'Is it that obvious?'

'To someone with incredible observational skills such as myself, absolutely.' He nodded in Nate's direction. 'Just look at him.'

Nate had turned his head toward her and, even though he wore sunglasses, she felt pinned in his gaze, making her the only other person on the crowded boardwalk. When he took off the glasses, the look he gave her was intense, hungry.

Her stomach fluttered. Just as Nate made her feel like the only person around, now she had eyes only for him.

What did she want, really? For much of her life, she'd had two main goals: be successful at her job and have her night of passion with the man making eyes at her over there.

Now she'd achieved both, and already the two were in conflict.

But it wouldn't last, she was sure of that. Despite their attraction and their passion last night (OK, and this morning, she acknowledged, unable to fight back a satisfied smile), she and Nate didn't have a future personally. He was bright lights and glamor, starlets and parties. She was behind the scenes, normal and maybe even a little boring. She wasn't his type, and that was fine.

She sighed. She didn't want a long-term relationship with him, but if she could do a kick-ass job as his publicist while continuing to enjoy his bed, why not? It was worth a try, at least.

Gina finished her shots, and Hannah crossed over to Nate.

This was professional time, she reminded herself, even as she smelled his shampoo and felt a flare of desire streak through her belly. It was all about balance.

'Like I said, let's give the press a few minutes,' she said. 'A couple of soundbites, quotable stuff. I'll set up longer interviews later.'

He nodded. 'You're the boss.'

Well, that made for some interesting – and very non-professional – mental images. Nate spreadeagled on the bed, muscles taut as he tested the strength of the leather straps that bound him . . .

Stop it. Just stop it.

The media shouted questions, microphones and mini-recorders held his way. Nate picked and chose the questions he answered, and Hannah stood ready nearby to step in if she was needed. She wasn't. His responses were quick, deft and constantly turned the topic back to his newest album and upcoming tour. He was good at this.

More than one reporter asked about his drug habit, and the accident that had put him in rehab. When the questions slowed, Hannah moved forward, thanking them all for coming. She passed out her cards, assuring them that she would be available later to answer further questions about Nate's future plans.

The interviews finished, Nate turned to the fans. They'd been polite and patient while he did his work, but they fairly vibrated with contained excitement the entire time. Hannah separated herself from the microphones with a final wave, and moved to watch Nate sign autographs.

'Hey, Helen, good to see you,' Nate said to a curvaceous woman with dark-red curly hair.

Hannah blinked. He knew their names? Were these women he'd been intimate with?

She missed whatever the fan had to say, but Nate had finished signing his name to an 8 x 10 and had moved on to the next.

'Karen!' he said to a pretty, slender blonde wearing glasses. 'How was your trip to – where was it – Santo Domingo?'

Holy crap.

At least he didn't know all of the ones who crowded forward. Still, he worked through the line, a model of patience as he signed, posed for photos, answered brief questions. She noticed Gina nearby, the digital camera in her hand recording shot after shot to be posted to his website.

Finally, most of the fans had left, although a few lingered to one side, having already gotten their moment with him but obviously not yet willing to miss a second of his presence. That's when a thin wavering voice said, 'Excuse me?'

The question came from a wide-eyed teenaged girl who clutched a piece of paper and a pen in her hands. The paper was slowly being strangled into an unrecognizable wad. Hannah wasn't sure whether to be amused by the awkwardly eager look on the girl's face, or embarrassed that the child seemed so much like she had been all those years ago.

A slow smile curved Nate's wide mouth, a mix of humor and sensuality. 'Hi. Would you like my autograph?'

'Oh God yes,' the teenager said in a breathy rush. She thrust the pen and paper at him, and then snatched it back, frantically trying to smooth the mangled paper.

Nate plucked the pen from her hand and stepped closer to her. He touched a spot just above his picture on her shirt. 'We can use this,' he told her with a grin. 'What's your name?'

'Miranda, but my friends all call me Mindy, which I hate so if you could sign it to Miranda that would be really cool.' The words came out in one jumbled sentence. 'I am such a big fan, I mean, I really am. I have all your CDs. I just got the new one and it's so good. Oh God, I can't believe I'm standing here talking to you. No one is going to believe me.'

Nate smiled at her as he scrawled his signature across the shirt and then handed the pen back. 'It was nice meeting you, Miranda. I'm glad you like the latest CD. You should come to the concert. The tour starts next week.'

'Oh, I will,' she said, backing away, not taking her eyes from him. It was only when she bumped into someone that she looked away, clutching her pen to her chest while she hurried back across the pier.

'That was nice of you,' Hannah said.

'I'm a nice guy,' Nate told her with a slow smile. It was funny, he thought, but he hadn't enjoyed signing an autograph as much as that one in years.

Maybe it was the way Hannah's eyes had softened while she watched. He wondered if she were remembering their first meeting. She'd been a lot like that young fan.

Of course, she'd grown up since, finding a poise she'd lacked then. But her mouth was the same sweet curve it had been that first time. He felt himself harden, remembering what that mouth had done the night before.

Andre and his minions were shooing the crowd away.

Nate caught Hannah's hand, drawing her away to the back wall of Castignola's where there was a modicum of privacy. He was puzzled by the wariness he saw in her eyes. He trailed his fingers over the smooth line of her jaw, letting them follow the delicate curve of her throat to where her pulse fluttered quickly.

'Nate,' she began quietly.

'Hannah,' he teased. He bent his head, allowing himself the pleasure of tasting her lips. He stroked his tongue along her full lower lip, relishing the soft sigh of need she made. Despite what he'd seen in her eyes, there was no wariness in the way her mouth invited him in. He ran his hands down her sides, teasing the swelling curves of her breasts with his thumbs before drawing her hips tightly to his. He wanted her to remember just exactly what her nearness did to him. The restless movement of her body against his made him groan, and he finally lifted his mouth from hers, knowing that if they continued, they might draw more publicity than he really wanted.

Hannah took a deep breath. 'I have to talk to you about something. Sam's concerned.'

'Yes?' Nate asked carefully. He'd wondered why Sam had drawn her aside, whether it had to do with the wariness.

'He reminded me – rightly so – of the need to be professional,' she said. 'My job is to get you back on top, and that has to be my number-one priority. I have to separate my personal and professional selves. I'll be honest with you, Nate. I've never slept with a client. Before or after.'

'I'll take that as a compliment,' he said lightly. But seeing the seriousness in her gaze, he added, 'I've never slept with a professional contact, either.'

'It was extraordinarily unprofessional of me,' Hannah persisted.

'And of me,' he said. His hands tightened briefly on her shoulders, not intended as a caress, but as a punctuation of his words, to let her know he felt the same. Still, just touching her was enough to rekindle the memories, the desires.

'I don't think any less of you,' he continued. 'We both agreed to it, as adults. I'm glad it happened. It was ... intense.'

'Yes, it was,' Hannah agreed. He felt her relax at his words.

'I'm not ready for it to end,' he told her, and felt her draw in a long breath.

'We didn't quite get it out of our systems like we planned,' she said. Her grey eyes were flecked with silver. They were eyes that held mysteries, eyes that would haunt his fantasies.

Nate grinned. 'You're right. We failed abysmally on that count. Let's go home and try again.' He slipped his thigh between hers, watching her eyes widen as he pressed against her sensitive mound. He could feel her heat through her clothes.

'Nate, I have to get to the airport. I have an afternoon flight out.'

The breathy sound of her voice, the dilation of her pupils, told him just how tempted she was. 'Then promise me it'll be soon.' His mouth brushed her cheek. 'Tell me you want to see me again.'

'I want to see you again,' she admitted. 'As long as it doesn't interfere ... Yes, yes, I do.'

He felt a surge of triumph. It turned into outright hunger when one of her slender hands stroked through the hair at his nape and pulled his mouth down to hers. He let her control the kiss, using every ounce of willpower he possessed not to take charge and kiss her senseless. He let her tongue flirt with his, let her explore the recesses of his mouth. When her tongue flicked across his lip, he thought he was going to lose it right then and there. He groaned and pulled her tightly to him, holding her still until she understood just what she was doing to him. Her wicked smile when she looked into his eyes told him that she knew exactly what she was doing.

This woman was trouble. He knew it, and it didn't seem to matter. He just knew that he wanted more of her, as much of her as she was willing to give. He wanted to see how far he could take her, what the limits of her passion were and whether they could reach beyond them. She intrigued him and aroused him in a way he hadn't felt before, and the knowledge was intoxicating and terrifying. He just knew that he had to see her again.

Have her again.

And again.

With a low moan, Nate eased her away. It was a good thing that Gina had disappeared with the camera or she could get some shots of his condition that would scare the holy bejeezus out of mothers everywhere and give his fans endlessly restless nights.

'What are you thinking about?' Hannah asked. Her fingers traced the line of his jaw, then wandered down the tendons of his neck. The touch raised shivers that chased down his spine.

'That I'm very glad no one has a camera pointed this way.' He looked down at the obvious bulge in his jeans. Hannah's gaze followed his, and she laughed softly. The sound made him grit his teeth. God, but he wanted to take her right here, to back her up against the railing and wrap her legs around his waist. To hell with anyone watching.

'It's still going to be too long,' he said.

Hannah smiled. He was glad the wariness was gone from her eyes. He still didn't know what had caused it. He kissed her one last time, thinking that his bed was going to seem even lonelier tonight than it usually did.

And the cravings he battled every night were going to have an entirely different cause.

Chapter Six

Traveling sucked.

Hannah dropped her suitcase on the floor of her condo. Not only had take-off in San Francisco been delayed, but by the time she'd gotten into LA, the 405 had been a parking lot. She was grumpy and her feet hurt.

Toeing off her shoes solved one of the problems. She padded down the hall, her cellphone pressed to her ear. Her voicemail was full and she accessed it while peeling off her sweater. The first message was from her mother. She rolled her eyes. Another crisis in the Forbes household. No doubt the latest housekeeper had quit.

The sweater landed on the bottom of the bed, followed by her pants. She was tempted to flop down and wrap up in her favorite antique Baltimore rose quilt, but she still had things to do. Pretending to be a contortionist, she pulled on a comfortable T-shirt and yoga pants while listening to the rest of the messages. Most were from friends, two from clients. The last message was from a guy she'd seen a few times in the last month. He'd been nice, but there'd been no sparks.

And now that she'd met Nate, she knew just exactly what was possible when there were sparks.

Hannah refused to think about Nate. If she did, she'd end up using one of the toys in the drawer next to the bed. Which would be a poor substitute for the real thing.

How on earth had she thought that having him for just one night would be enough?

'Call your mother, you know she worries,' Hannah muttered out loud. She'd get the call out of the way, and then she'd have a glass of wine. Maybe listen to some music. The thought of Nate's voice, all smoky velvet and sex, filling her living room, made her breath catch.

Better yet, have the wine first. The refrigerator yielded up half a bottle of her favorite vintage Zinfandel. She poured herself a glass.

'Call your mother,' she repeated sternly. She folded her legs into the corner of the purple-and-gold striped sofa and hit speed dial. The bright colors of the sofa were her personal rebellion against her mother's designer pastels when Hannah had lived at home. Now, she filled her own space with sleek lines and rich color.

'Hi, Mom,' she said when her mother answered. Definitely another housekeeper quitting. Her mother hated answering the phone.

'Hi, honey, are you back from San Francisco? I was beginning to worry.'

Almost eight years on her own, and her mother still fretted. Hannah sighed. 'The freeway was backed up. What's going on?'

'Alice quit,' her mother announced. 'I just don't know about people these days.'

Hannah made appropriate soothing noises.

'Oh, I mentioned to your father you were meeting with that Fox fellow, and he reminded me that you two had already met. Did you catch up on things?'

'He hired me to be his publicist, Mom,' Hannah said. 'I'll be going out on the road with him soon.'

'That's lovely, dear. I'm so glad you have a job. I seem to remember you had a poster of him in your room when you were younger. Did you tell him that?'

Hannah nearly choked on her wine. 'No, Mom,' she said when she finished coughing. 'I didn't tell him that.' Quick, change the subject. 'So am I still welcome for dinner on Tuesday?'

'Of course you are.' Her mother sounded offended. 'And you can bring a date, you know that.'

Oh right, like she'd ever consider taking Nate home

for dinner. Now *there* was a nightmare of supreme awkwardness. Between the reminder of their first kiss and her mother's blithe stories of Hannah's teenage crushes . . .

'I don't think so, Mom. I love you. Kisses to Dad, and I'll see you both on Tuesday.' She hung up quickly before her mother could continue the excruciatingly embarrassing conversation.

There was no way in hell she wanted to remind Nate that she was Everett Forbes' daughter. Nope. She wanted him to think of her as a grown-up sex kitten, not some frizzy-haired teeny-bopper groupie. She'd changed her image. It was going to stay that way.

Feeling restless, Hannah topped up her wine, then wandered into the study. The familiar mess greeted her. The crowded bookshelves, the desk scattered with papers and magazines and Post-it notes and cables for her BlackBerry and iPod, the faded comic strips taped to the wall next to the window.

On the wall opposite the desk, where she wouldn't be distracted when she worked, was the poster of Nate. It had seen her through a lot of lonely nights. Her fantasies had kept her company between boyfriends and, in some cases, even during.

Nate Fox, Fantasy Rock God, had set the bar for the men in her life. Whether she wanted to or not, she unconsciously made comparisons. She knew it wasn't fair, knew it wasn't right, but hadn't figured out how to fix it.

Of course, now she'd had the real Nate Fox. Her eyes skimmed the body preserved in the photo. He'd grown up too. He'd looked good back then, had fueled enough fantasies to start a forest fire.

But now. Oh now. There was something about the look in his eyes, the confidence in his stance. His totally hot body. How did he compare to the fantasy? He exceeded it, just by walking into the room.

My oh my. She'd had her one night. And a morning. She'd fulfilled her teenage vow. She sat in her beloved Aeron desk chair and spun around so she could stare at the poster.

She should be happier. She should be feeling triumphant. How many women had looked up on stage and fantasized about having sex with the rock star of their dreams? How many had had the fantasy come true? She was happy she'd fulfilled a goal, but somehow, it all felt empty.

Jet lag.

The devilish voice inside reminded her that she couldn't get jet lag flying from San Francisco to LA, but she ignored it. She could certainly blame it on not a lot of sleep last night . . . The memory of what – and who – had kept her up made her squirm in her seat.

With those thoughts came the rush of guilt mixed with the jealousy she'd felt when she'd seen him working the crowd at the Wharf. She wasn't allowed to feel jealous. She'd violated her professional ethics, but that didn't give her license to feel jealous when he looked at another woman. Guilty, yes. Jealous, no.

More importantly, her fling with Nate was far from serious. She had no claim on him, no reason to feel possessive. They'd have their fun, get it out of their systems and move on.

It was her job to put him back on top, where she knew he belonged. That meant being heard on every rock station in the country, being seen in every good entertainment magazine. Along with that was being seen with the right people. It was all about image. Being seen with the best implied that you were the best.

She was just going to have to get used to that.

Besides, the attraction between them was still there. They didn't seem to be able to keep their hands to themselves. And right now, no other woman could say that.

Focus on work. That was the ticket. Putting her back to the poster, Hannah opened her laptop. Gina had given her the memory card from the shoot and Sam had given her their webmaster's address, acknowledging that it was her job to get the photos online. There was the FoxFanatics website to visit, pictures to send. No room for daydreams today.

And definitely no room for the longings Nate's words had rekindled.

I want to see you again.

The house was too quiet. Nate flipped on the stereo. Low strains of heart-aching jazz filtered from hidden Bose speakers. With a grimace, he turned it off. OK, the silence was preferable to having libido-enhancing music filling the house. He didn't need any help feeling frustrated and turned on.

Nate wandered to the kitchen for a bottle of water. That was a mistake. The dishes from that morning's breakfast were still stacked in the sink. The apron he'd worn was crumpled on the floor. He looked at the granite countertop, remembering how it had recently been used, and groaned. At this rate, he was going to have to pour the cold water over himself rather than drink it. Grabbing a bottle from the refrigerator, he quickly left the room, eager to put some distance between himself and the last place he'd made love to Hannah.

Hannah. Lord, he could still feel the lush warmth of her body. Those long legs had trapped him tight, keeping him captive while they'd slaked their passion with each other. He was never going to look at his kitchen the same way again.

When he'd woken up yesterday he hadn't expected to end the day with the most incredible night of his life. And certainly not with the woman who had so intrigued him all those years ago.

He'd never forgotten that impulsive teenage kiss. She'd been too young. Her father had been his producer. But there'd been something about her . . .

He wanted her again. He wanted to see where it all led.

Needing to burn off some energy, he took the stairs two at a time. Nate went to the bedroom to change into sweats. The bed was still unmade, the sheets a tangled mess.

And damn, he could still smell her. Her scent lingered, softly intriguing, slightly exotic. He closed his eyes, breathing it in. He was instantly, painfully, hard. Another groan rumbled from his chest. The next few days were going to be the longest of his life. He was positive.

He was pretty sure he was going to explode long before he saw her again.

The need for her was almost like an addiction, and he had plenty of experience with that. But this felt different, better. Something good could grow from this.

Nate moved to yank the sheet up, covering the pillows. He found the comforter on the opposite side of the bed, lifted it, and saw something black and lacy drop to the floor. He hooked the item with one finger. Her thong. He crushed the tiny scrap of lace in his hand, and thought he might go out of his mind. He remembered peeling them off her, sliding them down those incredibly long legs. Pressing his lips to the sweet treasure they'd hidden.

The fact that she'd left his house bare-assed naked under her sexily professional skirt practically made his eyes roll back in his head.

The musky scent of aroused woman filled his senses. He held the cloth to his nose. Breathed her in. Allowed himself to be consumed by the fantasy.

Sinking down on the edge of the bed, Nate cupped himself through his jeans. The rasp of his zipper seemed too loud, but he imagined it was her hand freeing his swollen cock, caressing the sensitive flesh. With his eyes closed, he wrapped the fabric around his fingers and sheathed himself with it.

The combination of smooth satin and textured lace had him almost ready to come with one stroke. He slowed down, imagining Hannah cupping him, her slender fingers drawing the scrap of lingerie across his aching flesh. He moaned, spreading his legs, caressing himself while her scent teased him. He came in a sudden burst of pleasure that made him cry out, the sound fading to a throaty moan.

Nate's breathing slowed, but somehow the ache in his groin didn't seem any easier.

He laughed. Oh, he had it bad. He only hoped that she was as turned on by memories of their lovemaking as he was. He knew he'd see her again soon, but he wasn't going to kid himself that what he really wanted right then was to be in her bed.

Hell, the floor would do. Or they could check out *her* kitchen counters. Or maybe the couch.

Damn, this wasn't helping. He stared down at the panties still clutched in his hand. He was going to have to come up with something to make her pay for having this effect on him. Something sexy and outrageous.

The thought filled him with anticipation.

Nate grinned, heading for the bathroom. He was going to let his imagination have its own way, and see what it came up with. Then he was going to make Hannah as achy and needy as he was.

He couldn't wait.

Opening the door in response to the bell, Nate found Sam on his doorstep. The older man held up a cup from Nate's favorite coffee house. Sam arched his shaggy eyebrows in a silent question.

His arrival had been inevitable. Stepping back, Nate ushered his friend in.

'So what did you think?' Sam asked, glancing over his

shoulder as he preceded Nate down the hall to the kitchen.

'What did I think about what?' Nate asked carefully. He watched as Sam put the coffee down on the counter where only that morning Hannah's fine ass had graced the granite.

He picked up the cup. He forced himself to relax his grip before coffee exploded all over his hand.

'About the photo shoot this afternoon,' Sam replied. He took a long swig of coffee before heading over to the refrigerator and pulling it open. He pulled out a container of take-out Chinese. Peered at it suspiciously. Put it back.

'It seemed to go OK,' Nate said. He took the white container back out of the refrigerator and tossed it into the garbage. Then, because he didn't want to spend any more time in the kitchen with the counter that seemed to take up the whole room, he headed for the media room.

'It looked like it went more than OK to me,' Sam said. 'I think it was really valuable. Hannah did a good job bringing your fans out. The hardcore ones are the ones who'll spread the word about your grand return.'

Nate sprawled on the burgundy leather sofa, sinking into the deep cushions. 'It was good to see them again,' he admitted. He knew damn well who, in the end, paid his bills.

He appreciated his fans' unwavering support, craved the give and take of their energy at his concerts.

'Every little bit of flirting helps,' Sam said with a laugh. 'Speaking of which, I noticed the sparks flying between you and our new publicist.'

Figures. Half the time, Sam couldn't find the off-ramp they needed on the tour bus, but anything to do with women, and he was spot on. 'She was pretty hot.'

Tantalizing. Vibrant. Addicting.

Sam browsed through the CDs lining one wall, his

blunt fingertip sliding from case to case. 'She was that,' he agreed. 'Do you know what you're doing?'

'Hannah said you'd talked to her. I'm a big boy, Sam. I can take care of myself.'

Glancing over his shoulder, Sam grinned. 'Did I or did I not see the two of you making out after the photo shoot?'

'We weren't making out.'

'Only because it was the middle of the afternoon in a public place,' Sam said. He sat down on the sofa, put his feet up on the teak coffee table and crossed them comfortably at the ankle. 'It looked pretty serious to me.'

'So I kissed her. That doesn't mean it was serious.'

Sam snorted. 'Don't even try to tell me that you two didn't spend the night together. I'm not an idiot.'

'Never said you were,' Nate said. He took a sip from the cup. Wiped a spot of foam off his upper lip.

'Look, I want you to be happy, have some fun. I know it's been hard since . . .' Sam didn't need to finish the sentence; they both knew exactly what he meant. Sam had been there for Nate through the whole thing.

'I just don't want you screwing up a good working relationship,' Sam continued. 'She's great at PR and we really need that.'

Nate stared at his old friend. Always the bottom line for Sam.

'She'll be on the road with us,' Sam persisted. 'You'll need to decide how public you want a relationship with her to be.'

'There's no relationship,' Nate said.

Not yet. Maybe never. Maybe just lots of hot sex. But then why could he still taste her? Feel her around him?

Sam nodded. 'If you say so. Just keep your non-relationship discreet. I've got to run. There are a million things to do before the tour starts.'

Nate followed Sam to the door. It was good to see his friend and manager so positive again. He said as much.

'I could say the same thing for you,' Sam said soberly. 'Look, I know you've been worried about the tour, and the problems that could crop up. You've just gotta have faith in yourself.' The familiar evil twinkle started up in his eyes again. 'Or just keep thinking about your publicist, if that's what puts you in a good mood.'

Nate laughed and punched Sam on the arm. 'Get outta here.'

But by the time he'd finished his coffee, his thoughts were indeed right back with Hannah.

Despite the drink on his tongue, he couldn't seem to forget the taste of Hannah's skin. The desire to touch her again was almost consuming him.

Maybe just hearing her voice would ease the yearning ache. The need.

Or it would lead to other things. After all, he wanted her just as aroused and needy. His groin tightened at the thought.

He reached for the phone.

Hannah stretched, feeling her spine pop, the kinks dissipating. She'd logged off the last website and she was finished. Gina's pictures were perfect, as always.

She was struck by how good Nate looked in them. Not just his usual good, but healthy. She hadn't realized just how much he'd changed until she'd surfed some of the sites that had photos from his last tour. There'd been a gauntness to his face. Lines and tension that had aged him, which spoke of turmoil. Funny that she'd never really noticed it until now.

These new shots caught his edgy sensuality. They made Nate seem dark, mysterious and utterly delicious. Hannah sighed. Hunger coiled in her body, making her clit throb. Just thinking about the things he'd done to her made her shift restlessly in the chair.

The phone rang, and she jerked upright, her feet hitting the floor.

'Hello?' she said.

'Hello, Intoxicating.'

'Nate!' Her heart thudded in her chest, making it difficult to breathe. Or maybe that was just the husky voice in her ear.

'I wanted to call you. I wanted to say goodnight,' he said.

Hannah glanced at the clock and smiled when she saw that it was still relatively early. 'I don't usually go to bed yet,' she told him.

'We did last night,' he reminded her.

His low voice sent shivers through her. Her nipples beaded in response to the images that flooded her memory.

She felt herself grow moist.

'What are you doing?' he asked.

'I'm thinking about you,' she admitted. Hannah smiled when he reacted to the admission with a quickly drawn breath. It gave her the courage to go further. To allow herself the pleasure of listening to his voice just a little longer. 'I'm thinking about all the things I'd be doing right now if you were here.'

He groaned. 'Yeah, me too,' he admitted. 'I found your panties. You left them on the floor. They smell like you.'

Hannah found it impossible to answer. Her throat had tightened, along with every nerve in her body, sending rippling awareness to places she wished he were there to fill.

'I like them, the black silk and lace. I was wondering what color you're wearing now.' His voice continued to seduce her.

'I don't remember,' she admitted. Right now, she wasn't sure she knew anything at all.

'Check,' he instructed with a soft laugh. 'I want to know. I want to picture you in them.'

Hannah licked her lips. Of its own accord, her hand had gone to her waistband and was sliding it down. She stood up and shimmied out of the yoga pants. She kicked them under the desk. 'Blue,' she whispered. 'Slate blue.'

'Silk or lace?'

'Lace,' she said.

'Mm,' he said, encouraging her. 'Can you feel how wet you are through them?'

'How do you know I'm wet?' she asked, low and breathless. It was hard to talk.

'I know,' he told her. 'Touch yourself.'

'Nate . . .'

'Touch yourself,' he whispered again. His voice was velvet and magic, calling to the wild side of her that wanted so desperately to play.

She whimpered as her fingertips skated across the edge of the lace, slipping downward to where she throbbed. Shock waves rippled through her thighs when she brushed her clit through the lace.

'Are you wet?' he asked again.

'Yes,' she said, feeling the moisture gathering in the cloth. She flicked her nail against her clit. Pleasure made her moan. The pressure built unbelievably quickly. That his voice and a few simple words over the phone could do this was nothing short of amazing. Her knees trembling, she dropped back into the chair, waiting for his next instruction.

'I wish I were there,' he said softly. 'I'd touch you slowly, teasing you. Are you teasing yourself, Hannah?'

Her eyes were closed, her head tipped back. She could imagine his hand pushing aside the scrap of cloth, touching her hot slick flesh. She managed to moan a reply, knowing he understood by the sexy laugh that drifted down the phone lines.

'I'd slip a finger into you, and then another. You're so tight, Hannah. So hot and wet.'

'Nate,' she pleaded, her body aching for release. Her fingers had followed his instructions, slipping the lace aside to thrust into herself. Except that they felt like his and she swore she could feel his warm breath on her cheek when he spoke.

'Not yet, sweetheart,' he told her. 'With my other hand I'd cup your breast, caressing you until your nipple was hard against my palm. Will you do that for me, Hannah?'

'Oh God, Nate, please,' she moaned. She blindly reached for the phone's headset, tugged it into place and slipped her hand beneath her T-shirt. Her nipple pressed, aching, through the lace of her bra. She rubbed her thumb in light circles, feeling the pleasure beginning to spiral out of control. She pinched lightly, the sensation going straight to her clit.

She was going to come.

'That's it, baby,' he told her. 'Think of my hands on you.' His voice held her in thrall, controlling her release. 'You can come now,' he said.

She did, the pleasure bursting through her in wave after wave of exquisite release. She cried out his name, her hips bucking against her hand. Slowly, the sensations faded, the aftershocks easing until sanity returned. She whispered his name again, knowing that her voice held all the need she felt.

He laughed softly in her ear. 'Sweet dreams, Hannah.'

The soft click told her that he had hung up. Hannah smiled, relaxed and boneless in the chair. She wasn't sure if she was going to be able to sleep now or not, but she did know one thing.

It was going take more than a few orgasm-filled encounters for her to get enough of him.

Chapter Seven

Hannah paced the radio station lobby from the front door to the leather-and-chrome waiting area to the glass doors that led deeper into the building. She'd been up since four, eager to get ready, so hyped about seeing Nate again that she'd gotten little sleep the night before. Her inability to sit still had nothing to do with work-related nerves, though. It didn't have much to do with her job at all. Granted, this on-air interview was important, if not crucial for Nate. Her own reputation was on the line with this job. She had to get him back on top. The pressures didn't even register.

No, she was antsy because she hadn't seen him in a week. The thought of standing in his warmth, of seeing him and smelling him and touching him, was wreaking havoc with her panties.

They'd talked on the phone at least once a day. The calls had been long, sharing details, learning about tastes, dislikes. The hesitant sharing of two people getting to know each other. Interesting conversations that had inevitably ended with phone sex. Hannah had never been one for lots of talk during sex. But somehow Nate's smoky voice had drawn her from her erotic shell. Asking her what she liked.

Asking what she'd like to do to him.

Following her halting, breathy suggestions. Not afraid to moan in her ear as he touched himself, urging her on to bolder instructions until they were both sweat-soaked and sated.

Would the connection hold when he walked through the radio station's door? Hannah couldn't imagine it wouldn't. Just the thought of it hardened her nipples beneath her silvery-grey bra.

'New relationship energy,' Gina had called it. 'It won't last forever, but enjoy it while it does. And how could you not, with someone like the foxy Nate Fox!'

Hannah had given up protesting that it wasn't a relationship. Obviously it was, even if they hadn't defined its scope. It might not last longer than her job. It might not even survive that long.

But she agreed wholeheartedly with Gina – she was going to enjoy every hot, erotic, orgasmic moment of it.

Her new silk underwear teased her most intimate areas. Over that she'd slipped on a simple sleeveless silk top that caressed her curves. A handkerchief-hem flowered skirt swirled around her legs, long enough to imply competence but short and flirty enough to reveal tantalizing hints of her thighs when she moved. Pointy-toed pumps made her calves curve nicely.

Hannah forced herself not to glance at her watch again. She knew that she was annoying the receptionist with her pacing. She was beginning to annoy herself.

A blast of warmer air interrupted the air-conditioned chill, and Hannah turned. Andre, wearing his usual wraparound sunglasses and looking like the cover model for *GQ Goes Mercenary*, held the door open. The menacing look he wore warned the fans who had turned up outside the building that they would not be entering.

Nate was smiling at her as he walked through the door, clutching a giant-sized coffee cup from the nearby Coffee Bean and Tea Leaf in one hand and his guitar case in the other. The jeans that outlined the muscles of his thighs were faded, a small tear in one knee made her want to rip it wider. The black T-shirt he wore clung to every rippled inch of his torso. Despite the early hour, he looked so good even the receptionist sat up a little straighter.

'Nate.' Hannah held out her hand, her eyes flicking to the receptionist as a subtle signal that they needed to stay businesslike.

For the time being.

'Good to see you again, Hannah,' he said, taking her hand. The shake turned into a caress, and he used the contact to pull her a little closer. His lips brushed a chaste kiss across her cheek, a promise of more intimate caresses to come, and she shivered.

He saw her shiver and his smile became wicked, the look in his blue eyes meant only for her.

She dared a glance down. His jeans were faded at the crotch, and the paler mark made his interest all the more obvious.

The receptionist must have called the DJ while they were lost in each other, because she said, 'You can go through now – Jerry's waiting for you.' She buzzed them through.

Andre preceded them through the door into the inner sanctum of the station. His forbidding presence led the way through to the studio. The fluorescent lights gleamed on his freshly shaved head.

Hannah followed Andre down the hall, every sense aware of Nate close behind her. She wondered, if she stopped suddenly, would he smack into her? The temptation to test it, just to be in contact with his body, made her ache.

The DJ met them just outside the main studio, hand already outstretched. His sandy hair was drawn back into a ponytail, the freckles across his nose at odds with the crow's feet around his eyes and California-tanned-to-leather skin. The welcoming grin on his face added to the youthful effect. Jerry Kane had been a DJ on a small but influential station in the Bay Area when Nate was breaking out. He'd liked Nate's music so much that he'd played it every day for a month on his show, and the publicity had helped catapult Nate to fame.

Now in LA, his show was nationally syndicated. He was also the only DJ in the metro area enthusiastic about interviewing Nate again. Right now, everyone else considered Nate a has-been, had moved on to the newest and latest artist or stuck with the classic rock icons.

'Hey, Jerry,' Nate said. The two men engaged in a brief back-slapping hug. 'I really appreciate this.'

'No problem, man,' the DJ said. He wore jeans and a red Henley shirt with the station's logo on the breast. His voice was as smooth and mellow as it sounded on air.

'I'm thrilled you're touring again,' Jerry went on.

'I'm pretty excited myself,' Nate said. 'Jerry, you know my PR maven, Hannah Montgomery.'

'Hey, Hannah, good to see you.'

They'd met in passing over the years, working in the same music circles, and of course she'd set up this interview. If he was curious why she was on-site with Nate, he didn't ask.

'You too, Jerry,' Hannah said. 'Do we have a few minutes before we start?'

'Sure. I don't go on until six.'

They went to the sound booth where he'd be conducting the interview.

'I want to reiterate that we've got a few requirements,' Hannah said. 'Some topics are off-limits. While it's OK to positively spotlight Nate's rehab, no questions about drugs or his past drug use. We want to keep this upbeat. Highlight the new album, the new tour.'

'You know I'm on your side, man,' Jerry said to Nate, but Hannah sensed a slight hesitation. 'I only want the best for you. But if I ignore stuff . . . listeners are gonna wonder.'

Nate shrugged. 'The rehab's OK. If you have to talk about the drugs, then talk about my work with Options and their anti-drug campaign. I don't want a rehashing of the past, Jerry. I want to move on, focus on the future.'

'Those are our conditions,' Hannah said. 'Focus on the fact that Nate's clean and healthy and going out on tour again.'

The show's producer waved a hand, letting them know Jerry would be on in a few minutes. They settled in, slipping on headphones. When Hannah made the move to leave, Nate caught her eye and shook his head. He wanted her to stay. She crossed one leg over the other, aware that the handkerchief hem of her skirt played peek-a-boo with her thigh.

Jerry did his opening spiel, said Nate was coming up, took a trivia quiz call, and played a commercial before it was time for the interview.

'We have the legendary Nate Fox in the studio this morning,' he purred. 'Nate, we're thrilled to have you here. How've you been?'

'Doing great, Jerry,' Nate said. 'It's good to be talking to you again.' Beneath the counter, his fingertips caressed Hannah's thigh, teasing aside the silky fabric of her skirt.

Hannah bit her lip. It had been only a week, but far too long since she'd touched him, *really* touched him. She needed to feel him pressed against her ... She resisted the urge to scoot her chair closer so he had better access.

'I'm excited about going on tour again,' Nate was saying. 'I love playing live – I love the give and take with the fans, the feedback of energy we give each other. We're going to have a lot of fun with this one.'

Nate was good, Hannah realized. She'd never really thought about that before, how he handled the media. How he put on the public face. He knew what to say. He sounded good, positive, and it was all true.

She'd seen him on stage. It was obvious he loved performing more than anything.

'You're touring based on a new album, *Cannibal Eyes*,' Jerry said. 'A CD of cover songs – that's a new direction for you, isn't it?'

'That's right. It's an album of songs that influenced me when I was younger, songs that meant something to me, that made me want to do this crazy job.'

'Some of your fans are itching for new music,' Jerry said.

'We'll focus on that after this tour,' Nate said. His tone was easy, but he moved his hand away from Hannah's leg. 'The tour will be a combination of tunes from *Cannibal Eyes* as well as a lot of my hits – the fan favorites. I may even pull out a B-side or two. You'll just have to come out and see the show.'

'I plan to do that,' Jerry said. 'I never miss a Nate Fox extravaganza. Right now, we're going to play a track from the new album, *Cannibal Eyes*. This one's called "Panama," and I don't have to tell you who sang it originally, do I?'

They all slipped off their headphones for the duration of the song.

'I love your version of this,' Jerry said. 'It's a whole new take on the song, but it's still honest to the original. That's not an easy combination.'

'Thanks,' Nate said.

'Good thing to mention,' Hannah said, and Jerry did when they were back on air.

It was going well, Hannah decided. Jerry was enthusiastic, Nate well spoken. The songs spoke for themselves.

Jerry played 'Dragons of Winter,' one of Nate's biggest hits. She loved that one.

'So, Nate,' Jerry said. 'How are you approaching this tour? You've been through rehab, but being on the road must have its temptations.'

'One day at a time, Jerry, one day at a time,' Nate said smoothly. 'I've made mistakes, and I acknowledge them. But like I said, the real high of touring is being on stage and the interaction with the fans. I've missed them and I'm looking forward to the connection again. There are always some familiar faces out there.'

He glanced at Hannah as he spoke. She felt the heat rising in her cheeks. Did he remember seeing her in the crowd before? Did he know what his music did to her?

'Fantastic,' Jerry said. After playing another song, he went on, 'So, Nate, you're the fantasy of women worldwide. Is it true you haven't been in a relationship since Suzanne Cooper?'

Hannah choked on her own breath. Nate's face twisted in anguish, and she wanted to climb over the desk and punch Jerry in the face.

It was a low blow to bring it up. She thought they'd made it clear that Nate's past wasn't to be discussed.

Instead of following her first desire to smack Jerry into next Tuesday, Hannah went with another, stronger instinct. Beneath the desk, she put a hand on Nate's leg. Comforting. Reassuring. Letting him know she was there for him and that she understood.

'Suzanne's death changed a lot of things in my life,' Nate said, surprising her when he answered Jerry's question. His fingers twined with hers. The warmth of his grip reassured her.

The DJ's eyebrows went up. It was obvious he hadn't been sure if Nate would answer the question. Avoiding Hannah's angry gaze, he went on, 'You were never charged in the accident, were you?'

'I wasn't driving,' Nate said. 'We were both high, but she was behind the wheel. Since negligent stupidity isn't a crime, no charges were brought. I got off with hardly a scratch and she died.'

'And you went into rehab?'

'Yeah. Three months of hell, but it was worth every second of it.'

'Are you worried that the pressures of the road will make you slip? Sex, drugs, rock and roll, you know.'

'No,' Nate said. He leaned forward, his eyes holding Jerry's as if by convincing the DJ, he could convince the world. 'I'm clean and I'm staying that way. There won't be any other casualties in my life.'

Jerry nodded slowly. 'Thanks for being honest, Nate. But you still haven't answered one question. Are you seeing anybody now? If you're not, you're going to raise the hopes of your fans everywhere.'

His tone was light, as if he were trying to soften the previous blow. It was too little, too late, Hannah thought, but it was better than nothing. She still intended to strangle the man until he begged for mercy. And then a little bit longer, for good measure.

'Let's just say I'm exploring my options right now, Jerry,' Nate said. 'I'm not quite ready to bring my personal life into the spotlight. That's reserved for my music. The tour is my main focus, which starts in Las Vegas in two days.'

Good job, Hannah mouthed at him. He gave her hand a squeeze. Her reaction to his touch was entirely unprofessional, but she managed to keep it to herself.

'Let's take a caller,' Jerry said. 'Hi, you've got a direct connection to Nate Fox.'

'Hi, Nate,' a woman's voice said, 'this is Helen.'

Hannah pursed her lips. Why was that name familiar?

'Hey, Helen,' Nate said. 'What's up?'

'It was great seeing you in San Francisco last week,' Helen said.

Oh! *That* Helen. Was she some sort of stalker? Hannah wondered. But Nate seemed unconcerned, treating Helen as if she were a familiar part of his life.

'Thanks,' he said. 'It was great seeing you, too. Thanks for coming out. It's good to be touching base with the fans again. What's your question?'

'I was wondering about your choice of including "Renegade" on *Cannibal Eyes*,' Helen said. 'What kind of inspiration was Styx for you?'

If Hannah weren't kind of jealous of Helen, she might want to hire the woman. She knew the right questions to ask.

Nate talked more in depth about his early influences, and then Jerry queued up another song.

'Not cool, Jerry,' Hannah said as soon as the song started and they could take off the headphones. 'Bringing up the accident.' And Suzanne. She didn't want to think about Suzanne, and Nate certainly didn't, although for different reasons.

'I can't ignore what happened,' Jerry said. 'I told you that. I didn't ask about the accident, OK? Just about who he's dating now.'

'You could have left Suzanne out of it and just asked about the present,' Hannah snapped.

'It's OK,' Nate said. His face was a neutral mask that she couldn't read. She didn't like that one bit. 'It's over. Let's just move on.'

She wanted to distract him. She needed to. He was keeping up a fantastic public front, not letting the listeners know how he was really feeling. From a PR front, she couldn't ask for anything better.

On a personal front, however, she couldn't bear to see him this way.

'I'll be right back,' she said.

A quick trip to the ladies' room was all she needed.

Andre stood in the hall, leaning against the wall in a casual manner that Hannah knew was a front. He could snap her like a twig if he wanted to. She promised herself to always stay on his good side.

'Keeping the crazed fans at bay?' she asked on the way back from the restroom.

He smiled, teeth flashing. Definitely a man who'd had whitening done, along with his usual manicure.

'Well, one of the marketing people has walked by five times so far, but I think he's just attracted to the smell of my cologne.'

'Like flies to honey,' Hannah said.

'Don't you know it.'

Inside, Nate was playing something live on his guitar. His eyes were closed as he leaned toward the microphone. His shoulders were still tense, though.

She waited until the 'On Air' sign went off again and slipped back into the sound booth.

'Everything OK?' she asked, and both Nate and Jerry nodded. Neither looked unduly upset, which she hoped meant Jerry hadn't set off any more bombs.

'You OK?' Nate said quietly to her as she sat back down.

'I'm great,' she said, and palmed him her silk panties. 'You?'

His sharp intake of breath told her more than words ever could.

It was more daring than she'd ever been. Oh, she'd gone without underwear once on a boyfriend's dare, and once again when she couldn't find her thong after her night at Nate's. But her boldness in passing off her underwear to Nate surprised her.

And thrilled her.

Distraction had been her goal, to pull him out of the morass of bad memories and negative emotions. His arousal was just pure reward.

Even though her skirt was beneath her, she was more aware of the chair's leather seat, and certainly the sensation of her skirt's fabric on her ass. She crossed her legs, her clit tingling. She had managed to turn them both on.

The next caller wanted to know if Nate's tour would be coming to Cleveland, and the one after that asked about Les Paul versus Gibson guitars. Although Hannah couldn't see Nate's hand, she could tell from the way his bicep flexed that he was toying with the scrap of silk as he talked.

'We've got time for one more song,' Jerry said. 'This is

from the platinum album *Strange Desires*. I'm sure you'll all recognize the song of the same name.'

After the show, Jerry apologized again, citing the program manager's insistence.

'We got through it,' Nate said. 'I know you're getting pulled from both ends, Jerry. I appreciate the airtime.'

'Take care, man,' Jerry said. 'I'll be at the Forum show.'

'See you on the flipside.'

Hannah shook hands with Jerry, saying essentially what Nate had, and then they fell into step down the hall.

'Naughty girl,' Nate murmured in her ear. 'I've had panties thrown at me on stage before, but I've never had them passed to me during a radio spot.'

'I just wanted to distract you,' Hannah said.

'Oh, you did that, all right. In spades.' He leaned close. His breath against her ear, fluttering her hair, aroused her as much as his next words: 'I want you, Hannah. I need you. Soon.'

'Well, you'll just have to hold on to that thought,' she said, wishing just as desperately that they could be alone. She wanted to lick her way down his chest and, when he couldn't take anymore, climb on top of him and ride him until they were both sated. 'We've got two newspaper interviews and one phone call with *Rockdawg* magazine before noon. Then you have to meet the rest of the band for a rehearsal. And somewhere in there, Sam said something about last-minute wardrobe fittings.'

He groaned.

'I want you just as bad,' she admitted. 'Tonight. My place. I'll feed you.'

'And I'll eat . . . whatever you offer,' he said, and she would have stumbled if he hadn't caught her arm.

'Nice,' Nate remarked, following Hannah into her condo. The door led to an open floor plan, the large living room flowing into the kitchen and dining area. Plush rugs in bold colors covered areas of the shining wood floor. The last of the day's sunshine spilled into the room through glass doors leading to a balcony, beyond which he could see the Hollywood Hills.

'Thanks.' Hannah smiled over her shoulder while she dumped her attaché case onto the table by the door. 'Why don't you make yourself at home? I want to change and then get dinner ready.'

'Not yet,' he said.

Hannah frowned. 'You're not hungry?'

Nate laughed. Catching her wrist, he circled it lightly with his fingers, using it to draw her close. His mouth quirked into a smile, and her heart skipped a beat. 'I am very –' a brush of his lips against one corner of her mouth. '– very –' the other corner, the feathery caress sending a tingle of excitement through her '– hungry.' His mouth took hers, sending all thoughts of dinner right out of her head.

Nate's tongue flicked her lips, learning their shape, drawing a whimper of need. He laughed again. The sound was a low masculine growl that thrummed along her nerve endings. His tongue dipped in, swiping the slick flesh inside her bottom lip.

Hannah tried to catch his tongue with hers, but he drew back. One long-fingered hand stroked the length of her back, soothing her protest. He kissed her again.

Hannah's hands splayed on the soft cotton of his shirt, fingers curling tightly, wanting him to take the kiss deeper, to feel the connection her body longed for.

But he made her wait. Light caresses, the gentlest touch of his tongue to hers had her trembling with desire. Nate caught her bottom lip between his teeth. He nibbled until she felt the sensation echoed in her breasts, in the aching bead of her nipples. Still not giving her what she wanted, Nate skimmed the line of her jaw with his mouth. He explored the hollow beneath her ear, his warm breath teasing her flesh.

'Please,' she murmured. Her hands moved to his shoulders, feeling the hard ridge of muscle. He was making her crazy. When he slid a thigh between hers, Hannah moaned, rubbing against him. Nate eased his leg away, refusing to let her seek the pressure she craved. All the while, his mouth continued to explore the smooth skin of her throat.

'You smell wonderful,' he murmured, his tongue flicking against her earlobe.

She thought he did too, but she wasn't sure she had enough brain cells functioning to point it out.

'What are you wearing?'

Hannah licked her lips. He expected her to speak? 'Bergamot,' she said, tipping her head back so his mouth could suck lightly at the place where her pulse thundered. 'Lemongrass,' she added weakly.

'Mm,' he commented. His thigh rubbed lightly against her, tantalizing her with his nearness.

Hannah arched into him when his broad musician's hands curved along her ribcage. His thumbs teased the undersides of her breasts, and she thought she was going to die if he didn't take her soon. She squeezed the muscles of his arms, feeling the strength there, holding onto him when he nuzzled aside the edge of her shirt to lightly nip her collarbone.

'Do you know that my room still smells like you?' he asked. Nate drew back enough to look into her eyes. Hannah found herself fixated on the dark sweep of his eyelashes. She'd had more experience with men's eyelashes since she was a teenager, and Nate's really were amazingly sexy. 'I haven't had a decent night's sleep since you were there.'

'So you're saying you're too exhausted to function?' she asked with a quick lift of her eyebrows.

Nate laughed, the sapphire of his eyes lightening. 'Sweetheart, I don't think you'll have to worry about that.'

Then he kissed her again. Finally, his mouth devoured hers the way she had hungered for since they'd parted. Her own dreams had been haunted by his taste, and she reveled in it now. He tasted of mint and coffee, and she moaned as he filled her senses. Suckling his tongue, Hannah felt a surge of power when he growled in response. He cupped her ass, lifting her to settle her hips against him. Wrapping one leg around his thigh, Hannah moved against the hard bulge of his erection, sending tremors through them both. The pressure did little to ease the ache in her crotch. She couldn't seem to get close enough to him. Hungrily, she slipped her hands between them. Nate hissed when her fingers stroked him through his jeans.

'Didn't you promise me dinner?' he asked. His eyes were closed, his forehead against hers. Her fingers were plucking at his belt buckle.

'Are you hungry?' she asked breathlessly.

'Now we're back where we started,' he said with a laugh. A last kiss, his mouth clinging gently to hers, and then he stepped back. His hands remained on her hips. 'We have all night.'

'You started this,' Hannah pointed out. Her body felt empty, needy. She ran her fingernails across his denim-covered cock, making him twitch. The sharp intake of his breath made her smile in feminine satisfaction.

'I'm going to change, Nate. Make yourself at home.' Slipping away from him, she left him standing in the foyer. Hannah could feel him watching her, and she smiled to herself, putting a little extra swing in her hips.

Up until now, he had been the one in control.

Tonight was where she took it back.

Chapter Eight

Nate wandered into the living room. His jeans were unbearably tight. The woman could turn him on like no one else.

He closed his eyes, breathing deeply. The action only served to fill his lungs with her scent. It lingered in her condo, driving him crazy. He had to fight off the urge to follow her back to her bedroom, dinner be damned. Looking around for something to distract himself, his gaze settled on the mantel.

Photos graced the pale cream marble, interspersed with personal knick-knacks. He picked up a silver-framed photo showing Gina on the beach next to a surfboard, a wide smile on her face. In the photo next to it, the two friends were together. Gina still displayed her board while Hannah, curvy in a one-piece emerald bathing suit, her hair slicked back, flashed the hang-ten sign. The photo had caught the mischief in her eyes, even while her tongue was stuck out at the photographer. Nate smiled. She looked young, but not as young as the gawky teenager he'd first met.

Setting down the photo, he picked up another. It showed an older couple, the man's arm thrown around Hannah's shoulder. She wore a graduation gown, the cap at a jaunty angle. He recognized the couple as her parents. It had been a few years since he'd seen Everett Forbes, having switched labels after his second album, but Hannah's father had changed only a little. He touched a gentle fingertip to the young woman in the photo.

For whatever reason, Hannah didn't seem to want him to know that they'd met before.

Still restless, Nate wandered to the sliding glass doors. Hannah's condo was up high enough in the building that he could see over the palm trees. To his right he could see the rooftops of Hollywood, if he had his geography correct. The hills directly ahead were hazy, shifting to a darker blue-grey as the sun set.

'There's a blanket on the end of the couch,' Hannah said from behind him. 'Will you spread it out on the floor?'

'Planning on giving me a massage?' Nate asked as he turned.

His brief attempt at humor disappeared. He could only stare. The silk lounging pajamas were the same delicate purple as the sunset sky behind him. She'd left the bottom two shirt buttons undone, teasing him with glimpses of her flat stomach. She looked both totally hot and coolly untouchable.

It made him want to devour her.

She noticed his attention. Holding his gaze, she stroked one finger down the buttons of her shirt and slowly popped open another at the bottom. A flash of creamy flesh, the dip of her navel. He actually groaned out loud. He took a step forward, intent on ripping open the rest of those buttons.

'The blanket, Nate,' she prompted. The smile she gave him was full of wicked female confidence. She knew exactly what she was doing. She slipped behind the counter that separated the living room from the kitchen. She reached up to take Fiestaware plates from a shelf, her top's silky material pulling taut across her breasts. Her nipples were hard.

Nate felt his cock twitch again. She was killing him. He pushed the coffee table aside and moved to pick up the blanket. It felt incredibly soft in his hands as he spread the cream expanse over the gold looped-leather area rug.

'We're having a picnic,' she told him, carrying the

plates and wine glasses into the room. He stole a kiss as he took them from her. She smiled and ducked away. Her hair was caught in a French braid. He wanted to unwind it, to feel the waves spilling across his fingers. Instead, he knelt, setting the plates and glasses on the blanket.

'What kind of picnic?' he asked when she carried a wicker basket into the room. He took it from her. When he tried to peer inside, she lightly slapped his hand.

'Patience,' she told him, and then returned to the kitchen to retrieve a bucket of ice and a chilled bottle of sparkling cider. She settled in a swirl of silk at his side. Her knee nudged his. He wanted to slide the silk up her leg, press his lips against the warm skin behind her knee. He bit back a groan.

'Will you open the bottle?' she asked.

Since it gave him something to do with his hands, Nate obliged. He cursed the cork as he wrestled with it. She'd completely thrown him off guard, turning him into an adolescent boy on his first date. He felt shaky and unsure.

And totally turned on.

'Here,' Hannah said, leaning close to slip a grape between his lips. Her fingers brushed against his mouth. He felt the contact right down to his toes, and all the sensitive places in between. The grape burst between his teeth, flooding his mouth with its crisp taste.

When he poured their drinks, his hand trembled. Handing her a glass, Nate watched while she sipped. Her smoky-grey eyes held his over the rim of the glass. She touched the tip of her pink tongue to her bottom lip, and a groan escaped him.

She was in complete control, and knew it. He was going to have to do something about that.

Plucking a grape from the bunch she'd placed between them, he held it out. Stroking the cool globe across her lips, he leaned close. When she bit down, he kissed her, sharing the explosion of flavor on her tongue. He nipped her bottom lip. When she would have deepened the kiss, he drew back. He smiled at her soft sound of disappointment.

'I have a present for you,' he said. 'But you're going to have to wait for it.'

'Why?' Hannah asked.

'Because I'm hungry. What's on the menu?' he responded, surveying the spread of food she'd managed to arrange while he'd been opening the bottle.

'Finger food, for starters,' she said. The look in her eyes was a mixture of laughter and desire.

'Mm,' he murmured approvingly. Catching her hand, he lifted it to his mouth. The tip of his tongue traced a damp path from her palm up the sensitive inside of her index finger. 'My favorite kind.'

'Behave,' she told him.

'Or?' he prompted.

Hannah smiled, spreading something that smelled delicious onto a stone-wheat pita. 'Or you won't get dessert.'

He bit down onto her offering, the savory tastes of pesto, cream cheese and sun-dried tomatoes unfurling in his mouth. He watched as she took a bite after him. A dot of pesto clung to her lip and he swiped it off with his thumb, offering it to her.

'Finger food,' he told her with a grin. The grin faded as she swiped her tongue over his flesh, then curled it around the warm digit. When she sucked his fingertip into her mouth, he almost came.

'Damn, Hannah, do that again and we won't be eating dinner,' he warned.

She laughed, delighted by his reaction.

She fed him apple slices, their tart crunch a delightful counterpoint to the robust combination of the pesto and tomato. He fed her a spread made of lemon and artichoke, the citrusy scent tantalizing as he layered it on a cracker. He shared the taste on her lips, helpless to do anything other than cup her cheek with his palm while he supped on her mouth.

She was making him crazy. And oh, so aroused.

'Are you ready for tomorrow?' he asked, trying to regain a semblance of control. If he didn't, it was all going to be over too soon. And she'd promised him dessert.

'Sam had my luggage picked up already. I just have to throw the essentials in a bag.'

'Mm, I like a woman who doesn't wait until the last minute.' He eased aside the collar of her silk pajama top. The flesh of her shoulder tasted better than anything he'd eaten. He nibbled, feeling the shiver that ran through her.

'Keep up the compliments, Fox. You may get lucky,' she told him. Her voice was breathy. He was pleased to have made it that way. He looked forward to making her even more incoherent. As much as he'd loved listening to the noises she made when aroused through the phone lines, it had been exquisite torture not to be actively touching her, not see her grey eyes go unfocused.

Nate grinned. He dipped a finger into his glass, painting a wet line down her throat. He followed it with his tongue. Hannah moaned as his teeth grazed her skin.

Soft red hair tickled his chin as she dipped her head to kiss his temple. The touch of her mouth on his skin made Nate's hand clench into the blanket. When her mouth drifted lower, he closed his eyes, concentrating on sheer sensation. He was so hard it hurt. He wanted to grab her hand and place it on his crotch so she'd know what she was doing to him, but he made himself wait. Besides, he knew full well that she was aware of his every reaction.

Reaching out, Nate tickled his fingers along her instep, sliding her pant leg higher. She yelped, yanking her foot away, but not before he noticed that her toenails were painted a deep, sexy burgundy.

He dragged his finger through the lemony spread she'd fed him only minutes before, and caught her ankle. His eyes held hers, seeing the desire in her smoky gaze. With a light touch, he smeared the cool paste across the delicate bones of her foot. Still holding her gaze, he bent his head and slowly licked it off. He was pleased to hear her moan.

'What else is in that basket of yours?'

Hannah licked her lips. Her chest rose and fell, her nipples bold beneath the concealing fabric. 'We haven't finished the appetizers yet.'

'Yes, we have,' he told her. He licked her calf, tracing a wandering path across her flesh. Her scent was stronger here. His lips found the curve of her knee. She dotted her perfume there, in the crease of flesh he tasted so slowly. Up on his knees, he lifted his head and caught her mouth in a hot kiss.

The secret taste of her mouth filled him, more intoxicating than any wine could ever be. He chased her tongue through the slick warmth of her mouth, twining with it in an erotic dance. When her hands tugged at his shirt, he helped, not breaking the kiss until he had to. Her palms splayed flat across his chest, branding him with heat. He finished pulling his shirt from his jeans, yanked it over his head and flung it somewhere.

When he tried to ease her back onto the blanket, though, she twisted aside.

'Dessert,' she reminded him.

Nate made a frustrated noise and sucked in a deep breath. He didn't think he could take any more damn finger foods. Hannah straddled his thighs, and he took the opportunity to rest his hands on her legs. His thumbs stroked circles on her inner thighs and he felt her muscles tremble.

'You're making me crazy,' she murmured. Her palm

was warm against his chest and her teeth tugged lightly at her bottom lip as his fingers slid a little closer to their goal. Her eyes opened, the smoky grey bewitching him.

Nate yelped when she pushed him down. The blanket felt soft against his back, but the position put him too far from her lips. Hannah wiggled, moving into a more comfortable spot astride his hips. The contact was a tease, because when his hands tightened on her legs, she stopped moving. Her smile was wicked and he wondered what this woman had planned for them next.

'I thought we were having dessert,' he said. He was having trouble focusing on anything other than the heat between her thighs, feeling it right through the denim of his jeans. He wondered if she'd replaced the underwear she'd given him earlier, or whether she was naked and wet for him under the pajama pants.

'We are,' she said. Hannah reached into the basket and pulled out a bowl. The sweet summer scent of strawberries teased his nose. She took a ripe berry and stroked it playfully across his lips. Nate bit the fruit, watched as she finished it.

'I've never eaten dessert lying down before,' he pointed out.

Hannah's eyebrows arched. 'A dessert virgin. I've never had a virgin before.'

He grinned. 'Will you be gentle with me?' She rocked lightly against his hips, and Nate felt the ache in his groin intensify, making him catch his breath.

'Are you sure that's what you want?' Hannah asked softly.

'I want you,' he told her. He caught her gaze, watching as her eyes widened. Need darkened them, echoing what she saw in his. Nate watched as uncertainty warred with desire. Her lashes swept downward, hiding her feelings. When she looked at him again, pure mischief had replaced the doubt. She reached back into the basket and then tossed a foil-wrapped condom onto the blanket.

A bowl of chocolate joined the strawberries. Hannah swirled a red berry through the dark confection and held it over Nate's chest. He watched as a fat, cool droplet dripped onto his skin. Hannah leaned over and licked him clean. He closed his eyes as she painted a stripe of chocolate down the center of his chest, using the fruit as a brush.

'I didn't know you were so artistic,' he murmured when she continued the action, circling his nipples.

'There are a lot of things you don't know about me,' she teased. Hannah bit into the strawberry, using the red juice to add to the design she was creating.

Nate dropped his hands from her legs and clenched his fingers into the soft blanket. The need to touch her, to slide his hands up her thighs and drive her wild with passion was too strong. But if he continued to touch her, he would lose control. And he wanted to see what she would do next.

Chocolate pooled at the base of his throat. Tipping his head back obligingly, Nate moaned at the touch of her mouth. She nibbled his flesh, teeth drawing shivers of sensation along his skin. Her mouth moved lower, removing her artwork slowly. He felt her tongue sweep over the circle she'd created around his left nipple and he sucked in a sharp breath.

She flicked her tongue across him, and his hips left the blanket, rocking up against her. She laughed delightedly, her breath hot against his skin. Nate groaned, convinced that she would be the death of him.

Hannah dripped chocolate into his navel. He opened his eyes to watch her dip a strawberry into it. Sharp white teeth bit delicately and the enjoyment on her face nearly did him in. He opened his mouth when she held the strawberry to his lips and took a bite. He caught her hand, then licked her fingers clean. When he tried to trail his tongue along her wrist, she pulled away.

'I'm not done yet,' she murmured. She scooted down, her braid tickling his stomach. Lightly, she tongued his navel. The sensation was overwhelmingly erotic and his eyes closed again, losing himself in pleasure. When her fingers found the button of his jeans he moaned again, so close to exploding that he thought he wasn't going to last long enough to bury himself inside of her.

Nate lifted his hips and felt her drag his jeans and briefs down. She straddled his legs again, holding him still. Unable to resist watching, he opened his eyes to see her drizzle chocolate along the ridge of his erection. It teased his swollen flesh, sending a buzz of pleasure through him that made his entire body twitch.

Hannah's bottom lip was caught between her teeth and Nate couldn't decide what was more erotic: the anticipation of what she was going to do next or the expression of concentration on her face.

Hannah looked up. She grinned wickedly when she saw he was watching. Nate held his breath when she leaned over, waiting, but instead of his aching cock, she touched her lips to the smooth skin of his hip. Her tongue swirled over the tattoo there, a winged guitar wrapped in a banner bearing the words 'Rock & Roll Forever.'

'You're killing me,' he informed her, his breath coming in short pants when she traced damp patterns on his skin. Hannah laughed, her teeth grazing the point of his hip bone. Just when he'd become resigned to the thought that she might never give him relief, Nate cried out as the tip of her tongue flicked against the base of his cock.

She slowly licked the hard length of him. The feeling was indescribable, and his hands finally lifted to stroke her hair, needing to touch her almost as much as he needed his next breath. Her lips closed around him, the wet heat of her mouth slid down his length. Her tongue lapped at his flesh, seeking the chocolate, giving exquisite pleasure. She sucked, her tongue and lips stroking, tasting.

'Hannah, stop,' Nate said, knowing he wasn't going to last much longer. He felt as much as heard her laugh, the vibrations rippling through him. He gave in, hating and loving the loss of control – and then the pleasure became too much and exploded outward, taking his senses with it.

Hannah pressed her lips to his damp chest, smiling. 'I always was a big fan of dessert,' she whispered. Thinking him still lost in the pleasure she'd given, she leaned closer and brushed her mouth across his.

She was wrong. She yelped in surprise when he flipped her neatly onto her back, pinning her against the blanket with the weight of his body. His sapphire eyes were dark and dangerous.

'My turn,' he said. He sat up, slipping the last few buttons of her shirt free and pushing the edges wide. She shivered, her nipples puckering harder. Nate dribbled chocolate onto the taut flesh, smiling when he heard her soft whimper. Hannah bit her lip, feeling him drag a strawberry around her nipple, scooping up the rich liquid. He tasted the fruit, murmuring his appreciation, before licking the remaining liquid off her breast. His teeth tugged at her nipple and her clit fluttered in response.

She'd gotten incredibly aroused while playing with him; she was already more than ready for him. But she suspected that he was going to tease her as exquisitely as she'd teased him.

Hannah tried to remain still while he made a gooey trail down her stomach, but he nibbled lightly, his tongue teasing until she writhed impatiently. Nate laughed. His husky voice slid over stimulated nerve endings like velvet. He moved lower, the decadent path dampening her flesh.

Thumbs hooked into her waistband and he peeled her pajama bottoms down. The pants joined his shirt somewhere in the room. She was deliciously naked beneath them.

Chocolate drizzled over her nether lips and Hannah forgot how to breathe. When his tongue tasted her, licking the chocolate and mingled juices from her flesh, she cried out, the pleasure so intense she thought she might not survive it.

Nate parted her with his fingers and then Hannah felt something cool and faintly rough stroke across her clit. Trapped between curiosity and pleasure, she dimly realized he was teasing her with a strawberry.

As he circled her core, teasing her aching bud, she widened her legs and arched her back. Giving herself over completely to the sinful sensation of the fruit massaging her flesh.

The seeds bumped over her, stimulating as he circled and stroked. She cried out when he stopped. Cried out again when the heat of his mouth replaced the cool berry. He sucked her inside, his tongue flicking, and Hannah came. Waves of heat and pleasure flooded her.

Nate paused long enough to sheath himself in a condom and for her to be amazed at his recuperative ability, and then surged into her. Hannah gripped him tightly, her fingers digging into his back as he spread her wide.

He rocked slowly and Hannah matched his rhythm, feeling him hard and thick and deep. Desire pooled in her stomach, heat gathering again. She tried to quicken their pace, but now he was the one in control.

Nate held back, murmuring soft words against her throat, forcing the pleasure to coil tighter and tighter. His back was smooth and strong, and she ran her hands down his spine and then up again, then tangled her fingers in the thick dark hair at his nape. His mouth claimed hers, tongues thrusting in a dance that matched the movement of their hips. Hannah moaned.

When she came again, he swallowed her cries before matching them with his own.

Hannah didn't know, or care, how long they lay entangled on the blanket, their breathing and heart rates slowing. Proper post-coital bliss demanded no checking of clocks or concerns about schedules.

She let her mind wander, her insides fluttering in response to the memories of their most recent clinch.

Another thought wandered into her brain. 'Hey,' she said lazily.

Nate's warm breath fluttered a lock of her hair. 'Hm?'

'Would it be presumptuous of me to assume that this was the present you mentioned earlier?' She nuzzled the warm skin at the juncture of his shoulder and neck, letting her teeth graze lightly.

A slow grin spread across his face. A grin she'd lusted over in pictures and posters for years. She'd had to grow up before she understood the sensual, wicked thoughts behind it.

Amazingly, that sensual wicked grin was all for her right now.

'Ah, that,' he said. 'Actually, there is something else. Have you been good girl?'

She purred, running her tongue along his collarbone. 'I think you can answer that better than I.'

'In that case, I'd say you've been a bad girl.' The look in his eyes made her insides spasm. 'And bad girls deserve presents like this.' He disengaged from their embrace and walked naked to where his leather jacket hung on the carved teak stand by the door. Hannah propped herself on one arm to admire the taut muscles in his ass.

He returned, carrying a small iridescent bag tied at

the top with curly ribbon. He settled back onto the blanket, his body warm where it pressed against hers. Her nostrils flared at the spicy scent of their lovemaking. She reached out and groped for her glass, took a swallow.

'I've been thinking about you a lot,' he confessed. 'Thinking about what you might like. And, quite frankly, the fact is that thoughts of you have been driving me crazy.' He handed her the bag.

Her curiosity piqued, Hannah slid the ribbons down one side of the handles so she could part the top of the bag. She pulled out the item, wrapped in unassuming turquoise tissue paper, still entirely clueless as to what it could possibly be.

The tissue paper parted to reveal a black leather thong. But not an ordinary thong, she noted almost immediately. There was a rigid object in the crotch of the underwear. She hefted the cool, smooth panties in her hand and looked at him, head cocked in question.

He uncurled his fist to show a small white rectangular box. With his thumb he flicked a switch.

The thong in her hand buzzed and she nearly dropped it in surprise. 'Oh my!'

Nate was watching her intently, gauging her reaction. She felt a blush rising to her cheeks. Remote-controlled vibrating underwear wasn't something she'd ever played with before. She'd heard of it, but . . .

Now, the very thought of putting them on, of having Nate wielding the remote, of being helpless to control the situation, made her brain short-circuit.

'Shall I go put these on, then?' she asked.

Hannah saw Nate's shoulders relax and felt a thrill of pride that she hadn't disappointed him. To be honest, the very idea of wearing them was causing a resurgence of wetness between her thighs. He'd be in total command. He would be able to make her come whenever he wanted to, and she'd be able to do nothing about it.

'No.' His large hand closed over her smaller one, trapping the panties in her fist. 'Not yet.' His voice was hoarse. 'I want you to wear them at the first concert, in Vegas.'

Her breath caught in her throat. Mental pictures raced through her mind. She'd been to what? Ten? Twenty of his concerts over the years? Maybe more. Even as a teenager, she'd been aroused by his performance. One year, she'd finally admitted to Gina that the back of the seats in front of them had been at an awfully auspicious height ... and Gina had laughed, admitting that she'd often noticed the same thing.

Nate stroked the length of her side, leaving in his hand's wake a trail of hypersensitized flesh. 'Will you wear it?'

She looked from the naughty present to him. To the look in his eyes that dared her to say yes. She nodded quickly and was rewarded with a kiss.

Nate claimed her mouth, sucking her lower lip between his teeth and nipping gently. 'Good. I like the thought of you being in my control.'

Nate propped himself up on one elbow so he could peer over Hannah's sleeping form to see the clock. The large red digital numbers showed him it was 3.16 a.m. The faint glow also showed him the perfect symmetry of Hannah's smooth back, the sheet rumpled low on her hip. She lay half on her stomach, half on her side, the small of her back an erotic shadow.

He resisted the urge to run his hand along the curve of her hip. As tempting as she was, he didn't want to wake her. He had another need to tend to first.

The door to the bathroom was in the short hall that led from the bedroom to the living room, but he couldn't remember which door. He leaned into the first room he came to and found the light switch.

Not the bathroom, but Hannah's office. He hadn't seen it earlier, so he paused to glance around. It always fascinated him to see the details of someone else's life, someone else's home. Hannah, he saw, was neither incredibly neat – as made apparent by the languishing Starbuck's cup and the flurry of green and pink Post-it Notes decorating the wall near her desk – nor astonishingly messy – evidenced by the neatly labeled file cabinets and stacked trays.

He turned to flick off the light, and that was when he saw the poster.

Mentally he did the math and realized she'd probably had it all those years ago when they'd first met. It was worn around the edges, but lovingly framed. It was, he mused, worth a fortune. Pity he didn't have a few copies lying around his attic.

He scanned the poster with an impartial eye. He'd been younger then and his career had just been taking off. He'd been caught up in the wonder of it, of being able to share his music with such a wide audience. The money hadn't been a bad side effect, either. It was what he'd done with it. Tossing away a frightening amount on women and drugs. Lost in his own sense of self-importance.

He was very lucky that Sam had pushed him to invest a portion of it when he'd first hit the charts. If he never wrote another song, performed on another stage, he'd still be able to live however he chose.

But early retirement wasn't what he wanted. He wanted the edge back. He wanted the spotlight. He wanted a chance to prove to himself that he could do it all again.

Do it without fucking up again.

He wanted to prove to himself that he could still make music that affected people.

Nate wondered what his idealistic younger self would

have thought of who he'd become. He shook his head. It didn't matter, really. It had been a fun ride before the fall. He could only go forward from here.

The existence of the poster told him something else, though. If it hadn't been obvious before, it certainly was now: Hannah Montgomery was still a card-carrying Nate Fox fan.

Nate flipped off the light and found the bathroom. He wondered if she'd ever been backstage. If they'd ever met up at an industry party. Sadly, there were real holes in his memory. He could have met her a dozen times. He'd never know.

He only remembered the shy girl who'd seemed so normal, despite who her father was, how much money her family had. Not like one of the miniskirted, overly made-up women who gathered near the tour bus or bribed their way backstage. Her sweetness had been part of her allure. It was one of the reasons he'd remembered her after all these years.

The shyness was gone. Oh, there were flashes here and there, but he hadn't been the only one with an interest in seduction that first night they'd met. Today she'd plotted and planned an erotic picnic and been the aggressor, and it had turned him on more than he could have imagined. He wondered what else she might do, given free rein. He hoped he'd find out.

That sweetness was still there, though, part of the mystery. She intrigued him, mind, body and soul.

Realizing he was far too awake to crawl back into bed, despite the enticement of Hannah's naked body, he grabbed his jeans, abandoned in the living room, and tugged them on. He carried his guitar case out onto the balcony. City sounds interrupted the night, muted but ever present. Exotic scents drifted to him on the light breeze, night-blooming jasmine from the building's landscaping. He made himself comfortable on the outdoor loveseat, took his guitar into his hand and rested it on his lap. It fit him like an old friend. His arm automatically curled over it, the body so much like a woman's.

A soft strum released music into the night. A few twists of the pegs brought it into tune. He propped his feet up onto the railing and let his hands play across the strings. There was no plan, no mental command to make music. His body just did what it had done for nearly as long as he could remember.

Letting his mind drift, trying not to focus too hard on the need, Nate explored old songs, revisiting his own and others. He tried to trick his hands into new melodies, tried to open new paths in his mind. Tried to write something that he hadn't heard a million times before.

Tried to write anything new.

But as before, a few notes in, he froze up. Either trailed off or segued into something old and familiar.

He heard the slide of metal on metal behind him, the rustle of fabric, and he turned to see Hannah. The pale silky robe she wore was ghostly in the night, her hair a deeper shadow over her shoulders. The scent of her teased him, starting a slow burn in his groin.

'Don't stop,' she said softly, taking a seat next to him. She curled her legs under her, her knee bumping his hip.

He leaned over to kiss her, relishing the way she opened to him. He was dizzy with her when he finally pulled back.

Leaning her head against her hand, she observed him quietly. 'Were you playing something new when I came out? I didn't recognize it.'

Nate shook his head. His hands automatically shaped the chords, playing the tune she'd heard. It was simple, from a time when he was still learning to write music. Back when he was still able to. 'I wrote this years ago. It never made it onto an album.'

The sound of notes released into the night wrapped

around them. It was a secret time, no lights except for the few brave stars that shone through the ever-present haze, the stronger lights of the never-sleeping city.

There was an intimacy to the dark of night, and Nate thought back over the past week to all the conversations they'd shared. The long phone calls and the things they'd been able to say because they weren't face to face. It felt like that now, even though they sat close enough to touch.

It felt like he could tell her anything.

More importantly, he wanted to tell her. Almost needed to – to confess the one secret that represented a barrier between them.

He stopped playing and he realized his hands were trembling. He knew he was taking a chance. If he'd misread everything, if Hannah was interested only in him for his rock god persona, then his words would destroy her vision of him. He'd lose her.

But he had to have faith. Had to believe there was more between them than that.

Before he could change his mind, he spoke.

'I haven't written a new song in the last two years. I can't write anymore.'

Chapter Nine

He felt the sudden surprise that tensed her body. He couldn't look at her.

Refused to see the shock and pity he feared he'd see.

'Why not?' Hannah asked.

The question startled him because it wasn't what he'd expected. There was no condemnation, only quiet curiosity. He chanced a quick look. She was watching him intently, but the shadows hid her features and he couldn't read her expression.

'I haven't written a thing since the accident. It was like a switch in my brain turned off, and I've never been able to turn it back on.'

She set a gentle hand on his thigh. 'That's why you did an album of cover tunes,' she guessed.

'Yeah,' Nate said. He looked out over the view. 'I was contractually obligated to do one last album for the record label.'

'Who else knows?'

'Only Sam,' Nate admitted. He realized he'd been playing the same song over and over and forced himself to stop. A silence stretched between them. He could hear cars on the freeway a mile away.

'Wow,' Hannah said, her voice soft. 'I had no idea.'

'It's not because you're my publicist,' he said quickly, realizing she might interpret it that way. 'I knew I'd have to tell you eventually, once the tour was over and our focus turned to what I'd be doing next. But I wanted ... I wanted you to know. It's part of who I am.'

'Then I'm honored you'd tell me,' Hannah said. 'I'm ... really glad you feel comfortable enough to tell me.'

He put his hand over hers, and she turned her palm so their fingers could twine.

'Do you know why it's happened?' she asked. She was obviously picking her words carefully. 'Is it because of the accident?'

He sighed. 'I wasn't injured, really, and I don't think it was shock to my system. All I know is, when I got out of rehab, I was blocked. The last few CDs were written ... let's just say, I often had a little boost for my creativity. I know that my last album sucked because I was spending more time boosting than being creative.' He ran a hand through his hair. 'God, I listen to it now and can't believe I let some of those songs be recorded.'

'So maybe you just need some time?' Hannah asked. 'After all, you wrote your earlier stuff not being under the influence.'

'It's been two years,' he said, a knot in his stomach. 'I keep hoping, keep trying, though.'

'It's in there,' Hannah whispered. 'Inside you. Maybe it's been buried pretty deep, but it's not gone. I can't believe that. Music is too big a part of you.'

He leaned over, pressed his lips to her forehead, stroking her soft hair with his free hand. 'Thank you,' he said finally. 'That's what I hold on to.'

'Play a little more for me?' she asked, tapping a finger on the guitar. 'Anything you want.' His eyes had adjusted to the light enough that he saw the flash of her grin. 'I've never had a private concert before.'

He thought for a moment, then strummed the first chords to Guns 'n' Roses' 'Patience.'

When he finished the song, they both let the final notes fade into the darkness.

Then he said, 'It's quid pro quo time, sweetheart,' trying to inject a note of lightness into his voice.

'What?'

'I've told you my deep dark secret. Now you have to tell me yours.'

'I don't think so,' she said.

He put the guitar back into its case so he could turn toward her. 'Chicken.'

'I am not!' she declared hotly.

Nate merely stared at her. He could feel himself smiling.

'Oh, all right.' He could practically hear the cogs of her mind turning. 'We've met before,' she admitted.

'Really?' He feigned ignorance. 'When?'

She moved a little in the corner of the loveseat. The robe slipped from her shoulder, revealing smooth skin. He realized she wore nothing beneath the robe. It was more than a little distracting. Still, he did want to hear what she had to say.

'We met at my parents' house when I was younger.'

'Your parents?' He wanted to see how much she would reveal. He wanted to know why she kept so quiet about it.

Her arms looped around her knees. There was a long pause and then she blurted, 'My father is Everett Forbes. I fell down the stairs at your feet and made a total ass of myself.'

He tried to keep from grinning, but couldn't seem to help himself. 'That's not the way I remember it.'

'What?' The outrage that filled her voice made the grin wider and he knew he was in danger of laughing. 'You knew?'

'I recognized you.'

She smacked him hard in the arm. 'You jerk! I can't believe you didn't say anything!'

'You didn't seem to want me to recognize you.' Nate reached out to wind a lock of silky hair around his finger. 'How could I possibly have forgotten you, Hannah?'

'Sure, I guess it wasn't every day that you had a gawky seventeen-year-old fall into your arms and humiliate herself.'

Nate shook his head. 'I told you, that's not the way I

remember it.' He caught her hand and dragged her resisting body across his. She wiggled to try to escape, but he held her tight, enjoying the way her ass felt squirming on his lap. When she quieted, he was almost sorry. But he could see her now, see the pout on her lips, the indignant glare in her eyes.

'I remember the way you touched my hair, like you couldn't believe I was real. I remember the way you felt pressed against me, all curves and softness. And I definitely remember you kissing me.'

Her tongue touched her bottom lip and he had to force himself not to kiss her. He waited for her to process what he'd said.

'My hair was all frizzy and I had big ugly glasses on –'

'Your hair was curly and I wanted to wrap it around my fingers and kiss the hell out of you.'

Nate gave into the urge he'd been fighting since he'd pulled her onto his lap and teased her mouth with his. Lightly, just enough to make her moan a little when he drew back.

'But somehow, I didn't think it would be a good idea to have your father walk into the foyer and see the latest person he'd signed to his label making out with his little girl.'

Hannah looked up at his face and her fingers toyed with the ends of his hair, just the way he remembered her doing that day. It was erotic as hell. The silk of her robe was cool against his bare chest and, when she moved, the sensation against his nipples went straight to his groin.

When she moved to straddle his thighs, her robe fell open. He helped it, loosening the belt and sliding his hands inside to grip her hips.

'Here's something you don't know,' she said. Her hands were between them, flicking open the button on his jeans. He hissed, praying like hell she was careful as she eased the zipper down over his hard cock.

She put her lips against his ear. 'I made a vow that night to have you, for one hot night of passion.'

She was slick and hot, so ready for him as she took him inside of her. He hissed a breath at the nearly overwhelming pleasure. His hands dug into her hips and he pushed up into her. The sensation of her inner muscles clutching him tightly made him grit his teeth.

'It's always good to have goals,' he managed. He cut off her breathy laugh with a kiss and lost himself in the slick, sliding rhythm of their bodies.

Hannah sucked deeply on the straw shoved down into the icy mochachino. The espresso-laced chocolate drink slid down her throat. Nate glanced her way and she smiled, then curled the tip of her tongue around the top of the straw. He stopped speaking and Andre turned his head, following Nate's attention. Hannah smiled sweetly at them both and gave a little wave. She had to turn away before laughter overcame her.

Last night had wiped both her and Nate out and they'd slept later than either of them had intended. Consequently, they'd had to rush to be at the tour's departure spot.

It hadn't mattered. Sam had been held up in traffic. He'd only just arrived and was now simultaneously talking into his cellphone and going over a checklist with the tour's driver.

'That wasn't nice,' Nate said from behind her. His breath stirred the soft hairs at her nape.

She turned, her ponytail sliding over her bare shoulders. The kelly-green halter top she wore was designed for comfort. The intent behind wearing it and the dangling gold hoop earrings, however, was more about sheer enticement. Besides, it went well with her jeans and boots.

'I was just enjoying my drink,' Hannah said, trying for innocence and failing completely. The warm scent of his skin surrounded her. It was hard to resist the desire to lean into him, to tongue the ear lobe containing a small gold hoop.

Nate caught the hand holding her drink and took a long pull at the straw. His wicked grin made her thighs clench.

'Time to get on the bus,' he told her. 'I'll give you the tour.'

Hannah had been in tour buses before, but they never ceased to amaze her. How they could cram so much stuff into such a small space. Gina insisted it involved inter-dimensional pockets and Hannah wasn't sure her friend was wrong.

At the front there was the driver's area. Next was a lounging area with comfortable chairs and tables bolted to the floor. The small room contained a TV, a DVD player and a bitchin' stereo. A curtain separated a small kitchenette equipped with a fridge, a microwave, a cappuccino maker. A closet of a bathroom was opposite. A door led to a small sleeping area with bunks on each side of the bus. They were surprisingly roomy considering they were on a bus.

She tried very hard not to think about the roominess of the bunks, because that led her to calculating just how much space there was in a bunk for the various sexual positions she and Nate could get into.

And whether she could keep from screaming when they were doing so.

'Coming through,' the drummer yelled, a duffel bag held high. Scott gave them a wide grin, eyeing Hannah from head to toe. They'd met earlier, and she thought his sense of humor went right along with his T-shirt. The white shirt showed guys gathered around a barbecue, holding hot dogs on long forks. The caption read 'It's only fun until someone loses a wiener.'

Hannah patted one of the upper bunks. 'I'm sleeping up here.'

'In that case, I definitely want to be on the bottom,' Scott said.

Nate smacked him on the back of the head. 'Behave.' He caught Hannah's hand, leading her to another door. 'We're sleeping in here.'

'Here' was the last area on the bus. It could hardly be called a bedroom, despite the wide bed that dominated the space, but it provided privacy that the bunks lacked. Hannah plopped onto the bed, giving it a quick bounce. 'It's good to be a rock god,' she announced.

Nate sucked in a deep breath, watching her. 'Sometimes, it definitely is.'

This trip would be a relaxed one. They were driving from Los Angeles to Las Vegas during the day, which would take about six hours. They had the night to themselves and Nate had promised to show her around.

Tomorrow would be a stage rehearsal, going over last-minute lighting cues and sound checks, before the tour's kick-off concert.

Sam called out that they were leaving in less than a minute. She and Nate made their way back to the front. Hannah settled into a burgundy leather chair that seemed built for her body. The bus lurched forward and they were off, headed for the first leg of Nate Fox's comeback tour.

Andre was deep in conversation with Kenny, the bass player. Kenny was a tall man leaning toward heavyset. His shaggy blondish-brown hair was pulled back into a low ponytail. He didn't move much, but his playing was powerful. He was the only band member left from Nate's last tour. The others – Scott the drummer, Alan the keyboardist and Freebo the rhythm guitarist – had been handpicked by Nate to join the band for *Cannibal Eyes*.

'So you two are an item, then?' Freebo asked. His dark hair and goatee were trimmed closely. Chains decorated the black leather boots he had propped on the table.

'And it's not to go any further than here,' Sam said before either Nate or Hannah could reply. He gave them all what could only be described as a stern look. For a moment, Hannah had a flashback to high school and her sole visit to the principal's office, after she'd led a protest against the crappy cafeteria food.

'We want all the focus to be on the tour,' Hannah explained.

'OK,' Alan said. He pulled the sunglasses resting in his curls down over his eyes and settled back for a nap.

'Great,' Scott said morosely. 'The only time I get to live on a bus with a good-looking woman and she's already taken.'

'Down, boy,' Kenny said. 'We'll find you a treat in Vegas.'

Scott flipped him off.

Hannah decided that the next few months were going to be very interesting indeed.

A couple of hours later, the ride was already getting old. The endless expanse of desert provided very little in the way of stimulating landscape. She'd never been fond of mesquite or Joshua trees. Give her a good old palm any day, or even better, some shady sequoias. She'd already seen the movie the guys had put on the DVD player. Nate had wandered back to take a nap. Up front, the bus driver was singing about low women in low places. Nate was in no danger of losing his job.

Switching seats, Hannah settled down next to Andre. He pulled the earpieces out and shut off his iPod. He put down the book he'd been reading. Hannah took a glance at it. A delicious-looking man gazed moodily from the cover.

'You seem pretty relaxed,' Hannah said. It was true. The big man wore faded jeans and a silk pullover. The fact that the jeans were designer and probably cost as much as the iPod nano didn't escape her notice.

'Honey, I'm in a bus full of gorgeous men. I'm just pretending I don't know they're all straight.'

Hannah laughed. 'Andre, if I were a gay man, I'd be *so* after you.'

'Oh, please,' Andre said. 'All you and Nate have to do is look at each other.' He waved his hands. 'A girl could choke on the sexual tension.'

She couldn't help another laugh, utterly charmed by the huge dichotomy between Andre's professional bodyguard persona and his private, unrepentantly blatant self.

'Well, like we said before, we'd like to keep it as low-key as possible,' she said. 'It goes without saying that we're counting on you to help us with that.'

'I can totally sympathize, honey. If Nate swung my way, I'd be in the same predicament as you.'

'I really appreciate this,' Hannah said, relief flowing through her.

'There's just one condition,' Andre said.

Her heart sank. 'What?'

His grin was wicked. 'Indulge my fantasy. Boxers or briefs?'

Hannah howled. 'You are a naughty, depraved man – so of course I have to indulge you. Briefs, most of the time. Except . . .'

Andre leaned forward expectantly. 'Yes?'

'Except when he's wearing leather. Then it's nothing at all.'

With a groan, Andre pounded on the table.

'Is everything OK in here?' The curtain between the two lounges parted and Nate entered. His sleeveless T-shirt boasted a wraparound picture of a Magritte painting. Hannah tried not to drool over how the form-fitting shirt displayed his hard biceps. The fox-head tattoo on his upper right arm made her want to fall at his feet and beg to be his biker babe.

And that was just for starters.

'Just girl talk,' she told him with a smile. 'We're discussing fashion.'

It was Andre's turn to laugh, the deep sound seeming to vibrate the windows.

'We'll be in Baker soon,' Sam said, rejoining them from the front where he'd been keeping the driver company.

'Is that by your directions or his?' Nate asked. He looked at Hannah. 'Sam has a notoriously bad sense of direction.'

'Careful, boy, I know all your secrets,' Sam said. And then he smiled to show that he was joking.

Hannah stared at Sam, wondering if Nate had already told him that he'd confessed about not being able to write music. She glanced at Nate for a clue, but he'd become engrossed in the movie, one arm slung around her shoulders.

She still couldn't believe what Nate had told her. He hadn't written music in two years? That must be devastating for him. The fact that he'd trusted her enough to confide it left her feeling a little overwhelmed. They'd known each other so briefly, yet he'd felt comfortable enough to relate something that could potentially damage his career. He trusted her. She felt warm, happy.

And unbearably sad that he'd lost so much.

Baker sprawled across the desert, a huge thermometer commemorating the highest recorded temperature announcing its presence miles before the town streets were reached. Once merely a metal siding on the defunct T&T railroad, now it relied on tourism to keep its small population alive. Two-thirds of the way to Vegas, it was the most common place for travelers to fuel up, stretch their legs and get a bite to eat before the last leg of the drive to Sin City.

The heat baking up from the asphalt of the truck stop felt good after the chill of the bus's air conditioning.

That lasted about as long as it took to walk across the lot to Bun Boy. Then the cool air blowing from ceiling vents in the kitschy restaurant was sweet relief.

Scott held up a plastic replica of the 134-foot thermometer, the tallest in the world. 'Hey, Winks, you should get one of these for the dashboard.'

'Had one,' the rail-thin driver said. He adjusted the brim of his baseball cap. 'Last smartass that pissed me off had it put where the sun don't shine.'

'I think I've been threatened,' Scott said.

They all ignored him.

'We could eat somewhere else if you'd like,' Nate said. He was worried that Hannah would find the touristy restaurant too casual, not elegant enough. He was used to eating in places like this. At least there was the scent of cleaner nearly hidden beneath the smell of greasy burgers and burnt coffee. He'd eaten in some places a hell of a lot worse on the last tour. What he remembered of it, anyway.

'This is fine,' Hannah said. She linked her arm with his. 'It's a tradition to stop here. Or maybe a cliché.'

'The chocolate milkshakes are really good,' Andre said.

Nate hid a smile as he followed the broad back of his bodyguard to a table. Andre was a confirmed chocoholic. If you wanted a favor, a double fudge ganache cake went a long way to securing it for you.

'Oh my God! I can't believe it!' The high-pitched female voice squealing behind them was followed by the clatter of heels on concrete. 'Nate Fox! Oh my *God*!'

A feminine hand caught his arm and he swung around to avoid being pulled over. Andre stepped closer, but the woman ignored the implied threat.

'It is you! How have you been? It's been ages, hasn't it?'

Nate stared at the woman, trying in vain to recall if he'd ever met her. She certainly seemed to know him. He should remember her. The sleek black hair cut close to her head only accented the flawless skin, the red pouting mouth. And he'd be an idiot not to notice the curvy body in tight jeans. He was very aware of Hannah standing quietly beside him.

'I haven't seen you since we spent the night in South Beach. Do you remember how we danced naked on the hotel balcony?' Her words were accompanied by a hand resting on his chest, over the frantic beating of his heart.

'That's enough,' Andre said quietly.

'Oh don't be so stuffy,' she said. She edged herself between Nate and Hannah, wrapping her hands around his arm. 'I hear you're touring again. I would really love to join you for a while.' Big blue eyes flirted with him. 'I've really missed you.'

Nate was at a loss. He had no idea who she was. He darted a glance at Hannah, only to be met with a cool mask. Whatever she was thinking or feeling, it was completely hidden. He decided to play it off. 'We had some good times, didn't we? But this is a new tour, new shows. New everything.'

'New women?' she replied savvily.

Andre stepped closer, his big body crowding them. He angled himself so that Nate and the woman were hidden from view should anyone be watching from the restaurant. 'I said that's enough.'

'If you touch me, I will scream so loud cops will be coming from miles away.' She smiled sweetly as she said it.

Andre bared his teeth in a predator's grin. 'I remember you,' he said. His deep voice was quiet, but laced with menace. The light-hearted joker from the bus had vanished, replaced by top-of-the-line security. 'I remember the night you begged me to find you a fix. Are you still using, Lucy? What would we find if we took a look in your car?'

The hands clutching Nate's arm fell away. 'You're such a shit, Andre.'

'I'm sorry,' Nate said, not entirely sure what he was apologizing for. Maybe for not remembering her. Maybe for Andre having to do his job. He didn't know.

'Fuck you, Fox,' she said. She nailed Hannah with a bitter smile, vicious eyes. 'Don't get your hopes up. A month from now, he won't remember you, either. None of us could ever hold him.'

She walked away, her back rigidly straight. The jeweled belt she wore around her tiny waist caught the desert sun in a blinding glare.

'I'm sorry, Nate,' Andre said. 'I should have reacted quicker.'

Nate waved a hand in the air, dismissing the apology. In his line of work, there was no predicting who would approach. It was one of the reasons Andre worked for him.

Right now, his concern was Hannah.

The slender fingers he wrapped in his were cool. He wished he had an idea about what she was thinking, but she hadn't spoken a word from the moment Lucy had come up to them. Her face was a professional mask, unreadable, and he had the wildly inappropriate thought that she'd be great at poker.

'Let's talk,' he said, guiding her unresistingly back to the bus. Andre stayed outside. No one would get past him now. His pride had been hurt.

They had the bus to themselves. There was no telling how long that would last.

'Hannah, I'm really sorry about that,' he said.

'You don't remember her at all, do you?' she asked. The grey of her eyes was dark, serious. It spiked him with guilt.

'No.' He pushed one hand back through his thick hair. 'I don't remember a lot of the last tour.'

'Because of the drugs,' she said flatly.

He nodded. 'I was – am – an addict. I've been told the cravings will never go away. There were a lot of drugs.

There were a lot of women. I need you to believe that it's all in the past. I'm not proud of it. I wish to hell I could take it all back, but it is what it is. I'm done with all of that, Hannah.'

'How can you be sure? You just told me that the cravings never go away.'

He dropped down onto the couch. A tug of her hand brought her onto his lap. It told him a lot that she let him do it.

'I stay in control,' he said softly. 'It's worked for two years; I'll make sure that it works for the rest of my life.' He pressed a kiss to her temple.

'What about AIDS?' she asked abruptly. She looked into his eyes. 'You have no idea what you could have caught.'

'I've been tested,' he said softly. 'Tested and retested. I'm clean, Hannah, and I can show you the paperwork if you want. You don't have to worry about that.'

'How can I not worry? Your career –'

He stopped the words with his mouth, kissing her fiercely, until he felt the stiffness melt from her spine. Breaking away, he pressed his forehead to hers. 'This isn't about my career. This is about you and me. I *will* stay in control, Hannah.

'There won't be any more forgetting. I promise you.'

The regard of those solemn grey eyes was daunting. He realized how important it was that she believe him. That thought was startling, worried him a little. Trying to lie to himself that it was because she was his publicist was futile. The need for her trust ran too deep.

When Hannah nodded, curled her hand across his cheek and offered a small smile, the relief he felt was enormous.

Now he just hoped that he could live up to it.

Vegas held some deep shadows from his past.

Chapter Ten

The bus rumbled along the Strip. It had been a long while since Nate had been in Vegas. He hadn't been looking forward to visiting this particular casino again, but Sam had argued him down. The casino manager had offered the concert hall space and they would have been fools to turn it down.

'End of the line, folks,' Winks called out as the bus came to a stop beneath the VIP awning. Nate stood up, one hand rubbing at the knot of tension at the back of his neck. It had been there since Baker.

Andre was the first off the bus, dark eyes behind darker glasses sweeping the street and entranceway. It was only once he'd signaled that Nate and the others got off the bus. A doorman dressed in the casino uniform smiled a welcome. By his size, he no doubt also doubled as security. He spoke quietly into a headset and ushered them inside.

Chilled air wrapped around them and it felt good after the brief heat of the desert. Nate glanced around, noting that the place hadn't changed much since his last visit. It was quiet, the thick floral carpeting absorbing the sound of their feet. Leather couches invited them to sit, set into private oases surrounded by potted palms. Nate knew that somewhere in the casino, clanging bells, flashing lights and manic gamblers ruled the day. Here, there was quiet, a rich welcoming calm for the wealthy and the celebrity alike.

The attractive woman behind the highly polished check-in counter barely had time to smile before three men in tailored suits approached from a discreetly hidden door.

Victor Hernandez, casino manager, never traveled anywhere without his own personal guards. Andre had a momentary, testosterone stand-off with the body-guards. None of the security men removed their sun-glasses during the motionless assessment. Finally Andre nodded to Victor's men and stepped aside.

'Nate,' the center man said, moving forward and shaking Nate's hand. 'It's good to see you again.'

'You, too, Victor,' Nate said. Hernandez's hand was cool, the handshake holding just the right amount of strength. A chunky gold ring gleamed on his pinky. 'It's been a long time.'

Victor had lost some hair in the years since Nate had seen him last, but seemed to have compensated by the cost of the pinstripe suit he wore on his lanky body. A pale silk shirt and an Hermes tie showed off his rich olive skin tone. Nate thought he looked too smooth, a barracuda waiting for the scent of blood in the water before he attacked.

The handsome Hispanic man turned to Hannah. The smile he gave her was predatory, his teeth very white. Nate had a sudden urge to warn him off. The unex-pected jealousy surprised him. 'And this is your publi-cist, Hannah Montgomery. A pleasure.'

'Mr Hernandez.' She shook his hand crisply. If she noticed his appraising and appreciative glance, she said nothing.

Nate wanted to kiss her.

'I have your suite prepared,' Victor said to Nate. His glance took in the rest of the band. 'Your rooms are also ready. My staff will take care of your luggage if you'd care to follow them.'

With a wave of his hand, he indicated that Nate, Hannah and Sam were to accompany him. Andre was only a step behind. They walked out of the VIP area and into the casino's atrium. Sunlight fell from a skylighted ceiling, sparkling on the myriad pools and fountains scattered artlessly around the huge room. Through an arch, the sound of the casino proper intruded, the entrance filled with the ebb and flow of tourists and gamblers. Victor led them through another archway. The marble-tiled corridor was lined with expensive boutiques. They passed men smelling of pricy cologne, their arms adorned with women.

'Do you ever gamble?' Hannah asked Nate.

He shrugged. 'A little, here and there, just for fun. I've never been into the high stakes stuff.' He leaned closer to her, breathing in her unique scent. 'Right now I'm more interested in getting you up to my suite and into the Jacuzzi.'

Her smile was seductive, outshining the bright lights of the lavish casino. 'That sounds heavenly,' she said.

But first, there was the frustration of business. They reached the Cornerstone, a private club available by invitation only. It was darker here, quieter. The rich furnishings brought to mind a British gentleman's smoking room. They settled into a grouping of burgundy leather club chairs separated from the rest of the room by mahogany railing.

A curvaceous brunette in a fuchsia leotard, fishnets and high heels approached them.

'What's your poison?' Victor asked.

The question seemed loaded.

Vegas, this casino, held memories of too many excesses. Despite his craving for something to alleviate the tension that was beginning to radiate down his spine, Nate made himself order a Perrier with a twist of lime. Hannah asked for a lemon drop, Sam predictably went for a beer. Andre stood silently, his arms crossed over his chest. There was no expression on his face as he shook his head every so slightly to indicate he didn't need anything.

The cocktail waitress returned from the bar a few minutes later and distributed the drinks. Her fingertips brushed Nate's as she handed him the glass. The dark eyes and glossed lips hinted at availability. He thanked her politely.

Victor leaned toward Nate, leaving Sam and Hannah to peruse the publicity information that Victor had given them. 'Pretty, isn't she?'

Nate tried to maintain the easy-going smile. This place was his first and biggest hurdle. If he could handle himself here, the rest of the tour would seem easy in comparison. His eyes lingered on Hannah. The rich copper of her hair glowed under the subdued lighting. Pretty didn't even begin to cover it.

Nate started to answer in the affirmative, then realized with a start that Victor wasn't talking about Hannah. He meant the waitress. While her uniform was admittedly cute, her body shown to curvaceous perfection, she didn't really spark for him.

'She's available,' Victor said amiably. 'I remember you like brunettes. Or if she's not to your liking ... just let me know your requirements.'

'I'm fine for now,' Nate said. 'Thanks.'

Had he had a thing for brunettes? He tried to remember. Yeah, maybe the bulk of the women he'd been with had had dark hair.

Right now, however, he was into redheads.

'I can get you anything else you need,' Victor said, with a subtle nod. 'All you have to do is ask.'

Here it was. Nate had spent the last year training himself not to think about moments like these. Not to think about temptations and dark needs that kept him tossing and turning into the night. Victor's words, however, brought everything rushing back. Because Victor had said them before.

And Nate had always taken him up on the offer.

It would be so, so very easy to accept the quiet delivery in his room. Pass over the money. Give up control. Lose himself.

Trying to find balance, to find a sense of calm, Nate's gaze returned to Hannah.

She was talking to Sam. Something his manager said made her laugh and her face was radiant. She twirled her drink as she responded.

She must have sensed that Nate was looking at her, because she glanced over at him. When she saw he was watching, she plucked the glass swizzle stick from her martini glass and slipped it between her lips. The gesture was casual and yet somehow – and he knew, deliberately – suggestive.

Heat pooled in his groin. Minx. Any temptation he'd felt about drugs had been instantly and entirely replaced by desire for Hannah.

Naked. In the hot tub, her skin glistening wet, her hair in damp tendrils around her face as she lowered her mouth to his . . .

'Nate?' Victor's voice interrupted Nate's fantasy.

'Thanks for the offer, Victor,' he said. And the refusal came easily. 'You've always been good to me. But I don't need anything.'

The surprise on Hernandez's face gave Nate a feeling of power. 'Are you sure? A little –'

'No,' Nate cut him off. 'I'm clean now. I don't want any, and I don't want to hear that you've offered or provided any to the rest of the band or crew. OK?'

A pleasant mask slipped across Victor's handsome features. 'Of course, Nate. My job is to make sure you're happy. I'll do whatever you say.'

His smile was conciliatory, and Nate didn't buy it for a second.

He didn't tell Hannah what had transpired. She didn't need to know. He hadn't slipped, he hadn't accepted, and no one else had been privy to the conversation. Victor wouldn't risk his own reputation by repeating anything; he kept his job by ascribing to the see-nothing, hear-nothing philosophy.

Nate figured he might talk to Sam about it. Let him know that he'd handled the situation better than he had with the former PR asshole who'd made the same offer.

Just not right now. Right now all he wanted was Hannah.

She'd stripped and slipped into the bubbling tub before he'd made it out of the bathroom. The careless pool of her clothes on the floor was provocation in itself.

'Ecstasy,' she said as he slid in next to her. 'See, I knew being on the road was just like this.'

He laughed. It was rare to have down time like this, but right now he found himself hard-pressed to argue with her.

The Jacuzzi was on the balcony, but they were high enough that the harsh neon of the Strip didn't reach them. The setting sun sent streaks of tangerine and peach across the desert sky. Her eyes sparkled all on their own.

Officially, she wasn't sharing the room with him. Officially, she was two floors down. Tonight, she would probably go to her own room. He didn't want to sleep apart from her, but either of them caught sneaking out of each other's room would belie their public face of business only.

Right now, though, it wasn't just the view from the penthouse that made him feel like he was on the top of the world. He was high on his victory of resisting temptation and flying on the pleasure of having a beautiful, fascinating, unpredictable woman at his side.

He wanted to give her the world.

'After this,' he said, draping an arm across her enticingly wet shoulders; her skin was like silk, 'I'm taking you shopping.'

'Shopping?'

'I had Sam get us a reservation at Lorelei and, if you're going to Lorelei, you should go in a new dress.'

Hannah got a delightful look on her face: indignant outrage coupled with unadulterated interest. 'I don't need a new –'

'If you try to tell me you don't need a new dress and that you don't want to go shopping,' he said, indulging in his desire to lick droplets of water off her neck, 'I won't believe you. Every woman likes to shop.'

'That's just sexist! That's . . . oh, that's nice,' she said, threading her fingers through his hair and urging him to continue nibbling up the line of her jaw. 'No, wait, you're distracting me.'

He grinned, his lips sliding across her smooth flesh. 'That's my intention.'

'We have to talk about this . . . sexist . . . thing.' Her sentence ended in short gasps as his hand found her breast under the bubbling water.

'Later,' he said, toying with her nipple. Her body went rigid, and his cock followed suit, aroused by her reactions. 'All I'm saying is, I want to buy you pretty things. If you really have a problem with that, I'll have to find other ways –' he moved to straddle her so he could get both hands on her, '– to make you –' and between her thighs he found her slick clit '– happy.'

She shuddered and cried out, but he was only getting started.

After they were sated and showered, Hannah gave in to Nate's desire to take her shopping.

She was, after all, human.

The moment of panic she'd had in the hot tub had quickly fled. She'd known he'd been kidding, and she'd been joking right back about him being sexist. She just had to get past a quick, stupid sense of feeling like a kept woman. He was obviously in a good mood and obviously sincere in his wish to dress her up and take her out, and she was fine with that. After all, it wasn't unheard of for an artist to have a quiet dinner with his publicist.

She'd brought nice outfits, but nothing really right for a five-star restaurant, so she might as well pick something up. And there was something utterly decadent and indulgent about being waited on hand and foot in an upscale boutique, which had been closed at Nate's request so that she could shop in private.

Hannah slipped into a peacock-blue dress with a corset top, which nipped in her waist. The mirror revealed that the top showed off her cleavage to great advantage. The cut of the skirt swirled across her thighs in front, rippling down to mid-calf in the back. Her favorite pair of strappy heels would be perfect with it.

The look in Nate's eyes when she walked out of the dressing room was worth it. His expression clearly stated that all he wanted to do was peel her out of the dress and have his way with her from here to next Sunday. It made her knees weak.

Nate Fox was looking at *her* that way, and he meant it.

They left the boutique and turned toward the elevators when Nate reached out a hand and stopped an older woman passing by.

'Excuse me,' he said.

She stopped. Her nostrils flared slightly when she took him in, but if she recognized who he was, she was too polite to say so. 'Yes?'

'Your necklace is lovely. Did you get it here?'

She raised a hand to her neck, running her fingertips over the diamonds. 'Yes, actually, I did. Equinox, right over there.'

'Thanks.' Nate gave her a dazzling smile and, with a hand on Hannah's elbow, steered her in the direction of the shop.

'Nate, no.'

'We're just going to look,' he said.

No. Diamonds . . . shit, no. A dress was one thing, but diamonds were in a whole other category. Too soon. Too fast. Frantically she searched her memory for any information about etiquette when it came to diamonds. Surely her mother had had an opinion on them. Like, *if you give away the milk for free, you won't get any diamonds*. Or, *accept diamonds and you're in big, big trouble*.

She really wished her mother had said *something*. Maybe she should call her.

Except she really could imagine the awfulness of that conversation.

Gina. What would Gina say?

Nate Fox wants to give you diamonds, and you're asking me*?! Remember when you were seventeen and –*

She wasn't seventeen anymore. Hannah squared her shoulders.

And wilted only slightly as they entered the boutique and she was surrounded by mouth-watering gems.

In the end, it wasn't a necklace, or even diamonds, that he honed in on. It was a simple pair of drop earrings fashioned from stunning black pearls. Well, technically black. In reality they were shimmering, exotic shades of grey.

'They're the color of your eyes,' he said.

Still she protested. Even pearls were too much, too soon.

When he whispered in that husky voice of his that what he really wanted was to see her naked, lying on the bed wearing nothing but the earrings, open and wanting him, she relented.

Well, not so much *relented* as *had to prop herself up on the counter before she melted into a puddle of lust.*

The earrings were carefully wrapped in a custom box and scarlet-red shopping bag with gold tissue paper and ribbon, and would be sent to her room along with the dress.

'Thank you for indulging me,' he said.

Indulging *him*. As if.

She met Nate at seven at his room. She'd had just enough time to squeak in a booking at the salon, to have her hair shampooed and dried and pinned up, with corkscrew tendrils framing her face and caressing her neck.

He touched one pearl earring lightly. The way he'd looked at her had made the breathless rushing around worth it.

The way he looked kept her breathless. He'd given in to the convention that equated five-star dining with suit and tie. But his take on it made hunger curl low in her belly. A loose grey striped jacket over black pants showed off the breadth of his shoulders. The pale-grey shirt was open at the throat, a barely knotted purple tie pulled low. A black studded belt looped around his waist, hanging low over his hips. There would be no doubt just looking at him that he was a musician. Hannah found her fingers itching to slip through the dark gloss of hair that curled over his collar. Right before she slid her tongue along the hard column of his throat.

'Our reservation's for nine,' he said. 'Are you feeling lucky tonight?' He toyed with one lock of her hair, seemingly mesmerized.

If they hadn't been standing in the hall outside the elevator ... no doubt in perfect view of the security cameras. It was clear from the look in his eyes – and the thrumming of desire that shot through her – that if they were somewhere private, they both would be getting lucky immediately.

And repeatedly.

'I am at that,' she said, cocking her head and smiling at him.

'Good,' he said. 'So am I. Let's see what the Queen of Spades has in store for us.'

They took the private penthouse elevator down to the area of the casino reserved for celebrities, the very wealthy and high rollers. It wasn't much different than the rest of the casino – it still had the neon, the noise, the smoke. Only here the drinks were on the house and the bets started much, much higher.

Since they were staying in the private areas and Nate wanted this evening to be special, he'd given Andre the night off. Andre had gotten a gleam in his eye and Nate decided he just wasn't going to ask what the bodyguard's plans were.

Nate was offered entrance into a poker game, but he declined. 'Never really had a feel for it,' he told Hannah. 'How about roulette?'

'Sounds good to me,' she said, tucking her hand in the crook of his arm.

'What's your lucky number?'

'Forty-two. But since that's not an option, put a chip on twenty-four for me.'

They didn't win in the end, but they sipped drinks and laughed and watched their fortunes go up and down. They tried craps, playing at a table with at least one actress whom Hannah recognized, and possibly a director, and certainly someone who'd been to a recent dinner party at her parents' house. But if the latter man recognized her, he didn't say anything, probably because the much-younger woman on his arm was *not* the wife he'd brought to her parents' home.

'Here,' Nate said, handing her the dice.

She shook them in her hand, blew on them with pursed lips, looking up at him through her lashes. His hand on her hip tightened, just a little, and she smiled before tossing the dice.

They won a tiny bit more at craps than they lost at roulette, and Hannah stuck her card in a slot machine and made a whole three bucks, before it was time to head to the restaurant.

Lorelei had a futuristic warehouse theme, with lots of metal and glass. The entryway stairs wrapped around the restaurant's highlighted feature: a forty-foot tall tower of glass in which was stored all the wine.

'Ohh,' Hannah breathed when she saw it. 'I've heard about this.'

'Then be sure to order wine for yourself,' Nate said.

She was going to refuse, well aware that he preferred not to drink. She changed her mind when he covered the hand that rested on his arm, giving her fingers a quick squeeze.

The maître d' showed them to their table and their waiter appeared almost instantly to present the menus and describe the specials in mouth-watering detail before melting away. In a restaurant like this, Hannah knew, they wouldn't have to do more than lift a finger or glance in his direction to have him reappear; otherwise, they'd be left to their privacy.

Hannah perused the wine list while the wine steward hovered just out of range, prepared to offer suggestions. She didn't need any, though. She found the perfect wine in the list and motioned for him.

'I'll take the Rios-Lovell Petite Syrah. Just for me.'

'Excellent,' he murmured, and left.

'So how did you learn so much about wines?' Nate asked.

'At my father's knee,' Hannah said. 'My parents believe that knowing wine is an asset to business. They are also of the school that says you give your child a glass on special occasions to teach them about responsible, social drinking.'

Her mouth quirked in a grin at the memory. 'Actually, it really started when I was fifteen and "borrowed" a bottle of wine from our wine cellar. And my dad caught me.'

Nate favored her with a quick laugh. 'I'll bet he wasn't happy about that.'

'I tried to bluff my way out of it by saying he could take it out of my allowance. So he took me to his study, whipped out the calculator and showed me just how long it would take me to work off that bottle of wine. Because I'd chosen one that was just over a thousand dollars, last he'd checked.'

Nate laughed. 'And I'll bet you weren't happy about *that*.'

'Not in the least. I had no idea a bottle of booze could cost that much! The whole thing fascinated me,' she continued her story. 'What made wine so special that it could sell for four or even five figures? My father was happy to teach me, and I have to say I agree with him that the knowledge can come in handy.'

'Impressing the clients?' Nate teased.

'And getting to drink some mighty fine vino,' she said.

'You're a woman of many talents.' He slipped a hand over hers. The calluses on his fingertips grazed along her skin, and she felt the touch shiver through her, to her most intimate areas.

'You haven't seen the last of them yet,' she flirted. Her own boldness surprised her, excited her. He somehow brought out her adventurousness, encouraging her to play, to tease, to experiment and take chances.

'I imagine you're going to keep surprising me for a long time,' he said.

She turned her hand palm upward so she could caress his wrist. The clink of silverware, the low murmur of the other diners all faded into the background. He was by far the hottest man in the room. The subdued lighting threw shadows across the lean planes of his face. His full bottom lip tempted her enough that she had to keep herself from leaning closer to taste him. 'Hm, I think we should order quickly so we can get back to the room sooner.'

'Do you think they'll deliver room service?' he asked, and the plaintive note in his voice made her laugh again.

And made her clit quiver.

It took all of her concentration to focus on the menu. Finally, she decided on the handmade gnocchi in truffle sauce for her appetizer and duck for her main course. Nate ordered the chilled pea soup to start, along with the filet mignon.

'It comes with Parmesan fries,' he said after the waiter had taken their order. 'How could I pass up that?'

'You'd be just as happy at Burger King, wouldn't you?' she asked.

He shrugged. 'I like the fact that I can afford to come to a place like this and order whatever I want. I don't want to do it every night, but it's having the option that makes a difference.'

He'd told her earlier that growing up, he and his family rarely ate out, his parents considering it too much of a luxury. They hadn't been poor, but they'd had to make careful choices, and their main choice had been to send Nate and his older sister and brother to college. He'd only attended a year before dropping out to pursue his music career.

Suddenly, Nate frowned. 'What the hell?'

Hannah looked in the direction of his stare. A woman in a scarlet catsuit was clinging to the side of the glass wine tower.

'Oh, that's a wine siren,' she said casually.

'A *what*?'

'It's part of the shtick with the tower,' she explained with a laugh. 'They rappel down to get the wine. That could very well be our siren and our wine.'

She was right, because a few minutes later the steward was at their side, presenting her with the label to examine and the cork to sniff.

She let the wine slip over her tongue, savoring the

flavors of blackberry, liquorice and cassis. 'It's lovely,' she told the waiter, and let him pour for her.

When he'd left, she lifted her glass. 'To a successful tour,' she said.

'To a successful relationship,' he said, touching his glass of iced tea to hers with a delicate chime.

Did he mean *relationship* as in *working relationship*, or something more? Hannah wondered.

And was she ready for the answer to that?

No, it was too soon to think about it. Just enjoy the evening. Enjoy the fantasy – and the reality that she was out with Nathaniel Fox. She had his entire attention, and later . . .

Later she'd *really* have his attention.

Their appetizers arrived, delivered swiftly and efficiently. They lingered over them, exchanging tastes, sharing morsels off of each other's fork. The arrival of the main dishes was exquisitely timed to occur once they'd finished.

'What is it,' Hannah wondered aloud, feeling Nate's knee brush against hers under the table, 'about us and food?'

'Maybe it's our thing,' Nate said.

'We have a thing?'

'Seems like it.' He seemed content with the idea. 'Here, try a bite of this. It's so tender.'

He reached out with a forkful of filet mignon, and she obligingly opened her mouth. He teased her with it, pulling back just as she was about to close her lips. Giggling, she stuck her tongue out at him, then opened her mouth wide. He moved the morsel nearer.

A flash of light, blinding her.

'What the hell?' she heard Nate say, as he rose to his feet.

Dishes on the table rattled as she, too, leaped up, reaching in the direction of the man with the camera.

'Mr Fox – Ms Montgomery – we'll handle it.' The

maître d' held out a hand. 'We'll handle it. We're very sorry. This has never happened before.'

The photographer had bolted, but at least one waiter had gone after him. There was nothing they could do. The other diners went back to pointedly staring at their own plates.

Hannah looked at Nate. He was scowling, but he closed his eyes and took a deep breath. When he opened them again, he looked calmer, but he was still not entirely happy.

'Thank you for sending your staff after him,' he said to the maître d' when the man returned. 'I appreciate that. However, I'm disappointed that a paparazzo was allowed into your restaurant at all.'

'I understand, sir, and I must apologize. I checked, and he'd made his reservation under the casino manager's name, obviously to gain illicit entrance. Nothing like this has ever happened before, I assure you. Please, let us give you your meals free of charge, to make up for your dinner being interrupted.'

'The wine, too,' Hannah said.

The maître d' pursed his lips, then reluctantly nodded. 'Of course. Please, try to enjoy the rest of your time here. Carlos will bring you the dessert and coffee menu when you're finished.'

He moved away. Hannah and Nate sat. For a moment, they were silent. Then, Nate said, 'That was mean.'

She raised an eyebrow. 'What? Asking for the wine? Yeah, I suppose it was. But we deserve it.'

He looked down at his plate for a moment, and she wondered if he was angry. Then she realized he was choking back laughter.

'You know, I was having a really good night,' he said. 'And that asshole went a long way to screwing everything up. Thank you.'

He'd lost her. 'For what?'

'For . . . handling it with such grace.'

'I hardly think that insisting they cover the wine as well as the meal can be categorized as *grace*,' she protested.

'You didn't scream, throw a tantrum, cry or fling a shoe at anyone,' Nate said. 'That counts as grace in my book.'

'Well,' she said. 'Well. There may be screaming and shoe-flinging later, but only in the throes of passion.'

He raised his glass, and she clinked hers against it. 'I'll drink to that,' he said.

It had been a good day, a day worth celebrating. Back on the road, with the crackling energy and excitement that heralded the beginning of a tour. Facing and resisting his ultimate temptation. Quality time spent with an amazing woman. The only minor downside was that they'd agreed to spend the night in separate rooms.

Nate didn't want to spend the night away from Hannah. He'd hated watching her get up and get dressed. Hated the empty feeling of the room after she'd left. Hated even more the empty feeling of the bed. But at least he could fall asleep with the knowledge that he'd see her the very next day.

It had been a good, positive, life-affirming day.

The night went all to hell.

Chapter Eleven

Flashes of faces: Sam, the band, the crew; a parade of women, Suzanne one of many, blurring in and out of the crowd until her visage resurfaced, spattered with blood. He'd held her hand there, with the streetlight glittering on the rain-soaked pavement, not really sure where he was, when it was, only that it was dark and wet and he was dead and he was still flying high, torn between laughing and sobbing.

At that moment, he'd've given anything for a hit. He might have pleaded aloud to an unseen, unbelieved-in deity for Suzanne's life, but what he'd really wanted, what he'd needed and craved and would have sacrificed for was to get lit. To get even more lit. To take whatever was necessary to numb the fear and panic, the growing anguish at the searing knowledge of what had happened.

To find oblivion. Sweet, sweet escape.

Then there was Victor, all smiles and solicitousness, telling Nate that whatever he needed, Victor would provide. All Nate had to do was name it and it would be supplied.

And in his dream, Nate willingly – eagerly – took what was offered.

His harsh breathing filled the room, rasping into the night. Nate held his breath, just to make the sound stop, and listened to the hum of the air conditioning before he had to gulp air again.

Despite the air conditioning, sweat trickled down his temples, the sticky moisture gluing the sheet to his thighs.

He peeled the covers off. His eyes adjusted to the dim red glow of the clock's digits, enough light to help him navigate across the suite to one of the two bathrooms. He fumbled for the faucet in the dark, scooped water onto his face and chest, heedless of how it splashed throughout the room.

The combination of cold water and cooled air against his skin had him shivering uncontrollably.

The tremors reminded him of coming down from a high.

The nightmare flooded back.

God, what had brought that on?

Nate raked wet hands through his hair. He didn't care why, not right now, anyway. More important was the fact that he dreaded trying to sleep again. Dreaded returning to the dream.

He could think of any number of self-medications that would ensure him a dreamless sleep. His hands were trembling as he sat on the edge of the bed. He balled them into fists on his thighs.

It struck him then, the craving. The one that outshadowed all the others. The one that had saved him today.

He wanted to be with Hannah.

It was stupidly risky to go down to her room. Vegas never slept. Inside a casino the action didn't abate just because it was after midnight. Anybody could be wandering around. Anyone could see him.

Fuck it. He didn't care.

He dragged on jeans, not bothering with underwear. Found a T-shirt he'd discarded earlier. Eschewed shoes.

A hat and sunglasses could make him less noticeable, or they could be more obvious. He didn't want to waste time looking for them. In less than a minute, he was in the elevator, thankful it was empty.

Hannah looked bleary and confused when she answered the door, her red hair sleep-mussed. She'd thrown on a short peach-colored satin robe, which accented her long legs. Despite her confusion at his unexpected arrival, she understood his urgency and stepped aside as he pushed in.

'Are you OK?' she asked, reaching up a hand to touch his cheek.

The gesture twisted something inside him. For a moment, all he could do was echo the motion, feeling the softness of her skin beneath his fingertips.

Then his hands bracketed her head and he was pulling her into a crushing kiss.

When they finally broke apart, he said simply, 'I need you.'

And kissed her again, kissed her until they were both gasping for breath. He needed to taste her, touch her everywhere. Drown himself in her.

Lose himself.

After a moment's hesitation, no doubt borne on surprise, she matched him kiss for kiss, answering his intensity with her own. They may have made love in the Jacuzzi, then again after dinner, but it was as if they hadn't touched each other in weeks.

They made it to the bed by mutual unspoken agreement, still locked together. Her robe was easy enough to toss aside; he had his T-shirt off while she was still popping the buttons on his jeans. When she wrapped a slender hand around his already straining cock, he groaned aloud.

Pushing her down, he caught her hands and stretched them high over her head. He pinned them to the pillow with one hand while the other stroked her from thigh to breast and back again. She writhed under him, all heat and longing.

The kiss wasn't enough. She tasted of minty toothpaste and moonlight desires, and it wasn't enough. He sampled the skin of her throat, licking the salt from her flesh.

The breast that plumped in his hand wasn't enough.

He lowered his head, sucking the hard nipple, biting down. Hearing her startled cry, the moan of surprised pleasure.

It wasn't enough.

'Hannah,' he cried her name into her skin, the dream still clinging. The need to control the craving overpowered nearly everything else. But *she* was the craving. Her scent, her taste, her body.

Abruptly, Nate rolled over, pulling her on top of him. He let her wrists go and smoothed his hands down her spine. Her ass fitted into his hands perfectly. He didn't need to control her. He needed to lose himself in her.

For so long he'd fought to be in control.

Hannah looked down at him, her red curls wild around her face. Those smoky-grey eyes could see into him. See what he needed.

A movement of her hips, and he was inside. Her hands caught his now, meshing their fingers together. Everything else fell away.

He was safe. Safe to trust her. Safe to let go and give in to what he needed.

She clenched around him, shuddering. Nate allowed himself to give up control.

Later, when he was spent, sated, lying tangled with her and breathing in the scent of her hair, he knew he would finally be able to sleep in peace.

Hannah had done her best to whip up a media frenzy about this concert. It was the first show of the tour and had been set up for VIPs, friends, press, celebrities. Online and radio contest winners. The few tickets available to the public had been snapped up by fans who had come through and made it a sold-out show. Since on a level it was almost a private show, Nate knew a lot of attendees.

The pre-show meet-and-greet was therefore packed. Hannah had to mentally pat herself on the back, because she'd managed to arrange for a healthy number of reporters and photographers to attend the party and show.

Nate, clutching a mug of Throat Coat tea, moved through the crowd, not trying to talk over the hubbub of voices and whatever was playing over the sound system. Still, he had that hundred-watt smile going, and Hannah heard him give several pithy sound bites to the appropriate people.

'Nate!' A woman flung her arms around him.

He hugged her back. 'Marta.'

They disengaged. Marta looked a little disappointed. Or maybe that was wishful thinking on Hannah's part.

After all, Marta Ingersol was supermodel extraordinaire, and the shimmery little silver sheath dress she wore over impossibly high spike heels made it clear why she was in constant demand. That, along with the ski-slope cheekbones and flawless Scandinavian complexion.

'Marta, this is my publicist, Hannah Montgomery.'

Marta blinked and smiled sunnily, an expression that seemed more designed for a camera than a social situation. 'I'm very pleased to meet you, Hannah,' she said with a trace of an accent. Her waist-length blonde hair shimmered in the lights.

'It's nice to meet you, Marta,' Hannah said with just as much conviction, damping down the flash of jealousy and pulling up a veil of detached professionalism. Had Nate dated Marta at some point? Probably.

The niceties out of the way, Marta turned her attention away from Hannah and launched into some charming and amusing tale, which required she punctuate it by frequently touching Nate's arm or her own lips.

Ugh. Well, Hannah didn't have to stick around to witness this blatant attempt at seduction. Didn't have to stick around to fight the sudden feeling of inadequacy. The supermodel was his world, the bright lights, the paparazzi. Hannah was nights at home with a good book and a movie. Marta was slinky dresses. She was business suits. She didn't like to be reminded of that.

Looking for an excuse to leave, Hannah went to check that the media packages she'd put together were getting to the right people. The security at the door checked passes before ushering guests through into the room. A smiling hostess wearing one of the new tour shirts was diligently handing out the information to the press as they entered. Satisfied, Hannah snagged a glass of champagne and went back to see if Marta was succeeding in her quest.

She hadn't yet, although whatever she was talking about required her to toy with Nate's hair.

Hey, that's *my* fetish!

Hannah bit back a grin, almost embarrassed by how territorial she felt. She'd had time to get her feelings under control. Still . . .

Nate couldn't spend all night talking to the woman. This was a meet-and-greet and he had other people to meet and greet.

She moved close enough to be in Nate's field of vision, but hung outside the personal space so she didn't intrude on the private conversation.

Nate kept his eyes on Marta, nodding at something she'd said, but he reached out a hand to Hannah. She took it, feeling an absurd sense of victory, and he drew her to his side. He gave her fingers a quick squeeze and dropped them. As Marta paused to take a breath, he said, 'It's wonderful to see you, and I'm glad you're doing so well. But my public awaits – if I don't do my mingling duties, there'll be hell to pay.'

Well, damn. He'd read her mind.

Marta's lush mouth drew up in an insincere, joking pout, but Hannah sensed real regret lingered behind it. 'Very well, Nate. But you must call me, yes?'

'The tour's just starting, so I'm going to be pretty

busy,' he said. He gave her a charming smile. 'I'll do my best.'

They kissed on both cheeks (Hannah resisted the urge to roll her eyes) and then Marta walked away as if she were on a catwalk.

'She's very pretty,' Hannah said, knowing it was lame. Hating herself for her own insecurities.

Nate put his hand on the small of her back. She could feel the warmth of it through her shirt. She would normally have worn a suit to a client's press party, but the concert was right after, and she wanted to be comfortable. She wanted to blend in with the other fans.

'She is,' he said, his voice low and meant only for her. 'She also barfs up her dinner every night to stay thin. She's kind of nuts.'

Hannah smiled into her champagne.

'More importantly,' Nate continued, '*you're* the one wearing a present from me. You *are* wearing it, aren't you?'

Yes. Oh yes. Nestled between her legs, in an area already slick, was Nate's gift to her. The hard bullet of the vibrator pressed against her clit, stimulating her even though it wasn't turned on. The tight jeans she wore kept it tucked close, and she was aware of it every time she moved, shifted, walked . . .

She'd lost the ability to speak. The soft laugh he gave at her strangled response just made it worse.

'Good,' he said, his voice rough.

'Nate!' another female voice said.

This woman, thankfully, Hannah actually knew.

'Hey, Tani,' he said, giving the tall brunette a hug. 'Hannah, have you met Tani?'

'Of course!' It was Tani who answered, her usual breathless self. 'We've known each other for years. Hannah, it's so cool that you're working for Nate now. What a dream job!'

Nate raised an eyebrow. His blue eyes regarded her

carefully. 'Oh, now the truth comes out. How long have you been a member of the FoxFanatics?'

Hannah flushed. 'It's part of my job, Nate.' She side-stepped the actual question of just how big a fan she was. 'The FoxFanatics are one of the best-organized fan clubs out there. I've already been corresponding with Tani to get the word out about this tour, your appearances, anything to make sure there's an enthusiastic crowd.'

He knew she'd been a fan for a long time, given that they'd talked about their first meeting. She hadn't specifically mentioned the fan club because it seemed just a little too groupie. She was just annoyed that she couldn't tell by the light tone of his voice how he felt about it.

'That reminds me,' Tani said. 'We're doing a membership drive to coincide with the tour. Nate, would you be willing to do a welcome .mpg? Five or ten minutes talking to fan-club members about the tour, how you're doing, thanking them for joining.'

'I'd be glad to,' he said. 'Just check with Sam and Hannah. They're in charge of my schedule. I think we can record it in the next week or so – whenever we have a day off from the tour?' He directed the latter half of the sentence to Hannah, making it a question.

'Next week,' she said. To Tani, she added, 'Mention it to Sam and we'll make sure it gets sorted out.'

'Thanks!' Tani bounded off.

Watching her go, Nate shook his head. 'She's a trip. I don't know where she gets her energy.'

'She's got a good group of people helping her out,' Hannah said. 'But yeah, she's just really enthusiastic. You're lucky to have her on your team.'

'I'm lucky to have you, too,' Nate said. 'I don't think any PR guy I've had before thought to work with the fan club.'

'Word of mouth can be more powerful than the press,' she said. 'Which reminds me: MTV has a VJ here. Have you talked to him yet?'

Hannah fingered the laminated plastic of the backstage pass that hung from around her neck and peered out from the side of the stage at the audience. The concert theater was at full capacity.

Excitement thrummed through the air, thick and palpable and crackling with electricity. From her vantage point at the side of the stage, Hannah surveyed the audience. Most of the concert-goers – the ones in front, anyway – couldn't seem to stay in their seats. They stood, chatted with each other, fidgeted and stared at the stage. Many wore T-shirts from Nate's past shows and some wore the commemorative shirts from this tour, newly purchased in the lobby.

The smooth plastic of the pass was growing warm beneath her touch and Hannah realized that she'd been rubbing it slowly between her finger and thumb. There was something else she'd like to be rubbing, stroking . . .

She caught her bottom lip between her teeth. Forcing herself to drop the pass, she took one last look at the crowd. It looked as though they were barely containing their excitement. Nate Fox hadn't toured in two years. In a few minutes, they'd see him, whether again or for the first time, in the flesh.

She wondered where Nate had put the remote.

She wondered, for the millionth time, when he would choose to use it. And she shivered.

Sam had been stalking around the stage, barking at roadies and ensuring everything was nothing less than perfect. Now he turned his attention on her.

'If you want to watch the concert from down there, you'd better get going,' he said.

'Everything on schedule?' she asked.

He squinted and surveyed the stage. 'Yeah,' he said in a tone that implied that it probably wasn't, but he couldn't find the flaw and just had to live with it.

She grinned. 'Glad to hear it.'

Hannah threaded her way further backstage, stepping over the taped-down electrical cords, past the racks of guitars and basses, the monitors, the soundboards and the small army of technicians whose job it was to ensure every single piece of electronics worked without a glitch. One woman, wearing earphones, tuned a spangly green guitar. Hannah gave her a thumbs-up as she went by and the woman grinned.

As she passed by Nate's dressing room, she paused, wondering if she should tell him to break a leg. She blew a strand of hair back from her forehead, acknowledging to herself that she was just looking for an excuse to see him. She reached up a hand to knock . . . and the door opened before she could make contact.

Nate. All six feet of taut muscle, raven-black hair and striking blue eyes that she knew darkened to indigo when he was about to come.

Now, he smiled. 'I was hoping to see you before we got started,' he said. His low smoky voice curled around her, promising that she would enjoy everything that he had planned.

'I wanted to wish you good luck,' Hannah said. He looked incredibly sexy in his black leather pants. The fabric clung to the hard muscles of his thighs, cupping the heavy bulge of his groin. She wanted to touch, wanted to run her hands over his flat stomach hidden behind his tight T-shirt. Past concert experience told her that he would tear the shirt off toward the end of the concert, sending much of the audience into paroxysms of lust at the sight of his ripped body.

'I wanted to kiss you until you couldn't breathe,' Nate said. Taking her by the arm, he pulled her down a short hallway into a darkened alcove, crowding her body with his as he pressed her against the wall. His hands penned her in, resting on each side of her shoulders. He teased her, leaning in just far enough to let his chest rub lightly against her sensitized breasts. Warm breath heated her skin, his mouth only a sigh away from her throat. His dark hair tickled her cheek as he breathed in her scent.

'Are you ready for me?' he whispered. His hips brushed suggestively against her own.

Hannah couldn't have been more ready if he'd laid her down and licked every inch of her skin.

She tangled her fingers in his hair and pulled him in closer. Nate nipped her lower lip and she responded in kind. Their mouths met, lips against lips, tongue sliding against tongue. His kiss was a wonder, all wet heat and maddening friction.

'Still wearing it?' Nate asked, his teeth nipping her jaw lightly. His breath blew across her ear and Hannah shivered. Her mouth went dry, in contradiction to the wetness between her legs.

'Yes.' Her voice came out in a shaky whisper.

'Good.' He ran his tongue along her neck. Hannah gripped his shoulders to keep from sagging to the floor. She could smell his shampoo, a memory of the shower they'd taken together earlier. He rubbed one thigh between hers, lightly, not nearly enough pressure to satisfy.

'Good,' he repeated. 'Because I can't tell you how much I'm looking forward to watching your face when . . .'

Hannah moaned.

'Yeah, you'll sound like that. Or maybe you'll be screaming. You'll have to tell me afterward.' His hands slid from her hips, up her sides. She wore a dark-plum satin bra and a semi-sheer purple flowered camisole top over it. His thumbs caressed the underside of her breasts, the motion erotic against the satin. She felt her nipples harden beneath his ministrations, aching for more pressure.

'The hardest part –'

'I think I've found the hardest part,' Hannah teased, cupping her hand around the steely bulge beneath the leather of his pants. He caught his breath. The sound, and the knowledge that she caused it, sent a fresh thrill of arousal through her.

'Keep that up and the concert will have to be delayed,' he warned. The way he looked at her made her wish she could make the concert disappear, keep him entirely to herself.

'What's sauce for the goose . . .' she teased.

'The goose's arousal,' Nate said, 'is not as obvious as the gander's. Nor will the goose be standing on stage before thousands of people.'

'True,' she agreed, sliding her hand back to cup his tight ass and pull him closer against her. It was her turn to move against him, knowing by his ragged breathing that she had his complete attention. 'But I'll be the one making the scene, given your intentions with that remote control.'

He made a low rough noise in his throat. He took her hand and brought it to his waist. She could feel the remote clipped to his waistband. To someone who didn't know what it was, it would look like part of his stage gear. 'I don't know how I'm going to stand it, watching you come,' he admitted. 'It may be difficult for me not to join you.'

The fact that her arousal turned him on so much thrilled Hannah. It was as if they fed off of each other, bringing each other to new heights and getting dragged along at the same time, higher and higher until they went supernova.

'You deserve a little torture, given what you're putting me through,' she said.

'Is it really torture?' he asked softly, sliding his hand beneath her camisole and lightly pinching her nipple.

'Yes. Exquisite torture,' she managed between gasps.

'Good.' He pulled away, although even in the dim light she could see the reluctance on his face. 'I'll see you after the show.' He cupped her face with one hand. 'I'll be thinking about you.'

He disappeared back into the dressing room, no doubt to adjust himself before he had to appear onstage. Hannah took a deep breath, willing her heartbeat to slow. The aching between her legs wasn't going anywhere, however. She forced her trembling legs to move, always aware of the vibrator nestled between her lips. She knew she was flushed, trembling, her mouth swollen from kissing Nate. She probably looked like sex incarnate.

Hannah made her way to an exit that deposited her just outside the floor seats. The pass around her neck meant she had no problem getting to her front-row VIP seat. On her way she said hello to two fans she recognized as regulars at Nate's shows. Diamonds glittered from beneath Sheri's dark-red hair. Energetic Fran was stretching, preparing for a night of enthusiastic dancing.

Her seat was dead center, the place where Nate would be able to see every reaction she had when he played her body. She didn't have time to sit before the lights went down and the crowd was on its feet, already roaring its approval. She added her voice to the cheers.

A bass beat began. Drums pounded the rhythm.

An electric guitar wailed a melody.

An explosion of light in the background revealed the silhouette of Nate standing on a riser behind the drums. The screams of the audience intensified. Over them, into a headset microphone, he sang the first line of 'Luck Dried Up.'

The stage fell dark again, but the music pounded, giving the audience a lifeline. When the full lights came on, Nate stood at the front of the stage. His guitar was slung on a strap over his shoulder, his talented fingers drawing music from the metal strings. He launched into the song, the band chiming in on harmonies. Hannah could have sworn he winked at her.

Then she realized that she wasn't some anonymous audience member anymore. He *had* winked at *her*.

With a grin she couldn't have stopped even if she'd tried, she sang along with the chorus, dancing in place at the barrier a few feet from the stage. Seats had been abandoned, the fans energized and on their feet.

Over the years, she'd tried as a professional, as a publicist, to disassociate herself from her feelings about Nate and view his stage performance dispassionately. She hadn't entirely succeeded, but she'd managed to make some analyses. Seeing some of the rehearsals for this tour had solidified her theories. Every movement he made was calculated, planned. Of course, it didn't mean he couldn't be spontaneous. Certainly his between-song banter wasn't memorized, and he'd told her horror stories about the various things that had gone wrong on stage – earphones cutting out, guitar strings breaking, his pants splitting a seam right up the back . . .

But overall, he was in control. When he and the bassist ran over and circled the keyboard, they were all in sync, because they'd gone over it until they had it down to the second. When Nate ran across the stage and smacked one of the drum kit's cymbals, it didn't look like he'd make it back to his mark at the front of the stage on time – but he always did.

And he was in control, all right. During the third song (a heart-wrenching but otherwise innocuous ballad), he slipped long talented fingers over the remote control. Hannah hadn't even seen him do it. One minute she was singing along, lustfully admiring the trickle of sweat that ran down the side of his face, and the next, she was nearly leaping out of her skin when a subtle buzzing began between her legs.

The vibration wasn't strong enough to send her over the edge, but it was more than enough to make her voice falter even as her body lurched in anticipation.

And tremendous arousal.

Hannah felt her nipples snap into hardness again, pressing against the smooth satin of her bra. She knew the angle wasn't right and he couldn't see her reaction, but her expression had changed as well. Nate danced by and shared with her a wicked grin. Her fingers closed over the edge of the barrier for support. She pressed her hips against the hard wood in front of her, both for support and because it intensified the pleasure.

Hannah tried to pay attention to the concert; she really did. But the world narrowed, her focus tunneled, until all she could see was Nate, and all she knew was that whenever he was standing near her, at some point his hand would drift to the remote control.

He turned the control down and she nearly sobbed with frustration. The music pulsed inside her, her clit throbbing with every heartbeat.

Nate positioned himself in front of her, his legs spread. She looked up, knowing that he could see her arousal. She wondered how hard he was behind the guitar. His hips began to rock. Each thrust timed to the song, to the chord changes that flowed from his fingers. Hannah imagined she could feel him inside her, each rocking movement sending her higher.

Lifting her hands, she gathered her hair up, a stray breeze cooling the back of her neck. A sinful smile curved his sensual mouth. His hand stole to his waist. The buzzing, vibrating pleasure sped up just a little.

Hannah let out a moan. The crowd noise swallowed it up. Someone jostled her from behind. She barely noticed. He turned the control up again, just a tiny shift of intensity, and Hannah caught her breath, hanging on the edge of orgasm.

Lips parted, low breathy moans came from her throat. She was torn between desperately needing to come and the embarrassment of knowing it would be in front of thousands of people. They pressed against her from behind, from the sides, intimately close, yet none of them knowing what he was doing to her.

But to climax in public, like this, surrounded by people . . . He would be able to make her come whenever he wanted to and she'd be able to do nothing about it.

Nate spun away. The intoxicating buzz between her legs diminished, leaving her moaning with frustration. Her inhibitions were being whittled away with every tiny vibration. She'd never thought that she could ache so badly, be so close, so wet, and still cling to the edge.

The closeness of the crowd added to the thrill, the collective energy stroking over her skin. The fact that everyone was riveted, watching Nate on stage, meant that she could conceivably have a screaming orgasm and nobody would really notice.

Hannah had never considered herself an exhibitionist, wasn't sure if this counted, really. She was fully clothed. Nate wasn't even going to touch her.

But he did. With his eyes, as he ran by. With his fingers, as he stroked music from the guitar strings. With the titillating buzz that surged again and again. The world narrowed to just the two of them. The audience faded away.

The concert was nearing an end. Hannah knew that, because she was enough of a fan and had been to enough concerts to know the pattern of songs. The encore would be coming soon. Once she'd figured out the pattern, it had always caused her a brief moment of grief whenever she heard 'Dragons of Winter' live because it was a signal that all good things must come to an end, that the concert was nearly over, that she'd go home alone, to her empty bed, and relive the magic of the concert and dream of Nate Fox.

But now he wasn't a dream anymore, and even though the song still sent a pang of despair straight to the pit of her stomach, it was coupled with heart-fluttering excitement.

The concert was almost over. Soon it would reach its climax, and hopefully so would she.

The time for him to wield the vibrator's control was rapidly declining. Hannah couldn't remember having been kept on the brink of arousal for so long. Oh, she'd always been horny at his concerts, but this was very, very different. She could feel the hard egg of the vibrator against her vulva, pressing the lips open, leaving her ready and willing.

'Dragons of Winter' ended. Hannah hadn't been entirely aware of singing along, but she knew she had. The crowd around her screamed and cheered, and her own arms were in the air as she clapped and pumped her fist.

Kenny started a throbbing beat on his bass. Hannah stared at him, shocked at how well the rhythm was timed with the vibrations. Oh God, had Nate planned this that carefully? But no, it was the heavy bass making her sternum pulse, and her whole body was tuning into the hard-driving pound of the song.

She watched as Nate jumped up onto the keyboard. His hips rocked, the guitar an extension of his body. His head was thrown back, sweat trickling over his chest. His shirt was gone, and she imagined trailing her tongue along his taut flesh, chasing the sweat down his body. He howled the lyrics, and Hannah again pressed her hips against the wooden barrier separating her from the stage.

She hadn't seen his hand move, but she could swear

that the teasing egg nestled against her aroused flesh had sped up. Heat pooled low inside of her, tightening, drawing her awareness to it.

The song was close to its finale and her body echoed it. She didn't know if she could hold back for him. The cliff was waiting and she was ready to leap.

Looking down into her eyes, Nate sang the final words, 'your strange desires.'

He pulled his head up and gathered himself.

His fingers turned the remote control dial to maximum.

He leaped into the air off the keyboard.

The world exploded into a million shades of red. Hannah heard herself scream, her hips bucking uncontrollably as spasm after spasm consumed her. Heat pulsed outward from her clit, rolling along her skin, the buzzing egg sustaining the sensations. She came in waves that shattered her, wringing every last drop of pleasure from her aching body.

Looking up, Hannah saw Nate close, kneeling at the edge of the stage where he'd landed. His eyes glittered with dark satisfaction. The look was for her alone. He unclipped the remote, then pressed it to his lips before tossing it to her.

A souvenir.

A promise.

Chapter Twelve

The sun was hot, beating down on her shoulders out of a nearly cloudless sky. The sidewalk burned up through her sandals. Hannah ignored the discomfort. She was too busy patting herself on the back for the crowd turnout.

The CD signing at the Borders Books and Music in Phoenix had been her baby. The newspaper articles she'd engineered had been lukewarm. The charts had shown an upward trend for the CD, but not fast enough or far enough. Nate's remake of 'Born to Be my Baby' was receiving decent airplay, but it seemed stuck just outside of the Top 50.

Both Nate's and Hannah's reputations were at stake.

That was why she was so excited to see the long line snaking down the sidewalk outside the store.

'Pretty respectable,' Sam remarked. He handed her the extra bottle of water he carried.

'Thanks,' Hannah said. It was for more than the drink.

'Sales are up inside,' Sam said. He snapped the fingers of one hand, simultaneously beating out time on his thigh. He just couldn't keep still. 'It was a good idea to order in a supply of Nate's older stuff.'

'The manager's been great,' Hannah agreed.

Someone called out Sam's name and he raised a hand in acknowledgement. A lot of hard-core fans recognized him as Nate's manager.

Hannah scanned the crowd, seeing a few faces that she recognized. The FoxFanatics who'd shown up had been at the head of the line. They'd staked their places since early morning. Hannah had made sure she'd greeted them and thanked them for their support.

'How are the T-shirt sales going?' Hannah asked.

'I'm still not sure that was a good idea,' Sam said. 'I want to distance Nate's name from the drugs, not remind everyone of his addiction.'

'We've had this argument before,' Hannah reminded him. 'You know how he feels about it.'

'Shit, I know,' Sam said. He squinted up into the sun. His foot had taken over his internal rhythm, tapping restlessly. 'I just want him to maintain that bad-boy image. Being the poster boy for an anti-drug campaign just doesn't cut it.'

Hannah took a long swallow of the cold water. What she really wanted to do was hit Sam with the bottle. The two of them had clashed endlessly over this. 'Options is good for him. When they approached him about being a spokesperson, Nate was really excited.'

'Yeah, well, next thing you know, he'll be wanting to visit local schools to tell the kids to stay off of drugs.'

She frowned at Sam. She couldn't see why that was a bad idea.

'If he wanted to be a do-gooder, at least he could have picked a charity that didn't focus on drugs,' Sam went on.

As she'd told him time and again, people weren't going to forget Nate had had a drug problem. This was a way for him to turn the negative into positive publicity. He could still have a bad-boy image without drugs.

She knew Sam wanted only the best for Nate. The older man had been with Nate a long time and in many cases did know what was best. But he didn't have the PR training and experience that she had.

Patiently, Hannah guided the conversation back to her original question. 'So are the T-shirts selling?'

Sam ran a hand through his curly hair. 'The Options spokesperson here is thrilled. They've almost sold out of the large size.'

'See, it was a good thing,' Hannah told him with a cheeky grin. It had been her idea to feature the Fox band logo on T-shirts for the House. Borders was allowing them to be sold, with the proceeds going to the charity. Nate would sign them when fans brought them up to his table.

'I hate being wrong,' Sam muttered before marching off and leaving her to crowd-watch.

Hannah drifted along the sidewalk in the direction of the store entrance. She wanted to peek in on Nate. She loved to watch him work.

'It's her!' The excited shout had her looking around to see what was going on.

'Hannah!'

A woman was waving to her from the line, fairly bouncing up and down in her excitement.

Confused, Hannah walked over to her. Maybe they'd met at a concert. A sun visor hid a part of the woman's face and made it impossible to tell from a distance.

The woman elbowed a friend. 'I told you it was her!'

Sure now that she didn't know the woman, Hannah was about to say hello when a tabloid was suddenly shoved into her face.

'You're Nate's girlfriend. We saw your picture in here!'

There was suddenly a lot of people looking her way. Out of the corner of her eye, she saw someone holding up a cellphone, snapping a picture.

The woman was hurriedly flipping pages. 'Here,' she said finally, stabbing a finger at a picture. 'Will you sign this for me, please?'

Hannah's hands were shaking. Ignoring the pen shoved her way, she stared at the picture.

It was the paparazzo shot from Lorelei. The bastard had caught her at a highly unflattering angle. Her mouth was wide open, her eyes squinty, and Nate's fork poised there.

'A new low instead of his high,' the article began.

'Rocker Nate Fox was caught at a trendy Las Vegas restaurant sharing a romantic meal for two. Gone are the supermodel and starlet beauties of the past. Fox's new *amore* is his publicist, Hannah Montgomery. No longer on the A-List, is Fox reduced to dating his employees?'

Her stomach plummeted. The heat was suddenly unbearable. Her vision telescoped to a single point. The rest of the world was black.

Just the picture.

An ugly, accusatory picture.

Someone was shaking her arm. She looked up to meet the woman's excited eyes.

'Will you introduce me to him?'

People were pressing close, drawn by the excitement. Suddenly and unwillingly a celebrity, Hannah felt overwhelmed, sick. Pinned open and flayed alive.

'Ask her if he's good in bed!' The shout came from someone at the back of the crowd.

'Excuse me,' she said faintly. 'I have to go.' She tried to move away, but someone grabbed at her. The woman with the tabloid shook the paper, still waving a pen.

'Please, let me out,' Hannah said. She felt dizzy. Penned in.

Her mouth wide open, her faced squished up.

Reduced to dating an employee.

A new low.

'Please,' Hannah repeated.

A strong arm curled around her shoulders. A dark-brown hand closed over the pages of the tabloid, pulling it from the fan's grasp.

'Everyone step back now,' Andre said. The low rumble of his voice would have shattered a glacier.

What the words didn't do, the breadth of his shoulders and the utterly ruthless expression on his face accomplished. The crowd moved back enough to let them through.

Two of the guards that Andre had hired as extra security stepped in to regain control.

'You should be with Nate,' she said faintly.

'He's just fine inside,' Andre answered. He bent his head close to hers. 'I was told you were being accosted out here. What the hell is going on?'

They'd reached the store entrance, and Andre steered her inside. The shocking cold of the air conditioning was a slap in the face. She drew away a little, but let Andre keep his arm around her waist.

Everyone was looking at them. She could see them staring.

Not a supermodel.

Not a starlet.

Just a plain employee with her mouth wide open.

She was grateful when Andre took her back into the employee break room. She sank down into a hard chair and felt his hand at the back of her neck, pushing her head down between her knees. About to protest that she wasn't going to faint, Hannah kept silent when she realized that it was making her feel better.

A half-drunk can of Coke sweated on the table and there was a faint smell of tuna in the small room, probably emanating from some crumpled tinfoil in the full trash can.

A burst of static, and Andre spoke quietly into his walkie-talkie.

'Sam's on his way,' Andre said. 'Are you all right, honey?'

She looked up at him. He'd taken off his mirrored sunglasses and his dark eyes were concerned. 'Have you seen the picture in the tabloid?'

A glance down at the paper he still held in one hand and a quick shake of his head told her that he hadn't. His big hands flipped the pages deftly. When he reached the short article, he frowned. 'I'll find out who took this and arrange for him to meet with an accident.'

The fact that she couldn't tell if he were kidding or not was worrisome.

'What's up?' Sam asked. He stood in the doorway, looking from one to the other.

Wordlessly, Andre handed him the paper.

The frown that drew Sam's brows together changed the whole dimension of his face. 'Well.'

'I'm supposed to be helping Nate, not dragging him down.'

'I can't argue with that,' Sam said. A quick motion of his head sent Andre out the door. He stared at Hannah, his hands shoved down into his pockets. 'I thought you'd be good for him, but I have to say I'm not happy about this.'

She took the criticism in silence. Her misery couldn't go any deeper. She had enough self-confidence to know that she was pretty and sexy, but she also knew she couldn't compete with glamour girls. She knew that under her gloss and shine, she was still sometimes gawky. A little boring, even.

But she didn't need it in print for the world to see.

'What are you going to do about it?' Sam asked her. 'What kind of spin can you put on it?'

'I don't know,' she said. 'They wanted my autograph, Sam.'

He pulled out a chair and dropped into it. 'Great. So now you're a celebrity, too. Maybe you can sign some photos and sell them on eBay.'

She winced at his sarcasm. 'I'm sorry.'

'Too late for that now. I thought the two of you were going to be discreet.'

She glared at him. It was bad enough that she was beating herself up. She didn't need him to help. 'I didn't arrange for the paparazzi to be there, you know. The manager at Lorelei said he'd snuck in using another name. They're normally really good at protecting their customers' privacy.' She sounded defensive and she didn't care.

'I want you to fix this.'

'I will,' Hannah promised.

'I don't want to see any more articles with the words "new low" and "Nate Fox" together.'

'You won't.'

With a last hard look, Sam left the room.

Hannah dropped her head into her hands. She'd really screwed up this time. She'd jeopardized Nate's career, and probably jettisoned her own as well. Her work with Jenna Glenn, with Double Zero, with Simone DiPaolo, would be forgotten, eclipsed by her sensational failure here, as well as her sensational stupidity of getting involved with a client. Even if her actual publicity work for Nate was fantastic, from the outside it would look as if she'd been thinking with her panties, not her professionalism.

Fact was, she *had* been thinking with her panties, from the moment she'd gotten into the elevator with Nate.

And now it had turned around and bitch-slapped her.

Nate's fingers tightened. The paper crumpled in his fist. 'I'm sorry, Hannah,' he said quietly.

They sat on the empty tour bus. Nate had just finished a sound check. She hadn't wanted him to see the article until after the night's concert, but one of the local stage crew had shown it to him.

'I'm sorry, too,' Hannah said. 'I should have known better.' She couldn't bear to look at him. Couldn't bear to see the condemnation in his eyes. She was supposed to put him back on the top, not drag him down even further.

'What's that supposed to mean?' he demanded. 'Look at me, Hannah.'

She dared a glance up at him. The anger in his gaze seared her. Blinking back the hot burn of tears, she shook her head. 'I shouldn't have allowed myself to get involved with you. It wasn't supposed to be like this.'

'What was it supposed to be like?' He dropped to his knees in front of her. The hands that gripped her thighs sent heat straight to her core.

'I know you're angry –'

'Not with you, love,' he said softly. 'With the bastard that took the picture and the paper who bought it and the person who wrote that shitty article. But not with you.'

'You should be,' Hannah said. 'I should have known to keep it professional between us.'

'Fuck that,' he told her. 'I wouldn't change a thing about the past few weeks.' He smoothed back a lock of her hair, tucking it behind one ear. His fingers lingered on her cheek. 'I wouldn't change a thing about us.'

'I'm not what you need,' she whispered. Against her better judgment, she leaned into his caress, needing to feel his touch.

His hand cupped the back of her neck, urging her forward. 'You're exactly what I need.'

The kiss was gentle and sweet. It did what nothing else could have done, and swept her out of herself, away from the misery. There was only Nate and the joy of his mouth on hers. His scent, earthy and male, wrapped around her, drugging her. When he nudged her thighs apart, she acquiesced with a low moan. Gripping his tight denim-covered ass, she pulled him close and rocked against the hard length of his cock. The buzz of arousal began low in her stomach, increasing with each flex of his hips. She ached for him.

A sharp banging snapped her upright, pressing her back against the leather chair and away from the temptation of his body.

'Nate, we need you backstage,' Sam's voice came from just outside the bus. His fist against the door punctuated his summons.

'Yeah, OK,' Nate called out. 'I'm sorry,' he murmured to Hannah. He rested his forehead against hers, the midnight blue of his eyes dark with arousal. He took one last kiss, a sinful dip of his tongue into her mouth.

'We haven't finished this conversation,' he promised. A quick adjustment of his cock in his pants, a last piercing look and he was gone.

And Hannah was alone.

So very alone.

The heavy bass beat thrummed up through the floor, vibrating through her body. The concert was in full swing. Still in the bus, safe in the VIP parking area, Hannah closed her eyes. Nate would be seducing the crowd now, his voice filling the amphitheater. She could hear him, but the sound was distorted by distance. The roar of the crowd was hungry, predatory. She could imagine them eating him alive, taking everything that he gave and endlessly demanding more.

And there would be nothing left for her.

She scrolled through the phone numbers in her BlackBerry, selected Gina's and hit dial. If she'd ever needed her best friend, it was now.

The phone rang and rang. Rang again. Hannah crossed her fingers. 'Please pick up,' she murmured. 'Please, please.'

'This had better be good!' Gina's voice was breathless. 'I have a totally hot underwear model coming to my door in less than five minutes.'

Hannah closed her eyes. The phone was in danger of snapping in her grip. 'I'll try to talk fast.'

'So how's the tour?' Gina asked. 'How're the concerts? How's the *sex*?'

'Have you seen the *Weekly Word*?'

'You know I don't buy those,' Gina said, laughing. 'I just read them in line at the supermarket.'

'There's a picture of me and Nate in it.'

There was silence for a long beat. 'You don't sound too happy about that.'

She hadn't meant for the sob to come out. Once it did, the tears overwhelmed her, burning down her cheeks.

'Don't go away,' Gina said. 'I'll call you right back.'

There wasn't a single box of tissues on the bus. Hannah finally settled on a roll of toilet paper, blew her nose and tried to fight the tears. They wouldn't stop. Her chest was still hitching when the phone rang.

'I got rid of Sven. Talk to me,' Gina instructed.

'It's awful,' Hannah said. She related the episode with the paparazzo in Lorelei. The fans in line at the CD signing. 'I'd almost forgotten about it. It was over a week ago.'

'How bad can the picture be? You're gorgeous.'

'My mouth is wide open and Nate is sticking a fork in it. I look totally awful. That's not the worse part.' As quickly as she could, trying to maintain what little composure she had left, Hannah read her the article.

'That's harsh,' Gina said softly. 'But, sweetie, if you're going to date a rock star, you're going to have to toughen up. You can't let those rags get to you. You know the kind of spin they give stories just to sell the papers.'

'I know,' Hannah said. 'Of all people, of course I know. But Gina, how am I going to do my job when just by being with him, I'm sabotaging his career?'

'I think you're putting more weight on this than it deserves,' Gina said.

'No, I'm not. His career is at a vulnerable point right now and this does nothing to help it. I can't be objective about what he has to do to get back on top if I have such an emotional response to every little thing that's printed. I can't do my job *and* be Nate's girlfriend.'

There was silence on the other end of the phone and Hannah rushed to fill it.

'It was only supposed to be one night. Just one night to fulfill a stupid vow I'd made to myself. I can't believe how stupid I was to sleep with a client. And then I kept sleeping with him. And going out in public with him. On dates. What was I thinking? I am such an idiot.'

'Now you're being ridiculous,' Gina said. 'You're not an idiot. There was no way you could have stepped away from a relationship with him after that first night. I saw the two of you together the next day, remember? There was no way Nate was going to let you go.'

'I shouldn't have taken the job,' Hannah said. She barely heard what Gina was telling her, trapped in her own misery and guilt. 'I can't do the job properly if I'm this close to him.'

'Well, you can't quit,' Gina told her. 'You signed a contract with them. You're in this for the long haul, so you might as well get used to it. Don't think negatively – think proactively. How do you turn this around?'

She knew Gina had just manipulated her into using the problem-solving-obsessed part of her brain and she loved her for it.

'It's not too late to get this under control,' Hannah said. She sat up straighter in the chair. 'If they want to see him with models and stars, then that's what he needs to do. It's all about the image. See and be seen, and who you're seen with. I'm just his publicist. I don't have any star quality, but if Nate's seen with someone totally glamorous and popular, it will do wonders for his ratings. I promised to get him back on top.'

'Are you listening to yourself?' Gina asked. 'Girl, there is no way Nate is going to want to go out with some other woman when he has you.'

'Of course he will,' Hannah said. She was getting

excited now, the rest of her emotions shutting down. She pushed them away, far away. If she could keep focused only on Nate the client and not Nate the lover, she could do this. 'He wants to be successful. He wants the positive publicity that will put him back on top.'

The picture laying face up on the leather next to her gave her every reason to make this decision. 'I'm going to do my job and stop letting my personal life interfere. We'll all be much happier.' Hannah blew out a long breath. 'Thanks, Gina. For listening.'

Before Gina could interrupt, could try to change her mind, Hannah hung up.

Things would be OK.

Even if she had to lose Nate.

Even if she had to lose the man she loved.

Chapter Thirteen

The bus rumbled down the highway. The engines were muted, their sound partially dampened by the light soundproofing on the walls of the small bedroom he and Hannah shared. The soundproofing needed to be redone, though. Every so often, he could hear the sounds of the band up front laughing at something on the DVD player. The occasional squeal of the groupie that Kenny had picked up after the concert.

And Nate knew that if he could hear them, then they would be able to hear him.

He knew that the lack of privacy bothered Hannah, inhibiting her responses to his advances. They'd kept their nights on the bus chaste, sleeping curled in each other's arms. Frustrated, but together.

But he wanted her now. Wanted – no, needed – to take the sadness from her eyes, to ease the small line of tension between her brows. She was upset about the article in the tabloid. It wasn't the first time he'd been smeared across its pages. It wouldn't be the last. But to Hannah, it had to be embarrassing as hell.

She just wasn't used to being the one in the spotlight.

'Hey,' he said softly, running one hand up her arm.

She dragged her attention away from the laptop. 'I'm almost finished sending the new concert pictures to the FoxFanatics webmaster,' she said.

'You are finished,' he said, catching her hands and drawing them to his lips. He pressed a kiss into one palm, and then the other. The sudden catch of her breath, the way her nipples puckered against the silk of her camisole, made him smile.

He flicked his tongue against the fine skin of her

wrist, inhaling her exotic scent. The fluttering of her pulse tickled against his lips. His balls tightened behind the fly of his jeans, his cock hardening. She intoxicated him.

'I guess I am,' Hannah agreed. Her voice was breathy, and he'd already learned that meant she was turned on.

'Good,' Nate said. He licked a path up her arm and nuzzled the inside of her elbow.

Hannah's tongue dampened her lips. Unable to resist the temptation, Nate leaned forward and captured her mouth with his. She was heat and spice, rich as sin, and he reveled in her taste. He wound one hand in her hair, dragging her head back to deepen the kiss. His tongue thrust, anticipating the movements his body intended to make.

Hannah dragged her mouth from his. 'No,' she said.

He grazed the delicate skin of her throat with his teeth. He felt like he would come out of his skin if he didn't have her.

'No,' Hannah said, a little more forcefully. Her hands pushed against his bare chest and continued pushing until he was lying flat on the mattress.

One lock of hair draped over her shoulder, curling around the curve of her breast. It was fire against the cream-colored silk. He found the sight unbelievably erotic.

His cock ached, straining against the denim, and he threw one arm over his eyes. A deep groan left his lips. If she were going to deny him, then he couldn't keep staring at her. He just didn't think he had that much control.

The bed bounced a little, and he heard a rustle from the corner where a small bureau held their clothes. Nate concentrated on math equations. Anything to get his raging libido under control.

The mattress sank again when she returned. Nate peeked out from under his arm in time to feel her throw a thigh over his hips. She straddled him, her heat burning through his clothes. His cock hardened further and, with a naughty pout of her kissable lips, Hannah rubbed lightly against him.

Nate's hands caught her waist, intending to flip her over. Hannah shook her head, dangling a pair of cuffs from her fingers. The black leather studded with silver metal and rings was part of what he wore on stage each night. His interest piqued, Nate waited for her next move.

With excruciating slowness, she buckled them around his wrists.

'Have I ever told you just how sexy I find these?' she asked. Her tongue traced the line of skin just above one of the cuffs. Her teeth closed over the flesh beneath his thumb, sending sharp pleasure through him.

'If I'd known that, I'd never have taken them off,' Nate said. He wanted to touch her, push her silky top up and taste the nipples outlined so enticingly by the fabric.

He also wanted to see where she intended to go with this.

'I see them and they make me want to do wicked things to you.' She sucked one of his fingers deep into her mouth, stroking with her tongue.

Nate thought he might come unglued if she continued. He pushed his hips up against hers, groaning with frustration when she levered herself away.

'Behave,' Hannah said.

'Or?'

The wicked smile was back. She reached behind her, and showed him the silky red scarf she normally wore tied through her belt loops. 'Or I'll have to tie you up.'

She dangled it like a challenge between them. The ends tickled his bare torso and his stomach muscles contracted. She ran the silk through her fingers. He was enchanted. What man could resist a woman who wanted to have her way with him? He found her desire for control erotic as hell.

Nate held his hands out. The fingers that ached to caress her nipples remained still as she slowly threaded the cool fabric through the rings on his cuffs. Her teeth worried her bottom lip as she concentrated on tying a knot. Nate raised his head, wanting to steal a kiss, and found that he couldn't reach.

'I told you to behave,' Hannah said. Her husky voice held breathless excitement.

Taking his bound hands, she stretched his arms above his head. The motion pressed her breasts against his bare chest and he took the opportunity to taste the lace-edged skin between the soft orbs. He was so intent on her taste, the damp smooth skin, her unique scent, that he didn't realize she'd knotted the rest of the scarf through the handles of the cabinet above the bed until he tried to move.

Hannah sat back, wiggling a little against the steely bulge of his denim-covered cock. The motion sent pleasure through him and Nate moaned. Hannah dragged her fingernails down his chest, along the defined ridges of his abs. Her fingers came to rest lightly at his waistband.

Nate stared up at her, aware that he was breathing too quickly. She was beautiful, her hair tousled around her shoulders. Lace edged the camisole, plunged between her breasts. Tiny pearl buttons ran the length of the material, giving teasing glimpses of her hidden flesh.

'Now you're mine,' she whispered. Her fingertips stroked his chest, following the same path her nails had taken moments before. The soft sensation made him groan.

'Just tell me to stop and I will,' Hannah promised. Her nails traced a path around his navel. He heard himself whimper.

'You're going to have to be quiet,' she said softly. She leaned closer, her tongue flicking against his bottom lip. 'You wouldn't want anyone to hear us, would you?'

'The way I feel, I don't think I'll have much choice,' Nate admitted.

She bit his ear lobe and her tongue swirled around the whorls of his ear. 'Then I'd have to stop. You don't want that, do you?'

'No,' he said, his voice hoarse. Her nipples poked his chest through the silk of her cami. He pulled at the scarf, but she'd tied it too well. All he succeeded in doing was banging the cupboard doors a little.

'Naughty,' Hannah said. Her nails found his nipples and she plucked sharply.

Nate bucked against her. 'Ah, hell!' His shout seemed to echo in the room.

Hannah shook her head, her bottom lip in a delicious pout. 'I warned you about making noise. Now, I'll just have to stop what I was doing.'

She sat up, and he ached to run his hands up her sleek thighs to the silk-covered junction between them. The slinky shorts were damp with her arousal.

Hannah tossed her hair back. Her breasts strained against silk and lace. Running her hands up her own thighs, she unconsciously echoed his desire. She continued up her stomach, cupping her own breasts, thumbs stroking her nipples. She moaned softly, looking down at him.

One finger slipped a button free. An inch of creamy skin was revealed. She traced the deeper V with her nail. When he tried to push his hips against her, she lifted herself away. 'Enough of that,' she said. 'Or you won't get a peek.'

Another button popped free. Her fingers eased the fabric aside. The luscious curves of her breasts pushed against the lace. Hannah slipped one finger inside, flicking against her nipple. 'Mm, I'm imagining your hands on me. Your mouth,' she said, then licked a thumb to rub in slow circles across the other nipple. The silk darkened with her moisture.

Nate thought he was going to explode. His cock felt harder, tighter, than ever before. And if she kept up this slow tease, he might be forced to rip the cabinet doors from the wall.

Another button. One more. The cami parted, but still clung to her breasts, refusing to give him the satisfaction of seeing her. She continued to pleasure herself through the fabric, her breath coming in soft gasps.

'Let me taste you,' he said. His voice didn't sound like his own, so roughened with hunger and need.

Hannah shook her head. Her hair shifted around her shoulders. One thin strap slipped off, down her arm. Through the lace edging, he could see the deep rose of her nipple. The sight made him groan. His hands clenched into fists.

Slowly, Hannah slipped out of the cami, drawing out the seduction. Then, bared to his gaze, she gave him a sexy smile. Her hands cupped her breasts, fingers lightly squeezing the nipples. Her nails scraped, flicked, and she offered soft little moans. Her cheeks were flushed with pleasure.

'Hannah, please,' he begged. If she didn't get him out of his jeans soon, he might be maimed for life. The zipper pressing into him was sure to do permanent damage.

Leaning forward, Hannah scraped her nipples against his chest again. The sensation went straight to his groin and he felt a hot droplet seep from his cock. The woman was going to kill him.

Grey eyes gone dark with arousal looked into his. 'Will you behave?'

'I'll do anything you want,' he promised. 'Just get me out of these jeans.'

Hannah laughed, the sultry sound mingling with his

gasp when she lightly bit his bottom lip. Cupping her breasts, she offered him a taste.

Her puckered nipple was hard and he sucked it greedily into his mouth. He needed to make her as desperate as she was making him. Maybe then she'd give him some relief. His teeth scraped, his tongue soothed, trying for finesse but feeling his control falling away.

With a little moan, she drew back. Her flesh was damp from his attentions.

'Let's put that tongue of yours to better use,' she said. Her hands slipped beneath her waistband, easing the silk down over her thighs. With a little wiggling, and some moves she managed to make look graceful despite the awkwardness of her position, Hannah removed the tap pants, tossing them onto the floor.

Her pink clit peeked from between her nether lips, already taut with her arousal. Her musky scent teased him, and he was suddenly desperate to touch her, to bury himself so deeply inside of her that he would lose himself.

He tugged against his bonds, a frustrated snarl coming from his throat. He slammed his head back against the pillow. Cool fingers covered his, and Nate opened his eyes to find her close. Hannah's breath warmed his lips.

'Do you want me to let you go?'

Did he? The times he'd played bondage games before, he'd been the one in control. This was entirely new. The need to touch, to conquer, all denied him. He was a slave to her desires. It was exciting. The fact that it was Hannah made it doubly so. But, oh man, he didn't think he was going to survive this.

'No,' he admitted.

'You just have to say stop,' she reminded him.

He grinned up at her. The soft curtain of her hair surrounded them. 'Hell no,' he told her.

She rewarded him with a kiss. She nibbled and licked,

stroked and sucked, and drew back far too quickly. Before he could protest, she'd scooted back.

Deft fingers released the button at his waistband. The rasp of his zipper seemed incredibly loud, and he held his breath, hoping like hell his swollen dick didn't interfere with the metal. Thank God he'd worn underwear. He lifted his hips obediently, allowing her to pull everything off.

When the cool air hit his cock he moaned in relief. Hannah pressed a light kiss to the ridge of his hip. Her hair tickled his shaft and he arched up against her.

'Be still,' Hannah told him. She reached over, plucking something from beside the bed. 'I have a present for you.'

Nate stared at the narrow leather circle she was dangling from her finger. Metal studs decorated it. It reminded him of the wrist cuffs she'd said she liked.

It dawned on him what the leather band was. His gaze went from the suddenly very small-looking ring to her eyes and back again.

'Up to it?' she teased.

Nate didn't trust himself to speak. He gave her a quick nod and then hissed as her fingers stroked his cock. He felt the leather encircle him, snug against the base of his shaft. He winced as she tightened it, the pleasure–pain making him grit his teeth. When she was finished, he was harder than he'd ever thought possible.

Hannah rewarded him with a stroke of her tongue. When she teased the slit at his tip, his entire body twitched. Wet heat encircled him and Nate closed his eyes, reveling in the long slow suck that drew him into the back of her throat. He wanted to wind his fingers into her hair, to set a rhythm, but the silky scarf held him tight.

He was at her mercy.

Her fingers stroked, her palm squeezed and her mouth was a wonder of exquisite pleasure. His hips writhed against the sheets, bucking upward. The teasing flick of her tongue had him gritting his teeth. His balls ached with the need to come.

And then Hannah stopped.

Nate's groan of frustration hung between them.

Hannah smiled. She lifted her hair to cool herself, her lithe body arched above him. Her skin glowed creamy gold in the muted light. He'd intended to beg her to let him come, but looking at her took his breath away.

Hannah moved up his body. Soft thighs pressed against his bound arms. Her clit was only inches from his mouth.

'Taste me,' she demanded.

It was his pleasure to comply. Her fingers wound into his hair when his tongue flicked out. He traced her damp lips, avoiding the sensitive bud poking between. He pressed light kisses to the insides of her thighs. She was wet, her taste on his tongue. He almost forgot about the insane ache of his cock held tight by the leather ring.

Nate lapped at her honeyed juices, each little bounce of her body telling him that he was pleasing her. He thrust his tongue deep, fucking her with it. She moaned, pushing down harder. Her fingers tightened painfully in his hair.

The hard little pearl of her clit tantalized him. He swirled his tongue around it and was rewarded with a soft cry. He forgot about his own desires, concentrating on the hot musky scent of aroused woman.

A thrust, another, hard and then soft, a slow slide of wet tongue on wetter flesh. Hannah was writhing now, her cries filling the tiny bedroom, obviously so lost in her pleasure that she no longer cared who might hear. She cried out his name suddenly, a plea for release. He obliged by sucking hard, drawing her clit between his lips while flicking it again and again with his tongue.

She came, fast and intense. The spasms of her body

made her juices flow into his mouth and Nate drank her down, pleasuring her until she finally pulled away.

Hannah kissed him, licking her cream from his lips. Her teeth grazed his chin, his jaw. Bit hard into his earlobe. 'I'm going to ride you hard,' she whispered. 'Until you beg me to let you come.'

Nate didn't tell her that he was already close to that point. The leather drawn tight around the base of his shaft made every sensation that much more acute. When she straddled his hips again, her hand on his cock had him gripping the scarf. The wet sliding heat that slowly surrounded him, withdrew and then surrounded him again made him burn.

Gritting his teeth, Nate tried to hold back the cries that needed to escape as she rode him slowly. She squeezed him tight and then relaxed. Took him deep and then drew back until only his tip was inside her.

'You're enjoying this,' Nate said.

'Oh, God, yes,' she answered. Hannah worried her bottom lip with her teeth. Her hands came up, pinched and rolled her nipples. The sight of her pleasuring herself with his body was enough to send him over the edge.

Except that he couldn't come.

The cock ring constricted him, rocketing each sensation higher and higher, but allowing no release.

'Hannah,' Nate moaned. His body arched under her, desperate for relief.

'Beg me,' she said. Her tousled hair swung with each rocking motion. One hand moved to stroke her clit and Nate pulled hard against the restraints.

'I'm close,' Hannah breathed. 'Beg me, Nate.'

He was on fire. His balls ached, his cock strained for release and the pleasure was burning him from the inside.

'Please,' he begged. 'Hannah . . .'

Her deft fingers found the buckle. Flicked it loose.

The release was like a shaft of electricity had arced through his belly. Heat spasmed up through his sac, rolling outward. He came in hot spurts that seemed to go one forever, emptying himself inside of her. Her hand squeezed and caressed, milking his balls until he collapsed weakly back against the sheets.

Trembling from her own orgasm, Hannah managed to untie the scarf from the cabinet before she stretched out along his length. She nuzzled his throat and he smiled as her fingers wound through his.

He was never going to let her go.

The suitcase resisted. Cursing her haphazard packing, Hannah leaned her weight onto the bag until it snapped shut. She glanced around the small room. Everything packed away. Nothing left out on the bed. The closetlike bathroom cleared of all her things.

She was cleaning herself out of his life.

Arms slid around her from behind. Warm lips nuzzled the side of her neck.

'What are you doing?' Nate asked. 'You know this isn't a hotel night.' Although they'd had a few hours in a hotel that morning, after they'd reached Albuquerque, they'd be leaving directly from the venue for the next city.

Damn. She hadn't expected him to come in. She'd planned to have the cab waiting, her suitcase already in the trunk when she talked to him. It was the coward's way out, she knew that.

But the pain was so damn bad she didn't know if she could hold it together long enough to get through what needed to be said.

'I thought you were with Sam,' Hannah said. She turned, managing to step out of the warm circle of his arms.

Nate shoved his hands into his back pockets. The faded denim stretched tight over his crotch and she felt heat rush through her. She was never going to forget last night.

'He's busy dealing with the arena manager. Something about electrical outlets, I think. I thought we could grab an early lunch before the afternoon sound checks.'

'I can't,' Hannah said. Resolutely, she gripped the handle of the suitcase and lifted it from the bed. Staggered a little under its weight.

Nate caught her arm. He removed the suitcase from her hand. 'What's going on, Hannah?'

'I didn't want to do it like this,' she said. There was no way she could look into his eyes. She was only just barely holding on.

'Do what like this?' Suspicion and concern warred in Nate's voice.

Hannah licked her lips. It didn't help. Her mouth was too dry. 'I'm leaving,' she said.

The silence stretched. Hannah darted a glance upward. His face was taut, jaw clenched.

'You're not leaving,' he told her. He tossed the suitcase onto the bed. 'You can't leave.'

'I have to, Nate.'

'Why? You've been dealing with your other clients by phone and email. You've been handling it.'

'It's not that.' She reached for the suitcase, but he stopped her. He pulled her around sharply, but the hand that tipped her face up to his was gentle.

'You can't leave me,' he said softly. The huskiness in his voice held a note of panic that astonished her. 'I need you.'

Hannah shook her head, fighting to keep herself from reacting to the emotion she heard. 'No, you don't. You need someone glamorous, someone who'll raise your image back up to where you want it to be.'

'This is about that damned photo, isn't it?' Nate raked his hands back through his hair. A tiny silver fox dangled from his ear.

'I've thought it all out,' Hannah said with as much conviction as she could muster. 'You need to be seen with women on the A-list. Being seen with your publicist makes it look like I'm babysitting you. That's not good for your career.'

'We're not about my career,' Nate said. 'We haven't been for a long time now.'

The words cut her. She'd needed to hear them, needed to know that they were about more than hot sex. Needed to know that he might feel something close to what she felt for him.

But it was too late.

'I can't be both things, Nate,' she said softly. She touched his chest lightly, unable to keep away. His heart beat wildly beneath the warm cotton. 'I can't do my job like this. I can't be your girlfriend and your publicist.'

'Isn't it your job to be on the road with me?' Nate asked shrewdly. His midnight-blue eyes skewered her.

'I agreed to it,' Hannah said, 'but it's not actually in my contract. Sam will agree with me. Try to understand, Nate. I can't put you back on top if I'm pulling you down.'

Catching the hand that rested on his chest, Nate dragged it to his lips. He pressed a hot kiss onto her palm, breathing in the scent of her skin. 'Don't do this to me, Hannah.'

'I have to go, Nate. The taxi will be here any minute now.' The tears were so close. If he didn't let her go, she'd never make it.

His mouth tightened. 'So what was last night, then? One last bang before goodbye? You've had your fantasy fuck and now it's over?'

The words slashed at her. She'd meant for their last time to be something special and he'd destroyed it with his cruel words. She knew he didn't mean it, that he was lashing out, but the knowledge didn't ease the pain.

'I'm sorry,' Hannah whispered. She hauled her suitcase

off the bed. This time he didn't stop her. 'I'll keep in contact with you about interviews and things. I'll get you back on top, Nate.'

'Don't contact me,' he said harshly. 'You can deal with my manager. It's what a publicist does, after all.'

Hannah felt the sob hitch in her chest. She pushed out the door, dragging the suitcase down the narrow aisle between the bunks. His voice came to her softly.

'Was I ever anything other than a poster on your wall, Hannah?'

She couldn't look back. Couldn't answer. The tears threatened to spill. If she looked back she'd never be able to leave.

He'd been more to her than just a teenage challenge since the night they'd spent in her apartment. It had grown into something more powerful than she'd ever expected. Loving him meant understanding why she had to let him go.

Even if doing so killed something inside of her.

The pneumatic slide of the door closing carried through the bus. The only other sound was his harsh breathing. Hurt filled him. Panic. A fury so intense that he wanted to smash something. He wanted to follow her. Knew that if he did, he'd say more things that shouldn't be said.

Like, 'If you don't stay, I might self-destruct.'

Like, 'I love you.'

He'd had enough of begging.

Stalking through the bus, Nate smacked his fist into a kitchenette cabinet. The flimsy wood panel splintered. The sharp pain in his knuckles drew him up short. If his hand swelled, he wouldn't be able to play. He shook his hand out, cursing.

A car door slammed. Nate hurtled out of the bus in time to see a taxi accelerating through the parking lot.

She'd done it. She'd really left him. Their conversation

had had such a sense of unreality about it. The whole time she'd been trying to get her suitcase out of the door, he'd been waiting for the punchline.

Hannah had left him.

Hurt was a bitter taste in the back of his throat. He'd thought that there was more. That she understood him, saw him as something other than the stage persona he adopted in front of the fans.

He'd never thought she would run just because one sleazy tabloid published an unflattering photo and article.

He ground the heels of his hands into his eyes. The starburst of colors seemed too much a celebration. He felt dark inside. Empty.

Her absence was a desolation.

Oh God, he needed her.

He didn't want to, but he did. Needed her with an intensity that bordered on the insane. Needed her smile, her laugh. Her confidence in him. Even her conviction that she could put him back at the top of the charts.

Even if he didn't need to be there.

Even if he'd give all that up, just to have her see him as the man he was. And not as the image it was her job to promote.

The taxi had long since disappeared, taking with it the opportunity to talk to her. To apologize for the words he'd said in the heat of anger. He knew their relationship went deeper than sex. He'd said that only to lash out and now he felt like shit for wounding her.

Hurting in a way he hadn't since detox, Nate walked slowly back to the arena. She had her job to do and he had his.

Chapter Fourteen

Nate stepped out of the limo and into hell.

Cacophony of shouts and screams. Blinding lights. The heat of a summer night in LA.

He smiled and waved genially to people he couldn't see thanks to the unceasing camera flashes, then turned to extend a hand to his date.

Marta Ingersol slid gracefully from the limo, somehow not flashing her panties despite wearing a scarlet dress slit all the way to *there*. Once squarely balanced on impossibly high heels that brought her to Nate's height, she too favored the paparazzi and fans with a megawatt smile, then tucked her hand around Nate's arm so he could escort her properly inside.

It wasn't Marta's fault that Nate felt sick inside.

She wasn't a bad person. They'd had some good times together. It was just that she wasn't Hannah, and he missed Hannah like crazy.

He missed her more than he missed the ability to write music.

He was doing this for her. He didn't understand it, but unless he wanted to lie down and kick his feet like a toddler having a tantrum, he had to go along with it. Be seen at this swanky party with a supermodel on his arm.

As much as he didn't want to admit it, he did feel a trace of excitement, a shadow of what he felt when he first stepped on stage in front of a screaming crowd. He could feel the energy from the onlookers – mostly paparazzi, but a few fans as well – as their excitement washed over him.

But it wasn't the same. There was no music, no escape and joy in the creation.

So he smiled and waved, and made sure Marta was shown off to her best advantage, and then finally, blissfully, they were inside and the worst of it was over. Or so he thought.

There were a few photographers inside, but they were discreet. The camera crew from a local entertainment show filmed quietly, the trendily dressed reporter watching for opportunities to catch a word with any of the big-name celebrities she could snag. It was loud, not with screaming people but with pulse-pounding music blasting through speakers that shuddered in protest – and they hadn't even made it into the main room yet, where the stage was.

He felt a headache starting at the base of his skull.

It had been a long time since he'd been to a party like this. Two years. He found himself mentally stepping back, trying to figure out if he'd missed it.

He used to think these things were fun. He went to every party, every place where it was the place to be seen. He rubbed elbows with actors and musicians and producers and models and fashion designers and celebrities famous for nothing more than being famous. He soaked up the energy, a substitute for the energy he felt on stage.

But it wasn't the same as being one with the music. He realized that now. Before, he'd thought everyone was happy. Already he knew how wrong he'd been. Smiles were brittle, greetings were exchanged with a look deep in the eyes that assessed whether you were someone who could advance the other person's career.

Which was what Hannah wanted him to do. She'd arranged for him to be here to bolster his career.

'You need to be seen in the right places,' she'd said through an email to Sam, which listed the details of the hot new club's opening night bash. Then she'd sent over the clothes he should wear: blue silk shirt, brown leather pants and boots. Suggested a diamond stud in place of his usual gold hoop or silver fox, to imply financial success.

Nate had promptly tossed the shirt. Kept the pants and boots, but paired them with a T-shirt specifically designed to look as if it had been to hell and back. A belt slung low. He was a rocker, for God's sake, not a fashion model.

The kicker was when Hannah had arranged to have Marta Ingersol be the celebrity he'd be seen with.

He didn't need a supermodel to carry him to the top. He just needed Hannah, who made him feel like he'd already made it.

Marta was delighted to be there with him. He didn't know how to tell her it was just for show. He suspected she really thought he was interested in revisiting, maybe revitalizing their relationship. He hoped he could let her down gently.

They entered the main part of the club. Across the big room, on a stage surrounded by a dance floor, a local up-and-coming band played. They weren't bad, Nate mused, but they were still rough around the edges. Two levels of balconies ringed the room, with back rooms leading off them. There'd be sofas, food, tables, bars, Nate knew. The club may have been new, but the set-up wouldn't be much different from anywhere else.

'Look, there's Sandrine Moss and Ray Stark!' Marta said, pointing. 'We should go say hello.'

Nate wondered if Marta wanted to get into acting, because as far as he knew, she didn't know the red-headed starlet and her action-hero boyfriend.

'I don't think they're looking for company,' he noted. The pair were blocking access to one of the club's several bars as they necked passionately.

'Later, then,' Marta said agreeably. She clutched his arm, pressing her breast against him. 'Oh, hello,' she said to a reporter with a video camera who'd swung around and noticed them. She turned so that her upper body was slightly angled and one long leg was poised in front of the other. The official pose that was supposed to make women look thinner. Nate barely had time to register it all, but Marta was a pro, and had her hair swinging back and a smile on her face for the camera.

Well, maybe everybody would just think he looked brooding and sexy rather than grumpy and unprepared.

He really didn't care one way or the other. But he had a commitment to make this party work for him.

A commitment to Hannah.

Maybe if he pressed palms with the right people, let Marta cling to his arm, put up a good face, he'd get Hannah back. If he did the public thing and it boosted his career, then she'd be happy because she'd done what she was hired to do. He'd be back on top because of her, and then she'd come back.

God, he missed her. He raked a hand through his hair before remembering he'd gone to a salon – Hannah's suggestion, once again relayed through Sam – and had his hair trimmed, just a little, and styled, just a bit. How stupid was that? Not as stupid as forgetting you had product in your hair and messing it all up.

Maybe he could make it to the bathroom before any other photographers got to him.

'I'll get something to drink,' Marta said when he excused himself. 'Do you want anything?'

Twenty Advil and a pair of industrial earplugs. Aloud, he said, 'Just a club soda with a twist of lime. Thanks.'

Two steps and he was already accosted.

'Hey, Nate, how's it going? Long time no see!'

'Bobby, hey,' Nate greeted the grunge rocker. 'It has been a while.'

'Yeah. Hey, I didn't see you on the roster for tonight,' Bobby said. He smelled of cigarette smoke and whisky, and his Led Zeppelin T-shirt had a stain near the collar. He had no product in his hair. Largely because his dirty-blond hair was in dreadlocks.

Nothing looked dumber than a white boy in dreads.

But Bobby's band's latest single held the number-one slot in the charts.

'Roster?' Nate asked.

'Yeah. All the musicians on the guest list were asked to do a song at some point. Didn't see your name.'

'I'm in the middle of a tour,' Nate said quickly. 'Saving my voice.'

'Cool, man. Good to see you.' Bobby slapped him on the shoulder and wandered off.

No one had approached him about performing tonight. Apparently Hannah hadn't known, either, because she would have had him on the roster.

OK, he'd gotten on the guest list late. But still. It hadn't been so late that he couldn't have been squeezed in. He'd jammed spontaneously any number of times in the past. They could've tossed him up onstage with any of the other artists he'd seen here (except, maybe, the blinged-out rapper over there) and he would've done fine. Had a blast, even.

The hallway to the restrooms sealed the deal. Signed photos of rockers and rappers, all the hot bands and artists of the day, covered the walls. Nate had seen over half of them here tonight.

His photo wasn't among them.

Not important enough.

A has-been.

In the bathroom, Nate stared at his reflection.

Maybe Hannah's work was in vain. Maybe it was too late, he'd fallen too far. Maybe this tour was a fluke and soon he'd just be playing San Francisco clubs or touring as a nostalgia act. Doing Japanese commercials for booze or watches or cars.

It wouldn't be that bad, would it? He hadn't been completely stupid with his money. He'd snorted a fair amount up his nose, but with the investments he'd made, he could never perform another note and still live comfortably. He wasn't doing too badly. The pressure to succeed would be off. His relationship with Hannah wouldn't matter and he could get her back.

But it would also mean that Hannah had failed.

He knew, with a wrench in his gut, how that would devastate her. It ate at him in a way that the lack of his picture on the wall never could.

Back in the main room of the club, he couldn't see Marta anywhere. The local band was playing, currently fronted by Bobby.

Great. Ditched by his own date. The tabloids would have a field day with *that* one.

He checked the various side rooms, briefly chatting with people he knew, being reminded of how tenuous and vapid it all was. These may have been people he'd called friends in the past, but none of them had called when he was at his lowest point, not one had offered support. They were glad to see him now, but in a fleeting sense.

Part of him just wanted to get lost in that.

He headed upstairs, weaving his way through the throngs lounging on the open steps. In one of the rooms off the balcony, he didn't find Marta, but he found his past staring him in the face.

A past that tempted him, taunted him. Whispered to him of glory, ecstasy, escape.

Oblivion.

Money discreetly changed hands. He walked away with his addiction tucked into his pocket, his mind blank, his emotions numb.

Everything he'd learned about how to resist temptation had fled.

It was so easy. So very easy.

His hands were shaking. Nate stared at them, rather fascinated, before he remembered that if his hands shook, he couldn't play the guitar.

But he hadn't been asked to play or sing tonight so what did it matter?

Hannah mattered. The reminder was like the whisper of a song in his head. Hannah mattered, and the drugs in his pocket would change everything.

Or would they? Would she even care? Hannah might still believe in his career, but she didn't believe in *them*. She'd made it clear: his career and hers came first. If his career tanked, she'd failed in hers. If his career soared, she couldn't – wouldn't – be with him.

In Vegas, when he'd been so close, needed so much, the need for her had outstripped everything else. He'd been able to lose himself in her, in the taste and smell and feel of her, in the strength of her.

He'd lost her now, though. She wasn't there for him to turn to.

Had she ever been? Really? Or had it all been a grand illusion, a fantasy for her. Her number-one-fan obsession finally fulfilled. The poster come to life.

If any of it had been real, then how could she have walked away so easily?

Private. If he was going to do this, he didn't want to do it in front of anybody. If he was going to fail spectacularly, go down in flames, he didn't need an audience.

He ducked into an alcove. It was still loud here, but the music was muffled by walls and floors between here and the stage. Just a steady thump that made the paneling vibrate.

The pain in his chest needed to be eased. The screaming in his brain needed to be quieted. He couldn't go on wanting without doing something about it. Wanting the drugs. Wanting Hannah. He had to have one of them.

He reached into his pocket.

Pulled out his cellphone and dialed.

Nate closed his eyes and hoped.

Hannah's husky voice filled his world, washing over him. Like an ocean wave, surrounding him and cleansing him. Safety, security.

Passion and desire.

'Hi, you've reached Hannah Montgomery. I'm sorry I'm not available to take your call right now, but if you'll leave your name, number and a brief message, or text me with that information, I'll get back to you as soon as I can. Have a great day.'

A woman's shrill laughter heralded her approach.

Nate hastily thumbed the phone off before the recording option started. He didn't want anyone around when he said what he wanted to say.

The woman, clutching two companions – one male, one female, as near as Nate could tell – stumbled by him. The man (he was pretty sure) glanced at him and grinned triumphantly as if to say 'Look what I've got.'

Yeah, whatever.

It had only been Hannah's voicemail recording. Disappointment gnawed at his gut. But it had been her voice. That was something. So much of something.

He slipped his hand into his pocket, pulled out the packet. Stared at it. It didn't seem to hold as much allure now.

His fingers tightened around it into a fist. Holding it. Protecting it. He didn't need it as much now, but he was loathe to give it up. There was something to be said for having it around, nearby, just in case.

Nate closed his eyes, his hand squeezing the sweaty plastic bag. Oblivion was just a decision away. Then he could forget everything.

Even Hannah.

With a sudden, startled laugh, Nate opened his fist, staring at the packet on his palm.

He didn't want this. Didn't want any of it. Hadn't for years now.

All he wanted was the music and his fans' reactions to it. The joy he got from writing and performing. That was what he needed to feel like he'd succeeded in the business.

That, and Hannah at his side.

It was time to make his runaway publicist aware of that.

Without letting himself think anymore, feel anymore, he dropped the drugs in a trash can and resumed his search for Marta.

When he found her, he claimed a migraine and said he'd send the limo back to pick her up whenever she was ready to leave. She pouted about his leaving, the mouth that had sold endless tubes of expensive lipstick curving prettily. He apologized, brushing a kiss against her cheek.

Flashbulbs went off. The brown-bobbed reporter he'd seen earlier moved in but he turned his back. He didn't care. He just wanted to get out of here.

Favorite cotton pants with the little hearts and cross bones. Check.

Favorite tank top washed to silken softness. Check.

Favorite flavor of Ben and Jerry's. Check.

Hannah curled up on the couch, ready to spend a quiet evening alone. She dug her spoon into the ice cream, scooping out a huge chunk of cookie dough. It was a little like hitting the jackpot.

Of course, if she didn't quit eating the ice cream, she wouldn't be able to fit into the new jeans she'd bought. And they were killer. Worth every penny for the ass-defining fit alone.

Not that anyone was going to be ogling her ass anytime soon.

Feeling the ridiculous burn of tears, Hannah deliberately swallowed another spoonful of ice cream, letting the cold sweetness melt slowly against her tongue.

There was no way she was going to start in with the tissues again.

She was tired of crying over him.

The past week had been as full as she could make it. She'd scheduled lunches or dinners with every client who was in town. She'd touched bases with promoters, reporters, music executives. She'd spent evenings scoping out the hottest clubs, looking for the newest trends, finding the places to see and be seen. Every minute had been rigorously accounted for. Every waking hour filled with work.

It was the nights she'd come to dread.

They stretched endlessly. There was no one to kiss goodnight. No one to curl against. No strong arms to cradle her. No heartbeat to lull her to sleep.

No wild, screaming-orgasm sex to wear her out.

Just an aching, empty loneliness filled with thoughts of Nate.

She'd had to take down the poster. Every look brought a heart-deep pain. Every glimpse brought the memory of his final words to her.

Had he ever been anything more than a poster on her wall?

So many times she'd wanted to pick up the phone and call him. To tell him that she'd fallen in love with him. Nate Fox, the guy who made her laugh, whose smile could make her feel safe, happy and wildly turned on all at once.

She'd wanted to call to take away the raw hurt that had been in his voice. The despair that he would forever and always be an adolescent poster fantasy.

That no one would look beyond to see the incredible man he was.

She entertained wild, impossible fantasies that they could be together but keep their relationship totally secret from the media, the fans, everyone. Then reality would set in and she'd know it could never happen. She couldn't live hiding in a tour bus, sneaking into hotel rooms, waiting at home so he could creep in under cover of night.

The reality of being with Nate was both glorious and impossible.

The phone calls she'd made had been to Sam instead. Nate had told her not to call him. She'd ached to ask Sam how he was doing, but she kept it to business. The cordial, professional tone in Sam's voice didn't allow anything else. Hannah was pretty sure that he'd been glad to see her leave the tour, after the fiasco of the tabloid article. So she'd talked to him about CD signings, radio interviews at each of the tour stops. Phone interviews with *Guitar* and *Rolling Stone*.

No mention of the photo and article that had led her to leave. No mention of the phone calls she'd received from reporters wanting to interview her. Wanting to dish the dirt. Hear about any current tour excesses. Hot bedroom details.

She'd kept all of that to herself.

And the last call, about the opening of the Paradise Club. She'd wangled Nate an invitation to opening night, knowing that the publicity would be tremendous. She'd sent explicit instructions about how he should look, even chosen his clothes. She'd needed so desperately for him to get positive exposure. A phone call to Marta Ingersol's agent had gotten her a phone number.

That had been the hardest call she'd ever made. The spiteful triumph in Marta's voice when Hannah had asked her to be Nate's date to the club had just about done her in. Even the memory of Nate telling her that Marta threw up to stay thin didn't cheer her.

And tonight was the opening. Nate would have the supermodel on his arm. A gorgeous woman who would help his career, not drag him down. A woman who would put him in *People* and not the *Weekly Word*.

A woman who wasn't Hannah.

Pulling up a depth of willpower she was only just beginning to realize she had, Hannah put thoughts of Nate and other women from her mind. She picked up the latest thriller from her favorite author, determined to lose herself in the intrigue. Before she could get past the prologue, her intercom buzzed. Buzzed again. Kept buzzing.

Only Gina would play that particular rhythm to get her attention. The drumbeat from her first and favorite Nate song cut off abruptly. Hannah didn't bother checking to see who it was, hitting the button that released the downstairs lock. She held the door open, confident that it would be her friend who exited the elevator.

'I'll have to start ringing your bell like normal people,' Gina said, the elevator door barely open before she scooted through.

Hannah waved the implied apology away. 'I'm totally over him,' she lied. The snort that Gina gave told her just how unconvincing she was.

'What's with the champagne?' Hannah asked.

Gina's eyes shone and she was fairly vibrating with excitement. She pulled two flutes out of Hannah's cabinet and leaned one hip against the counter.

'What's the one thing that I've wanted more than anything else?'

'Sex with Brad Pitt?'

'OK, the other thing I've wanted,' Gina said with a laugh.

Hannah thought about it, and then her eyes widened. 'You got the cover?'

'Next month. A layout in *Vogue* and the cover shot. I'm flying to New York at the end of the week.'

Hugging Gina, Hannah congratulated her. Gina had been working toward that goal nearly as long as Hannah'd had her goal of sleeping with Nate. Now they'd both accomplished their dreams. She just hoped that Gina's ended better than hers had.

'Stop thinking about him,' Gina warned. 'And before you can deny it, I can see it all over your face.' She thrust a flute at Hannah and then lifted her own. 'To never looking back.'

'To you,' Hannah said. 'And to taking the most kick-ass pictures in the fashion world.'

'Yeah, I totally rock,' Gina said in smug agreement. She carried the champagne bottle into the living room, throwing herself onto Hannah's purple and gold couch.

Picking up the ice-cream container, she glanced at the contents. 'I'm going to do you a favor, and not let you eat any more of this,' Gina said.

'Great, so I'm going to drink my sorrows away,' Hannah said.

'No, you're going to celebrate my awesomeness and we're going to watch old movies on TV all night. And then tomorrow, we're going to pamper ourselves at the spa so we look totally hot for your dad's birthday party.'

Hannah settled into the corner of the couch, willing to let Gina's plan take away her need to make decisions.

Gina picked up the remote control and started flipping channels. She passed a seemingly endless selection of how-to shows, sports channels, syndicated dramas and cartoons, looking for just the right movie.

Hannah's cellphone rang. She stared across the room at it. She'd meant to turn it off. This late, it had to be one of her clients having a crisis. She debated answering it and then told herself that, just this once, she deserved a night to herself. Expensive champagne, old movies and her best friend. When it stopped ringing, she looked back at the TV and noticed that Gina had stopped at their favorite entertainment show.

The show was one of the most informative, tracking the trendy and the 'in.' It also had the benefit of being on late enough that she could catch it on a regular basis.

'I want to watch this first and then there's a Vin

Diesel movie on that we haven't seen.' Gina toed off her boots, topped up their glasses and settled back, dropping the remote on the sofa between them.

The celebrity break-ups passed in a blur as Hannah tried to pretend she didn't empathize with every damn one. The fashion segment made Hannah shake her head in bewilderment, although she did make a note of a designer she liked. Then the show went live.

The perky reporter smiled at the camera. Her brown-bobbed hair gleamed in the flashing lights of the club.

'This is Fiona McAllister, reporting live from the Paradise Club. It's a wild night here. Everywhere I look there's a famous face.'

The rest of the woman's report went unheard.

In the background was Nate, walking into the frame. He looked totally hot, his hair spiked a little in front, tousled. Like they'd had wild sex and Hannah'd run her fingers through it. He'd worn the leather pants and boots she'd sent. The shirt was faded and torn and it wasn't the one she'd chosen. A moment's irritation stole through her and then she realized just how hot he looked. She wanted to reach through the screen and rip the T-shirt off of him.

To stroke the sleek warm skin and muscle beneath.

And then his hand curved around Marta's slender waist. He leaned in, nuzzling her cheek. The model's face said it all. Pouting allure. Desire.

Numb fingers pressed frantically at the remote. Finally, the TV responded by clicking off.

'Are you OK?' Gina asked. Then, 'I'm sorry, that was a dumbass question.'

'I set them up on the date,' Hannah said. Her voice was hollow. 'It's my fault.'

He'd forgotten about her so quickly, obviously more than ready to take things up again with Marta as if Hannah had been nothing more than a mindless dalliance.

'Let's tack a picture of him on the wall and throw nasty things at it,' Gina suggested.

Hannah tried to laugh, and couldn't.

Her phone started ringing again.

Chapter Fifteen

The fluorescent lights were too bright. Everything about the diner was too bright at this time of night. She glanced up at the door again, but it still hadn't opened. At the counter, the waitress held up the coffee pot, and Hannah shook her head. She'd already had two cups and was beginning to feel a little jittery. The coffee had the consistency of wallpaper paste.

She was waiting for Andre. He'd called an hour and a half ago. And then kept calling until finally Gina had answered for her.

She'd left Gina at the apartment, preferring to respond to Andre's urgent demand for a meeting alone. She was afraid to find out what he'd do to her if she refused. The champagne in her system had long since evaporated.

And now here she was, waiting in this late-night diner for him.

'Honey, I am *so* sorry I'm late!'

Andre's voice dragged her out of her reverie. Hannah stood up and found herself enveloped in a steely-armed hug. The light fragrance of his cologne tickled her nose.

'Big kiss! Mwah mwah!' he said, air kissing each of her cheeks.

Hannah laughed in spite of herself and gave him a real kiss on his cheek. His skin was shaved baby smooth.

'Talk to me,' Andre instructed, sliding into the booth. 'You look like my worst nightmare.'

Self-consciously, Hannah put her hand up to her hair. She'd tried to sleek the curls, but hadn't really had the heart to work very hard at it. Instead, she'd drawn them back in a ponytail. She was pretty sure that something akin to a poodle tail was popping out of the back of her head.

'You're so good for a girl's ego,' Hannah told him.

'Girlfriends don't lie,' he said.

The dichotomy of his flamboyant personality off duty and his enforcer bodyguard persona when he was working still caught her off guard.

'Seriously, honey, I'm not sure who looks worse, you or Nate.'

'He looked pretty good on TV.'

Andre waved one hand dismissively. 'Window dressing. He's a wreck.'

The waitress came by and poured coffee into Andre's cup. She refilled Hannah's automatically. Andre ordered pastries for them both.

'I'm really not hungry,' Hannah said.

'Don't worry, the calories don't count if you eat them with a friend,' Andre confided.

The comment brought a startled laugh from her.

'Better,' he said. 'You left the tour so quickly, you didn't even say goodbye.'

'I'm sorry,' Hannah said.

Andre squeezed her fingers gently.

Hannah stared at the man sitting opposite her. When they'd first met, she never would have thought that she and Andre would become such good friends. She could talk trash, fashion and men with him without batting an eyelash. It was a lot like having Gina around, except that she could walk down a dark street in a bad neighborhood with him and not have to worry about being mugged. (Then again, Gina could kick some serious ass.)

'So why did you call?' she asked.

Andre took her hands in his. 'You need to help Nate.'

She tried to pull her hands away, automatically shaking her head.

Andre's big hands clamped down, not enough to hurt

her, but enough to keep her from getting free. 'He's self-destructing.'

'He's using again?' Hannah asked, shocked. She'd truly believed he was over the drugs.

'No,' Andre assured her. 'But I wouldn't be surprised if it eventually led to that. Let me tell you what's been going on with your man this week.'

'He's not my man,' Hannah protested.

Andre ignored her. 'He's become a tyrant. When he's not moping around, he's snarling at people and picking fights. He and Alan just about came to blows two days ago. And while I'm all for watching hunky men wrestle around, it's not good for the tour. The concerts are suffering. You have to talk to him.'

'I can't.'

'Why not? I don't understand what happened between the two of you.'

'The article –'

Andre snorted. It sounded a little like a bull getting ready to gore an unsuspecting victim. 'You're a publicist; you know how the game works. Not everyone is going to love you. Not every photo is going to be flattering. You have to develop a thick skin.'

She knew that. Lord knew she told her clients that often enough. But this wasn't the same thing at all – she wasn't supposed to be the one in front of the camera – and she told him so.

'This was personal. I've never been the actual cause of a client's bad PR before. They said that dating me was a new low, Andre!'

'So you had your feelings hurt,' he said. 'Was that any reason to up and leave the man hanging?' He squeezed her hands one final time, then let go. He took a deep drink of the coffee, grimacing at the bitter taste.

The waitress slid two plates onto the table. The warm smell of sugar floated up. Hannah looked at hers and silently pushed it across the table to Andre.

'I don't mean to be so hard on you, honey,' Andre said softly. He forked a big piece of cheese Danish into his mouth. 'But I've known Nate for a long time and I haven't seen him this low since he was using.'

'He's hardly low,' she said. 'He's on a date tonight.'

'You arranged that,' he pointed out.

'I didn't arrange for him to kiss her.'

'That was for the benefit of the camera.'

'He wasn't paying any attention to the camera.'

'You're jealous,' Andre observed. 'He was doing what you wanted him to do and now you don't like it.'

Looking away, Hannah fixed her gaze on the potted plant hanging over a nearby table. Its drooping fronds trembled in the air current generated by a ceiling fan.

'He's falling apart. And that has nothing to do with Hannah Montgomery, the publicist, and everything to do with Hannah Montgomery, the woman.'

'He'll survive just fine without me,' Hannah said. The question was, would she survive without him? The answer had to be 'yes.' She just had to put on her big-girl panties and deal with it.

'Surviving isn't the same as living,' Andre said. 'I'll tell you something you don't know.'

Hannah raised her eyebrows in a question.

'He left the party early tonight.' He paused, gauging her reaction. 'Alone. I know, because I was in the limo with him.'

The news hit her hard, the relief that surged through her making her dizzy. He wasn't with Marta tonight. They weren't in a hotel room. He wasn't driving another woman wild with passion.

Forcing herself to be the professional she knew she had to be, Hannah shrugged. 'I'm his publicist, Andre, not his girlfriend. It doesn't matter to me if he leaves alone or with a dozen groupies. In fact, it would have been better if he'd left with Marta or a dozen groupies. It would get him more publicity.'

'You can't tell me you don't care,' Andre said.

'It doesn't matter if I care. He wants to be on top. He deserves to be there. And he won't be if he's not seen at all the parties, with all the right people. Being seen with an employee just won't do it for him.'

Andre looked about to interrupt, and it was her turn to stop him.

'It's what he wants, Andre. Right now, his pride is hurt because I left him and not the other way around. He'll get over it and move on, because he wants to be number one again. It's what he's always wanted. It's my job to get him there.'

'And that's all?' His voice actually went up in pitch. Holy crap, she'd shocked Andre.

'That's all,' Hannah said firmly. 'That's what I was hired to do.'

She'd do her job, get him back on top. She'd do what he wanted.

Even if it meant her heart would never forgive her.

The ringing of her cellphone pulled Hannah out of layers of much-needed sleep. Not again. Groaning, she made a mental note to change her ringtone to something other than a Nate song, and squinted at the display.

Oh yeah, it was *way* too early.

Gina had been asleep on her couch when she'd stumbled in from meeting with Andre. She'd tossed back the dregs of warm Pouilly-Fuisse and tumbled into bed. Thankfully she'd been exhausted enough to fall asleep quickly, but that had only been, what, three hours ago? Ow.

The phone's display also informed her that the caller was Sam. As tempting as it was to let the phone go to voicemail, pull a pillow over her head and pray for more sleep, she knew she had to take the call. Her professionalism made her do it.

She made a mental note to stop being such a damn professional, because it was obviously ruining her life, and said hello.

'Did you see the entertainment news?'

'Good morning to you, too, Sam.'

'Sorry.'

Sam didn't sound very sorry, but she let it go. 'Yes, I saw the news. Nate got some prime air time.'

'You did a good job getting him into that party,' Sam said. Before she could relish the flush of pride, he continued, 'But he told me that other artists were invited to perform and he wasn't.'

Ow. 'I got him in last minute. There probably wasn't time.' She really needed to be more awake for this.

'And there were celebrity photos everywhere, but none of him.'

Hannah lay back against the pillow and prayed for a double-shot espresso and a super-sized bottle of Advil to appear. It didn't.

'That probably had to do with the last-minute bit, too,' she said. 'But I understand what you're saying. I'll call the club owner and chat him up, tell him what a good time Nate had, how it was good publicity for the club for Nate to be there.'

'Do whatever you have to do,' Sam said.

Anger boiled up inside her. She was too tired and headachy and heartachy to take Sam's snippy orders right now. 'What do you want me to do,' she snapped, 'sleep with him, too?'

As soon as it slipped out, she regretted it. On so many levels. Into the silence left by Sam's lack of response, she said, 'I'm sorry, Sam. That was really uncalled for. I had a shitty night and I'm not thinking straight. I'll get some coffee in me and call Harry Z and straighten things out.'

'Thanks,' Sam said. This time he sounded like he meant it.

The gratitude surprised her – and made her feel even worse. 'Look, it really was great PR for Nate to be seen there. This is going to help him, I promise.'

'You're doing a great job,' Sam said, and hung up.

Hannah held the phone away from her and stared at it suspiciously.

Hannah sat at the dressing table in her old room and slipped on her favorite strappy black heels. She didn't really need to touch up her make-up or her hair – the spa people had done wonders – but she was aware of the irony of the situation. In her old room, prepping to go downstairs to one of her parents' parties ... how could it not remind her of nine years ago?

Instead of staring into the mirror, she closed her eyes and tried some meditative breathing. She had to stop thinking about Nate.

Everything was different now anyway, entirely different. She felt a hell of a lot better about herself, inside and outside. No longer shy, no longer awkward and wallflowerish.

Even the room was different.

Her mother had gone through an Asian phase and the furniture was all sleek straight lines, black and red lacquer. However, because it was her mother, there had to be something astonishingly overdone and fussy, and that would be the walls: she'd covered them in Chinese silk, red and woven with golden dragons.

Hannah told herself it did *not* remind her of the Japanese restaurant they'd eaten at the first day she met Nate. The restaurant where they'd flirted so hard she'd almost come in her seat (and she suspected he'd been just as close).

She'd been high as a kite that night, not from any substance other than a glass of wine, but from the heady knowledge that her adolescent fantasy was coming true, that she was going to have her night with Nate Fox.

Well, she'd had it. It had been outstanding. Now it was done and it was time to move on.

She opened her eyes and stood, smoothing the folds of fabric along her thighs. The midnight-blue halter dress brushed just above her knees. It dipped low in the back and had a spray of sparkling crystals in the front that drew the eye to her cleavage. Her hair and make-up were impeccable and she looked good enough to kick ass and take no prisoners.

It was her father's sixty-fifth birthday and by God she was going to help him celebrate.

Focus on the positive. Her father's party, catching up with Gina yesterday and today, a job well done with Nate at the club. Just think about Nate as a client.

She left her room, headed down the hall, and started her descent.

As she rounded the sweeping curve of the staircase, she looked down and saw him.

Her stomach plummeted even as the rest of her body betrayed her by tingling with sexual anticipation. He looked good enough to nibble on, in a dark suit that emphasized his broad shoulders, the lean, strong lines of his thighs. He wore a pale shirt, open at the collar. No tie. She wanted to taste the column of his throat, push the shirt aside to bite his collarbone. She knew how his skin would taste, how it would feel against her lips. His hair still curled over his collar, and even from here she could tell that his eyes were just as blue as they had been when they'd caught sight of each other all those years before.

He made her *want* just by standing there.

He spoke first. 'I was kind of hoping you'd fall into my arms again.'

She finished walking down the stairs, slowly and deliberately and gracefully. 'I'm not seventeen anymore,' she said once she was standing in front of him. 'I don't get flustered by adolescent crushes.'

'No, you're definitely all grown up.' His gaze wandered south. Hannah felt a flash of bitchy feminine pride that her cleavage was significantly more impressive than Marta-the-supermodel's.

'I didn't expect to see you here,' she said. God, was that really her? She sounded so stiff, so formal.

'Your mother invited me. After all, I am one of your dad's former clients.'

Hannah decided she would slowly kill her mother tomorrow. It was just like Joanne to decide that Hannah's boyfriend should come to the party. Ignoring the fact that Nate wasn't Hannah's boyfriend.

And never was. He'd been a fling, nothing more. That's all she'd planned on all those years ago, and it was all she and Nate had agreed to.

Falling in love with him had been her own damn fault.

Dammit, she wanted to kiss him again. Wanted to wind her fingers through his hair and pull his face down to hers and kiss him until they both forgot everything that was wrong.

'You're early,' she accused. She refused to notice the way his dark lashes framed his eyes. The sensual curve of his bottom lip.

'I was hoping we'd have the chance to talk.'

'From my end, it looks like everything's in order. Sam told me about the club snubbing you by not asking you to perform and not having your picture up. I talked to Harry Z and he definitely wants you to autograph a photo for the wall.'

Harry had, in fact, been hugely apologetic. He'd had a space on the wall but hadn't had time to corner Nate. There was a great photo of Nate and Marta that would be perfect, he said.

'Wow, that's great,' Nate said. 'You're on top of everything.'

They stared at each other. Hannah knew he was probably thinking the same thing she was: the last time she'd been on top of him. Sexual heat warmed her from the inside out.

'I wanted to thank you again for arranging all that,' he went on. 'I think it really did help. The press certainly won't have anything to complain about. Except maybe that I left early.'

Despite Andre's insistence that Nate had left alone, Hannah had trouble believing he wasn't interested in Marta, not after that kiss.

'We can spin that so they eat it right up,' she said. She wasn't going to bring up Marta, not right now.

'You really think so?'

She nodded.

It was all about business. He was making that clear.

'Look,' he said. 'About the ... what I said about you just wanting a fantasy fuck – it was really out of line. I know that's not –'

She shook her head. 'Don't worry about it,' she interrupted. 'I caught you off guard. But we both knew it was time for me to go. We agreed to get it out of our systems, right? We let it go on too long, because it should never have affected your career. I was unprofessional in that regard and I appreciate your keeping me on as your publicist despite that ... misstep.'

'You're the best there is,' Nate said. She heard the compliment in his voice, but his expression was guarded, unreadable. 'I'd be stupid to let you go.'

The words twisted her stomach. If only he were saying those words about her personally.

'Thank you,' she said. 'It wouldn't be going so well if you weren't putting your all into it, too. I'll know we've succeeded when you're on top.' Before he could respond, she said, 'Guests will be arriving soon and I need to help my mother. Why don't you go into the living room and get yourself a drink? My father's in there and I'm sure he'd love to see you.'

She needed to walk away from him before she said anything else, before she went all unprofessional over him again.

Keep it to business.

Nate nibbled on a toast point topped with caviar and the tiniest dollop of sour cream, and watched Hannah across the room. The party was a glittering who's who of the music world, all turned out to celebrate the birthday of one of the top producers in the business. Hannah was making the rounds, spending a few minutes chatting with each of her parents' guests. He liked how she made them comfortable, encouraged them to be at ease, with a light touch on their arm or shoulder, with a joke, with her open body posture. It wasn't forced or insincere, either, and he suspected that was one of the reasons she was so damn good at her job. She did it because she cared, not for the money or power or prestige.

He'd been that way about music once upon a time. Back when writing and performing were a simple, sheer joy. He still loved performing, still loved that feedback from listeners.

The writing . . . well, it would come back eventually.

But Hannah wouldn't. She'd made that clear in their conversation by the stairs. She wanted it to be all business. He'd done what she wanted him to and she was glad he had.

Then why weren't either of them happy?

He knew she wasn't happy. He could tell that by

how rigid her back had been, how she'd held herself away from him. Miles different from the way she curved and curled around him in bed, how she laughed and flirted, how she danced when she stood in front of the stage.

Somehow, he had to tell her that it didn't matter, that he'd rather be with her than be on top. That in the end, it was his music that would make or break him, not how many pictures he was in or how many interviews he landed. And when she was gone even his music was less. He had to tell her she was brilliant at what she did, but he'd rather she go put someone else on top.

She might not understand. But he had to try.

He stared at the remainder of the toast point. Did he even like caviar? He put it in a cocktail napkin and deposited it on a passing waiter's tray.

He was torn between staying here and watching her, like a creepy stalker across the room, and leaving, to go back to another lifeless hotel room. He couldn't talk to her here, that much he knew. He didn't know what to say, for one thing. And he didn't want to take anything away from her father's special night.

He'd go, he decided. He needed to think.

He said his goodbyes to her parents, hoping as he had when he'd said hello that he didn't telegraph 'Hi, I adore screwing your daughter seven ways to Sunday,' and fled the party.

At the hotel, he found a package in his suite. The photo from Harry Z for him to sign. He opened the padded envelope and slid out the print.

Oh God.

It was of him and Marta. It must have been taken when he was hugging her goodbye last night. Because even though he knew damn well it hadn't been anything more than a friendly kiss on the cheek, the angle was such that it looked like he was all over her.

Even Sam had commented, having seen coverage of the club opening on TV, that Nate and Marta had looked quite cozy. No wonder. No wonder Hannah was so frosty, too.

She thought he'd gotten her out of his system.

Unable to sit still, he paced the suite. In the sitting area, a black baby grand sat against a bank of windows that looked out over the Los Angeles skyline.

Angrily he slammed the piano open, not caring if anyone heard. He was in the penthouse suite anyway; probably nobody could hear.

He wanted the music to carry him away. Take with it his pain and worry and conscious thought. He started with Journey's 'Open Arms,' one of the first songs he'd picked out on the keys when he was learning to play, and went on to other songs, mostly his own, just letting whatever music wanted to happen, happen. No thoughts of Hannah. No thoughts of anything else.

Gradually, though, he came to realize two things: that he was playing something new, something he'd never learned or heard before . . .

. . . and that it was all about Hannah.

As the music formed, he saw her in his mind's eye; it pulled him back to her even as her image, as memories of her drew the music out of him.

It was a song for her.

It was her song.

Hands stilled on the keys. The music still surged within him. The melody, the words, all coming together. It was a feeling Nate had all but forgotten. The sense that everything was right, that he'd somehow tapped into something *other*. Something that pulled the music from his soul, releasing everything he felt inside.

Hannah had given that back to him.

He wanted to share it with her.

He wanted her to see how much he needed her.

How necessary she was in his life.

He played through the last few lines again, then grabbed a pad of hotel stationery and started to scribble. In moments, the page filled, lyrics and chords and snippets of melody.

The hair prickled at his nape, the sense that he was being watched. Nate turned around on the piano bench to see his manager leaning against the door frame. Sam must have come into the suite when he'd been playing, oblivious to the sound of the door opening.

'Is that new?' Sam asked.

'Yes,' Nate said.

The look of triumph, excitement, that lit Sam's eyes plucked at Nate.

'It's Hannah's,' Nate said.

'I thought you two had broken up.'

Bending his head, Nate played the first few chords of the chorus. He didn't want to hurt Sam, but there were things that had to be said.

'You'd be happy if we weren't together, wouldn't you?'

'What are you talking about?' His manager came further into the room, bushy grey eyebrows drawn together into a frown.

Nate turned around on the bench so he could face Sam. The music called to him, but he knew it would wait. For the first time in two years, he was confident that it would be there when he needed it again. 'You pushed us together, hoping she would keep me from falling back into old addictions. But the minute our relationship became public, you went from praising her to damning her.'

Sam threw his hands up in the air. 'I couldn't care less about your relationship. It was the bad PR I had a problem with.'

'And you let her know that.' Nate didn't mean for it to sound as accusatory as it did.

'Of course I did. It's her job. If she can't do the job properly when she's with you, then she needs to be away from you.' Sam's eyes dared him to contradict that.

'What about what I need?'

'You need to be at the top of the charts. You need to recapture –'

'I need Hannah,' Nate said, cutting off Sam's words. He watched as his friend opened his mouth to argue, and then closed it again, changing his mind.

Sam went to the wet bar and opened the refrigerator to remove a bottle of Evian. It was a stalling tactic. When the older man turned around, he was ready to speak.

'You're just feeling hurt because she left. Once a little time passes, you'll realize that I'm right. She's one of the best PR agents in the business and that's what she needs to stay.'

Nate stood up and moved to the floor-to-ceiling windows that looked out over the lights of LA. When he spoke, it was soft enough that Sam had to move closer to hear. 'I need to make music. I need to perform. I need to see the fans pressed against the stage and realize that I'm giving something back to them.'

He swung around, his hands shoved into the pockets of his favorite jeans. 'I don't need to see my name in *Billboard*'s number-one slot. I don't need to have my picture in every magazine. I don't need to have every starlet-of-the-moment on my arm.'

Nate watched as Sam sat down in one of the overstuffed designer chairs grouped around the glass-and-steel coffee table. The frown was still in place, but he could tell that his manager – his friend – was listening.

'I don't need the drugs anymore, Sam. I don't have to be high to be happy. I've already made it. I have fans, a lot of them. They love my music and they love me.

That's what I need. I'll put out new albums, and I'll make new fans along the way. I'll lose some, too, but that's OK. I'll still be making music. It's what I am.'

Feeling the call of the music, he moved back to the piano. 'But what I do need, more than anything else, is Hannah. I need her in my life or the rest of it has no meaning. She gave me back my music. She gave me back the joy in it.' His fingers drifted across the keys, the ghost of a song answering him. 'I love her.'

Sam smoothed his hands back along his hair before dropping them into his lap. 'I had no idea that you felt this way. Why didn't you tell me all this ages ago?'

'I've only just realized some of it myself. You've always wanted what's best for me. I know that, and I'll never forget what you've done for me. You took a raw young musician and taught him what he needed to know to make it big. Somewhere along the line, though, we both forgot that the music is what's important. Not the money or the fame. Sure, it's nice to have those, I won't say it's not. But it's not everything there is. We forgot that, Sam.

'I got lost in drugs, and you've focused so hard on dragging my ass back from the brink that neither of us noticed that I'm not there anymore.'

'You scared the hell out of me when you told me you couldn't write anymore,' Sam admitted quietly. 'All I could think about was that something inside of you was broken, that the drugs and the accident had killed your creativity. I've pushed so hard to get you back on top because I thought it would help you get that drive back, jump-start your music again.'

'Hannah did that,' Nate said. 'She makes me happy.'

Sam nodded, slapping his hands onto his knees. 'Then tell me what I can do to help you win her back.'

A slow grin curved Nate's mouth. For the first time in a week, he felt optimistic.

Chapter Sixteen

Hannah clicked the mouse with her right hand while she balanced a large banana-berry Jamba Juice with extra wheatgrass in her left. A new day, a fresh start. Out with the junk food, in with the healthy stuff. Seeing her father, hale and hearty at 65, had inspired her. That and the reminder of her hot new skinny jeans.

Sucking up a mouthful of the thick smoothie, she scrolled through her email. There was a big after-show get-together tonight, and given that it was LA, execs from Nate's record company would be there. She had to make sure they saw how far Nate had come. How well the tour did wouldn't matter if the execs still thought he wasn't worth investing in anymore.

Her father had taken her aside at the party at one point, put his arm around her and told her he was proud of her.

'You're doing a bang-up job, Peanut,' he said. 'Your boy is generating a lot of buzz down the grapevine. There's even talk that we'll sign him again, if he's interested in coming back with us. That's just between you and me and the wall, of course.'

'Of course, Daddy,' she said, hugging him. 'And thank you.' His words really did mean a lot.

It did concern her that Nate wasn't writing new music. In the past, his strength had been the combination of his creativity and his performances. So far, however, the fans had been willing to follow him on this covers album and tour. There were a hell of a lot of amazing songwriters out there, and if Nate found someone whose music he clicked with, it would be fine.

And if Nate signed a great new recording deal, she'd

really know she'd succeeded in what she'd been hired to do: put him back on top.

And then, maybe . . .

Maybe she could quit.

After her father's party had wrapped up, Hannah had taken a long drive, wandering down Mulholland, cruising the canyons, ending up on PCH somewhere north of Malibu. By the time she parked at a deserted beach and rolled down the windows to hear the surf, she'd had a fair amount of time to think.

To push back the emotions and focus on the rational, the logical.

To come up with a plan.

Seeing Nate at the party had shaken her equilibrium. She'd thought it would be one night when she wouldn't have to think about him and then there he was, gorgeous and sexy and reminding her of the passion and the emotional connection they'd had and lost.

After their conversation by the stairs, he'd left her alone, but it hadn't mattered. She'd spent the evening not looking at him, trying to focus on her parents and their guests and the celebration, but she had been constantly, painfully aware of his presence the entire time.

She'd come to the realization that it would be like that for a long, long time. If she worked for him, she could avoid him for only so long. Sure, she could do the bulk of her work at home, but there would be times, like tonight at the after-show function, when they'd have to meet.

And every one of those times would be like picking a scab off the wound.

She was bound by a contract and she was too professional to break it. But it occurred to her that maybe she could find a way out of it. If she got him back on top, the work would be easier. Maybe she could turn the job over to a junior publicist, someone up and coming in the business who could take the reins from her.

By the time she got home, she had several names in mind. She would talk to Sam about it tonight if they had a free moment during the after-show party, provided the record execs seemed happy.

She didn't harbor any hope that no longer working for Nate would mean she had a chance with him. He'd made it clear that it was over.

It would simply be the easiest and best way to cut him completely out of her life, except as a successful highlight on her CV.

Hannah took another drink of Jamba Juice. There'd be good press coverage tonight, and she followed up with several contacts about that. Gina would be there to take more photos, which several quality magazines had already expressed an interest in.

She ticked that off her To Do list, then opened up the FoxFanatics website. Tani had emailed to let her know the boards were humming with positive feedback about Nate's recent shows, and Hannah liked to keep up with what the fans were saying.

A banner scrolled across the home page, urging visitors to check out the latest poll. The webmaster ran them on occasion, questions like 'What's Your Favorite Fox Album?' and, when Nate had announced the covers album, 'What Song Should Nate Cover?' Much to the fans' delight, Nate had, in fact, included the number-one choice, Bon Jovi's 'Born to Be my Baby,' on the CD.

The current question, oddly enough, was 'Who Was Born To Be Nate's Baby?'

What the hell did that mean? Hannah investigated.

'Who,' the subtitle read, 'should Nate date? Voting ends at midnight tonight, so cast your final votes! Click here to see if your favorite choice is winning.'

Hannah snorted. Unlikely that Nate would take the

fans' recommendation on that one. Still, she had to wonder who his fans thought he'd make the most beautiful babies with. (She voted for Angelina Jolie. Nate could totally take out Brad Pitt, and besides, that would leave Brad free for Gina.)

She clicked.

She set the Jamba Juice down on the desk, carefully, before she dropped the Styrofoam cup and the remains of the smoothie exploded all over her office.

The fan response was *not* what she expected.

Four percent chose Marta Ingersol.

Eighteen percent voted 'Me, of course.'

The clear winner, by a landslide 78 percent, was Hannah Montgomery.

Staring at the screen, she fumbled for her phone, looking away only when she needed to find Tani's number.

Breathless as always, the fan-club president answered. 'Isn't that fantastic!' she said when Hannah managed to choke out the words 'poll' and 'what the hell.' 'I knew you'd get a lot of votes, and I told Helen we should get you a plaque or something, but she said we should focus on getting the application in to the Hollywood Walk of Fame for Nate's star, but we can talk about that tonight – oh, that reminds me, I have to call Fran and Sheri – hold on, I'm about to go through a tunn –'

The line went dead.

At the backstage entrance, Hannah flashed her 'All Access' laminate at the guard. The LA night air brought a muffled bass beat on its mellow breezes. She couldn't actually identify the song from the sound before the door shut behind her, but she was pretty sure it was 'Dragons of Winter.'

She'd deliberately timed her arrival with the end of

the concert. Her presence wasn't required for it, and she hadn't wanted to hear it, much less see it. She knew that someday she'd be able to listen to Nate's music again with enjoyment rather than sorrow or grumpiness. But that was going to be a long time from now.

Tonight, she just needed to be in the private Cyclorama Club by the time the press and the suits started streaming in. They'd show up after the concert ended, while Nate was backstage showering.

Oh. Hell. That was the *last* mental image she needed.

'Darling!' Andre's voice rang out.

'We've been looking for you,' Gina said, right on his heels.

'Hey, guys,' Hannah said distractedly, reaching into her purse for her BlackBerry.

'You need to come with us,' Andre said. She realized he was standing at her side, one meaty hand gently cupping her elbow.

On her other side, Gina linked arms with her.

'What's going on?' Hannah tensed. 'Is something wrong?'

'Nope,' Gina said.

She tried to resist, but even the light pressure on Andre's side drove her forward. 'I have work to do – I need to get over to –'

'You need to hear this,' Gina said in a voice that brooked no argument.

They pushed her through the door to the wing of the stage. Sam, who was standing by one of the monitors with his usual 'something is bound to go wrong, I'm sure of it' frowns on his face, glanced up and nodded at her. In the dim light, she thought she saw him smile.

The final bars of 'Dragons of Winter' were pounding through the arena. Hannah refused to look at the stage, refused to see Nate poised at the edge crunching out the guitar licks.

Refused to think about the concert where he'd played her body so well and the triumphant look on his face right before she'd shattered into orgasm.

She turned to flee, but Andre was blocking the exit, his feet planted firmly apart, trunklike arms folded across his chest. She gave him her best puppy-dog eyes, but he just shook his head at her, expressionless. Her flamboyant friend Andre was gone; he had gone entirely into threatening, scary-Andre mode.

The song was over; the crowd's screams and cheers were dying down. But Nate wasn't leaving the stage.

Instead he stood in front of the center mic, just him and the guitar, as the rest of the band slipped away. A roadie tossed him a towel, which he used to wipe his face. He tossed the towel into the audience, and there was a brief scuffle before someone shrieked in victory and waved the towel over her head.

A single spotlight narrowed down to frame Nate. The metal rings on his wrist cuffs glinted as he ran his hand up and down the neck of the guitar. The leather pants he wore showed off his perfect ass. His black hair curled over the collar of a sleeveless vest and the fox tattoo on his bicep wore a sheen of sweat.

'We're going to do something a little different tonight,' he said. 'I've got one more song for you and then I'm going to say goodnight. I'm sorry there won't be an encore, but this is actually going to be something special.'

Random screams from the audience.

Hannah frowned. 'No encore? What's he doing?' She turned to Gina. 'What's going on?'

'Just shut up and listen,' Gina said.

'I went through hell a couple of years ago and thankfully came out the other side,' Nate said. 'It was a long road, but I'm back, thanks in part to all of you.'

More cheering. Nate raised a hand, waving them down.

'This tour, I've focused on my past, songs that inspired me to become a musician and songs of mine that you've made into hits over the years. But now, it's time to start looking to my future. When the tour is over, if all goes well, I'll be recording a CD of new music.' He paused, then shouted, 'Do you all want to hear some new music?'

The audience shrieked with delight.

Nate was writing again? Hannah's stomach lurched. She whipped around to look at Sam.

Sam was definitely smiling. He nodded at her to pay attention, but he didn't have to. She was already turning back to stare at Nate.

The audience had no idea how momentous this was.

'I've just written a new song,' Nate said, 'and I want to play it for you tonight. It may not be as polished as it ought to be, so bear with me. This is a song about what's really important in life. Believe me, it ain't the grand illusion you see up here on stage.'

He caressed the guitar, then picked out a complex melody in a minor key.

Hannah held her breath. She'd been wrong. Nate signing a new record deal wasn't the greatest measure of success.

This was.

You were there when I first found my wings
Watched from afar when I ascended
Top of the heap
Everyone's star
Music the wind to make me fly

But like Lucifer I grew too cocky
And like Lucifer I fell from grace
The depths of hell
No one to believe
No music to mend my broken wings

The music swirled around her, surged through her. It was beautiful. Nate Fox was back.

That was the only thought Hannah could manage. All she could do was listen as he continued.

> You were the one who didn't turn away
> You brought the music back to me
> Repaired my wings
> Healed my soul
> Now fly with me
> Come fly with me
>
> Just you and me
> You're all I need
> Fly with me . . .

The crowd erupted in screams and applause as the final chords died away. Nate slipped the guitar strap from over his neck, raising one hand to the audience, and quietly left the stage.

Somehow, he was standing in front of her, his eyes searching hers. His hair was spiked with sweat, his vest hanging open over his hard chest. A droplet of moisture ran down his breastbone.

'That was beautiful,' Hannah managed. Her heart was pounding so hard she thought he might be able to use it as the bass line on the song.

'It's yours,' he said softly, looking at her with an intensity that stole her breath. 'You gave me back my music.'

He put his hand on her waist to guide her to one side. A roadie hustled by, coiling cords. Nate's hand lingered, burning through the fabric of her shirt.

Hannah tried to remain professional. But somehow the song's lyrics had slipped past her guard. That, and the words he'd just spoken. He credited her with helping him find his way past his writing block.

Still, she had come here to do her job. She had to remember that.

'Say something,' he said.

'I'm glad you're writing again,' she tried, and immediately felt guilty. It wasn't what he wanted to hear, she could tell by the disappointment that shadowed his eyes. She couldn't bear it. 'Did you mean it?' she asked. 'What you said in the song?'

'Every damn word of it,' he said softly. 'You *are* all I need. Not the fame or fortune. Just you.'

'But your career,' she protested. 'People will say –'

He kissed her, effectively cutting off the words. Oh God, how she'd missed the feel of his lips on hers. She felt like she'd been drowning and he was the air she needed. One hand cradled her head; the other stroked down her spine, urging her closer until she was pressed against him. Nate teased her bottom lip with his tongue and she opened her mouth on a moan. She felt the velvet thrust of his tongue against hers all the way to her clit.

One last kiss. Just one. And then she would have the strength to pull away. Sliding her hands beneath his vest, she curled her arms around him. He was warm, his muscles hard beneath her questing fingers, his skin slick with sweat. She held him tight, trying to memorize his feel, his taste.

From some dim faraway place, she could hear applause. It yanked her back to reality.

'Nate,' she said, breathing his name against the temptation of his mouth.

He rested his forehead against hers. 'I've missed you. Being without you is not the way I want to live.'

She'd missed him, too, but she had to say goodbye. It was unfairly cruel that she had to say it again, but it had to be done.

But before she could tell him, he responded to her earlier protest.

'I don't give a damn about what people will say or think,' Nate said. 'The only people whose opinions matter all seem to think we should be together.'

That was the applause. Hannah looked over Nate's shoulder to see Gina grinning like an idiot. Andre clutched his hands to his chest, practically swooning. Sam gave her a quick thumbs-up, his nod telling her he approved before he turned to bark orders at the roadie breaking down the drum kit.

'I'm not good for your career,' she protested. She was going to kill her friends later. Maybe. Or maybe she'd thank them. She was rapidly losing track of how she should be feeling, what she should be thinking. Her resolve crumbled around the edges because she couldn't remember why she was supposed to be resolved.

'Sweetheart, you set my career back on the path to the top,' Nate told her. 'You did something truly amazing and impressive. But I'd walk away from all of it if that's what it took to be with you.'

She stared at him, shocked. 'You can't do that!'

'Coming through!' The warning was followed by a crew member wheeling a crate-laden dolly.

Muttering a low curse, Nate grabbed her hand and wove his way through the backstage disorder. She followed, trying to assimilate everything he'd been saying. He'd give up his music for her? That was crazy talk.

But it was sweet, too. And a small ember of hope flared a little brighter in her chest.

Nate tried the handles of a series of doors, finally finding one that was unlocked. He pulled her inside, simultaneously flipping a light switch. It was a storage room, stacked high with boxes and chairs. There was no lock on the door, so he grabbed a chair and wedged it up under the knob.

'We can't be back here,' Hannah said. 'There's a roomful of people waiting to see you!'

'If they want to see me, they'll wait. You're more important.'

He filled the small room with his scent, his presence. When he backed her up against the wall, Hannah couldn't help but respond to the hard pressure of his body against hers. She touched his cheek, stroking the lean planes of his face. When she traced the sensual curve of his bottom lip, he caught her hand in his. His tongue curled around her fingertip before drawing the digit into his hot mouth. She felt an answering rush of moisture between her thighs.

'I love you, Hannah,' he said softly. 'And I have no intention of letting you walk away from me.'

He loved her? Really? Something cracked inside of her, thawing in the warmth.

'I don't have to be at the top of the charts to know that I'm successful,' he said. 'Sure, being there is fun, but it's the music that matters. I'd lost the music and you gave it back to me. I've done everything you've wanted me to do to get back to the top, but unless you're there with me, it doesn't mean a damn thing.'

'Wait a minute,' she said. 'Everything *I've* wanted?'

'Giving you up, taking Marta to the Paradise Club, posing for pretty pictures.'

'I thought that's what *you* wanted. You hired me to put you at the top of the charts, to generate buzz about your comeback. Positive buzz, not –'

'I just want to play music, Hannah,' Nate said. 'My music and my performance should be enough for people. As long as the fans are happy, my career will be fine. If the media doesn't like me, or me with you, then screw 'em.'

He leaned close enough to brush his lips along her jaw. Warm breath tickled her hair. The sensation was maddening. Her eyes closed, her head resting against the wall. His teeth grazed her skin, his tongue soothing the spot. The throbbing between her legs intensified and she rocked her hips against his. He laughed, a low growly sound, and rocked back. The hard length of his erection pressed against her, a clear erotic sign that he wanted her just as much as she wanted him.

'Tell me you love me,' he whispered.

She opened her eyes to meet his gaze. The blue-black of his eyes drew her in, and she knew that no matter what happened, she didn't want to be apart from this man. 'I love you, Nathaniel Fox.'

The quick triumph that flashed in his eyes, the cocky grin that curved his mouth, she could forgive all of that, because he kissed her with an utterly focused possession that drove everything else from her mind.

They'd only been apart for a week and yet she felt as though they hadn't touched for years. The desire was as strong as the first time they'd had sex, back in his house in San Francisco. She couldn't get enough of the taste of him, the feel of his mouth on hers and his hands roaming restlessly over her body.

This was no time for drawn-out pleasure, for languid stroking and teasing, for romantic foreplay and slow joining. She wanted him. He wanted her.

Now.

Desperate for skin-against-skin contact, Hannah pulled her shirt from her waistband, wriggling the material up along her torso. Nate's hands immediately went to her ribcage, skimming along her, his calloused fingers digging into the muscles in her back. He pulled back from their kiss just long enough for her to pull the shirt over her head and toss it away. Then he was kissing her breathless again.

He worked his hands between them to take her pouting nipples between his fingers, rubbing the lace of her bra against her tender flesh.

'Jesus, Nate,' she gasped, her knees almost buckling as the sensations shot through her. She reached behind her and gripped the shelf she was leaning against. A plastic bottle of cleanser tumbled to the floor.

He tugged the cups of her bra down. Her full breasts spilled out of the lace. He bent to capture one nipple in his mouth. The first slow suck had her throwing her head back, crying out. Nibbling her with his teeth, he slid his hands down her sides. Capturing the hem of her skirt, Nate tugged it up, pulling it over her hips. His fingers grazed against her damp thong and she shuddered.

'So hot,' he murmured. 'So wet.' He raised his head and kissed her again. 'So intoxicating. Intriguing . . .'

She fumbled with the lacing of his leather pants. The knot caught, tied twice to keep an avid fan from reaching up and pulling it free. Her curse made Nate laugh, but didn't stop him from pulling her thong aside and slipping one long finger into her folds.

'That's not helping,' she ground out, riding his hand as he slipped a second finger into her. Heat spread inside, weakening her limbs. His thumb nudged her clit. Hannah gritted her teeth, determined not to come until he was buried deep inside of her.

But he knew exactly what he was doing, and each little bump of his finger against her notched the pleasure higher and higher.

Finally, her plucking fingers released the damned laces and she slipped her hand into the leather pants. He was gloriously bare beneath, and she was gratified to hear him groan when she pulled his erection free. He didn't give her any time to stroke or play, however. He spun her around, tugged her panties down. She kicked them off one foot and grabbed hold of the shelves, praying they were bolted to something solid.

Looking back over her shoulder, she saw that Nate had stopped just to look at her. Her long legs were spread, her feet still in the stiletto heels. She wiggled her hips, doing a slow bump and grind. His eyes were riveted on her ass. She reached back, gave herself a light slap on one cheek.

'Fuck me, Nate!'

The low growl that came from his throat made her wiggle her ass again.

Nate nudged the head of his cock against her slick opening. She felt him separating her, teasing. She tried to push back, to take him inside, but strong callused fingers held her hips tight. His tongue traced her spine, his teeth lightly biting the back of her shoulder.

'I love you, Hannah,' he said, his breath hot against her cheek. He reached around and stroked along her needy clit. She was suddenly at the edge. 'I want you. I need you.' He nipped at her ear and whispered, 'Come for me.'

She wanted to tell him again that she loved him, but words were impossible as she succumbed to her orgasmic convulsions. 'Nate!'

She was still shuddering through her climax when he drove into her, coaxing her up and over a second crest. Clinging desperately to the shelf, she pushed her hips backwards to meet his strokes. Her inner muscles clenched down hard on his erection, urging him to join her.

A flurry of thrusts, and then he groaned her name when he reached his release.

Nate rested his cheek against her shoulder, arms wrapped tightly around her. She could feel his heart beating, matching her own pounding pulse. Hannah relished the feeling, the sense of belonging and homecoming.

When she could move again, she turned around, seeking his mouth in a long slow kiss.

'As much as I want to stay here with you,' he said finally, 'I don't want to keep you from your job.'

'*Our* job,' she said. She gave him a playful pat on his butt. Such a cute butt. She was feeling awfully possessive of it right now. 'We both have to go out there and shmooze those music execs.'

He pulled her against him and kissed her hard. 'Thanks to you, I'll have some new songs for them to produce in a few months.'

He handed her the lace thong she'd kicked across the floor, held her shirt while she shrugged into it. He stroked his fingers through her hair, straightening the waves that tumbled down her back.

Every touch told her how much he cared.

They opened the storeroom door.

Sam, Andre and Gina waited for them across the hall.

'Are you two finished talking things through?' Gina asked. She didn't move her hands, but the air quotes were clear in her tone.

Hannah cleared her throat. 'We've definitely come to an agreement,' she said. A quick glance at Nate showed her that he was grinning, the joy so apparent in his eyes.

'Good,' Sam said. 'Now, don't you have some work to do?'

Andre simply fluttered his hands. Hannah noticed, however, that as they walked away he tilted his head to check out Nate's ass. She caught his eye, saw the query there. She nodded. Yep, leather pants meant no underwear. Andre rolled his eyes in delight, falling into step behind them.

Nate would wow the record execs. Offers would be forthcoming. She'd done her job and she'd continue to do it.

But this time, she wouldn't give a damn what the rest of the world thought.

The fans wanted them together. The FoxFanatics poll had proven that.

More importantly, Nate wanted them together. It was what they both wanted, and needed.

She opened the door to the meet-and-greet, her fingers firmly twined with Nate's.

They would fly together in the future.